Cities need people like us,

those who go after things the cops can't catch and keep the streets from boiling over. We handle nonstandard exorcisms, Traders, hellbreed, rogue Weres, scurf, Sorrows, Middle Way adepts . . . all the fun the nightside can come up with. Normally a hunter's job is just to act as a liaison between the paranormal community and the regular police, make sure everything stays under control.

Sometimes—often enough—it's our job to find people that have been taken by the things that go bump in the night. When I say "find" I mean their bodies, because humans don't live too long on the nightside unless they're hunters. More often than not our mission is vengeance, to restore the unsteady balance between the denizens of the dark and regular oblivious people. To make a statement and keep the things creeping in the dark just there—creeping, instead of swaggering.

And also more often than not, we lay someone's soul to rest if killing them is just the beginning.

Praise for Lilith Saintcrow:

"No one does gritty and paranormal better than Saintcrow."
—*Romantic Times* (Top Pick) on *Saint City Sinners*

"Dark, gritty, urban fantasy at its best."
—blogcritics.org

BOOKS BY LILITH SAINTCROW

JILL KISMET NOVELS

Night Shift

Hunter's Prayer

Redemption Alley

DANTE VALENTINE NOVELS

Working for the Devil

Dead Man Rising

The Devil's Right Hand

Saint City Sinners

To Hell and Back

Dark Watcher

Storm Watcher

Fire Watcher

Cloud Watcher

The Society

Hunter, Healer

NIGHT SHIFT

LILITH SAINTCROW

www.orbitbooks.net

New York   London

Copyright © 2008 by Lilith Saintcrow
Excerpt from *Hunter's Prayer* copyright © 2008 by Lilith Saintcrow
All rights reserved. Except as permitted under the U.S. Copyright Act of 1976, no part of this publication may be reproduced, distributed, or transmitted in any form or by any means, or stored in a database or retrieval system, without the prior written permission of the publisher.

Orbit is an imprint of Hachette Book Group USA, Inc. The Orbit name and logo is a trademark of Little, Brown Book Group Ltd.

Orbit
Hachette Book Group USA
237 Park Avenue
New York, NY 10017
Visit our Web site at www.orbitbooks.net

Printed in the United States of America

First edition: July 2008

10 9 8 7 6 5 4 3 2 1

For Nicholas Deangelo,
who never asked why.

The most terrible thing to face is one's own soul.
—Anonymous

NIGHT SHIFT

Prelude

Sit. There."

A wooden chair in the middle of a flat expanse of hardwood floor, lonely under cold fluorescent light.

I lowered myself gingerly, curled my fingers over the ends of the armrests, and commended my soul to God.

Well, maybe not actually commended. Maybe I was just praying really, really hard.

He circled the chair, every step just heavy enough to make a noise against bare floorboards. My weapons and my coat were piled by the door, and even the single knife I'd kept, safe in its sheath strapped to my thigh, was no insurance. I was locked in a room with a hungry tiger who stepped, stepped, turning just a little each time.

I didn't shift my weight.

Instead, I stared across the room, letting my eyes unfocus. Not enough to wall myself up inside my head—that was a death sentence. A hunter is always alert, Mikhail says. Always. Any inattention is an invitation to Death.

And Death loves invitations.

The hellbreed became a shadow each time he passed in front of me, counterclockwise, and I was beginning to wonder if he was going to back out of the bargain or welsh on the deal. Which was, of course, what he wanted me to wonder.

Careful, Jill. Don't let him throw you. *I swallowed, wished I hadn't; the briefest pause in his even tread gave me the idea that he'd seen the betraying little movement in my throat.*

I do not like the idea of hellbreed staring at my neck.

Silver charms tied in my hair clinked as blessed metal reacted to the sludge of hellbreed filling the ether. This one was bland, not beautiful like the other damned. He was unassuming, slim and weak-looking.

But he scared my teacher. Terrified him, in fact.

Only an idiot isn't scared of hellbreed. There's no shame in it. You've got to get over being ashamed of being scared, because it will slow you down. You can't afford that.

"So."

I almost jumped when his breath caressed my ear. Hot, meaty breath, far too humid to be human. He was breathing on me, and my flesh crawled in concentric waves of revulsion. Gooseflesh rose up hard and pebbled, scales of fear spreading over my skin.

"Here's the deal." The words pressed obscenely warm against my naked skin. Something brushed my hair, delicately, and silver crackled with blue sparks. A hiss touched my ear, the skin suddenly far too damp.

I wasn't sweating. It was his breath condensing on me.

Oh, God. *I almost choked on bile. Swallowed it and*

held still, every muscle in my body screaming at me to move, to get away.

"I'm going to mark you, my dear. While you carry that mark, you'll have a gateway embedded in your flesh. Through that conduit, you're going to draw sorcerous energy, and lots of it. It will make you strong, and fast—stronger and faster than any of your fellow hunters. You'll have an edge in raw power when it comes to sorcery, even that weak-kneed trash you monkeys flatter yourself by calling magic."

The hellbreed paused. Cold air hit my wet ear. A single drop of condensation trickled down the outer shell of cartilage, grew fat, and tickled unbearably as it traced a dead flabby finger down to the hollow where ear meets neck, a tender, vulnerable spot.

"I'll also go so far as to help you keep this city free of those who might interfere with the general peace. Peace is good for profit, you know."

A soft, rumbling chuckle brushed against my cheek, with its cargo of sponge-rotten breath.

I kept my fucking mouth shut. "Stay silent until he offers all he's going to offer, *milaya*." *Mikhail's advice, good advice. I was trained, wasn't I? At least, mostly trained. A hunter in my own right, and this was my chance to become . . . what?*

Even better. It was a golden opportunity, and if he thought I should take it, I would. And I wouldn't screw it up.

I would not let my teacher down.

So stay quiet, Jill. Stay calm.

I kept breathing softly through my mouth; the air

reeked of hellbreed and corruption. Tasting that scent was bad, as bad as breathing it through my nose.

I just couldn't figure out which was worse.

Something hard, rasping like a cat's tongue, flicked forward and touched the hollow behind my ear, pressing past a few stray strands of hair. If I hadn't been so fucking determined to stay still, muscles locked up tighter than Val's old cashbox, I might have flinched.

Then I probably would have died.

But the touch retreated so quickly I wasn't sure I'd felt it. Except that little drop of condensation was gone, wasn't it?

Shit. I was now sweating too bad to tell.

The hellbreed laughed again. "Very good, little hunter. The bargain goes thus: you bear my mark and use the power it provides as you see fit. Once a month you'll come visit, and you'll spend time with me. That's all—a little bit of time each month. For superlative use of the power I grant you, you might have to spend a little more time. Say, five or six hours?"

Now it was negotiation time. I wet my lips with my tongue, wished I hadn't because I suddenly knew his eyes had fastened on my mouth. "Half an hour. Maximum."

Bargaining on streetcorners taught me that much, at least—you never take the john's first offer, and you never, ever, ever start out with more than half of what you're willing to give.

Sometimes you can pick who buys you, and for how much.

That's what power really is.

"You wound me." The hellbreed didn't sound wounded.

He sounded delighted, his bland tenor probing at my ear. "Three hours. See how generous I am, for you?"

This is too easy. Be careful. "An hour a month, maximum of two, and your help on my cases. Final offer, hellbreed, or I walk. I didn't come here to be jacked around."

Why had I come here? Because Mikhail said I should.

I wondered if it was another test I'd failed, or passed. I wondered if I'd just overstepped and was looking at a nasty death. Bargaining with hellbreed is tricky; hunters usually just kill them. But this wasn't so simple. This was either a really good idea or a really bad way to die.

A long thunderous moment of quiet, and the room trembled like a soap bubble. Something like masses of gigantic flies on a mound of corpses buzzed, rattling.

Helletöng. The language of the damned. It lay under the skin of the visible like fat under skin, dimpling the surface tension of what we try to call the real world.

"Done, little hunter. We have a bargain. If you agree."

My throat was like the Sahara, dry and scratchy. A cough caught out in the open turned into a painful, ratcheting laugh. "What do you get out of this, Perry?"

That scaly, dry, probing thing flicked along my skin again, rasped for the briefest second against the side of my throat, just a fraction of an inch away from where the pulse beat frantically. I sucked at keeping my heartrate down, Mikhail warned and warned me about it—

"Sometimes we *like* being on the side of the angels." *The hellbreed's voice dropped to a whisper that would have been intimate if the rumbling of Hell hadn't* been scraping along underneath. "It makes the ending sweeter. Besides, peace is good for profit. Do we have a deal, little hunter?"

Christ. Mikhail, I hope you're right. *I didn't agree to it because of the hellbreed or even because the thought of that much power was tempting.*

I agreed because Mikhail told me I should, even though it was my decision. It wasn't really a Trader's bargain if I was doing it for my teacher, was it?

Was it?

"We have a deal." *Four little words. They came out naturally, smoothly, without a hitch.*

Hot iron-hard fingers clamped over my right wrist. "Oh, *good.*" *A slight wet smacking sound, like a hungry toddler at the breakfast table, and he wrenched my hand off the arm of the chair, the pale tender underside of my wrist turned up to face cold fluorescent light. My heart jackhammered away, adrenaline soaking copper into the dry roof of my mouth, and I bit back a cry.*

It was too late. Four tiny words, and I'd just signed a contract.

Now we'd see if Mikhail was right, and I still had my soul.

1

Every city has a pulse. It's just a matter of knowing where to rest your finger to find it, throbbing away as the sun bleeds out of the sky and night rises to cloak every sin.

I crouched on the edge of a rooftop, the counterweight of my heavy leather coat hanging behind me. Settled into absolute stillness, waiting. The baking wind off the cooling desert mouthed the edges of my body. The scar on my right wrist was hot and hard under a wide hinged copper bracelet molded to my skin.

The copper was corroding, blooming green and wearing thin.

I was going to have to find a different way to cover the scar up soon. Trouble is, I suck at making jewelry, and Galina was out of blessed copper cuffs until her next shipment from Nepal.

Below me the alley wandered, thick and rank. Here at the edge of the barrio there were plenty of hiding places for the dark things that crawl once dusk falls. The Weres don't patrol out this far, having plenty to keep them occupied inside their own crazy-quilt of streets and alleys around the Plaza Centro and its spreading tenements. Here on the fringes, between a new hunter's territory and the streets the Weres kept from boiling over, a few hellbreed thought they could break the rules.

Not in my town, buckos. If you think Kismet's a push-over because she's only been on her own for six months, you've got another think coming.

My right leg cramped, a sudden vicious swipe of pain. I ignored it. My electrolyte balance was all messed up from going for three days without rest, from one deadly night-battle to the next with the fun of exorcisms in between. I wondered if Mikhail had ever felt this exhaustion, this ache so deep even bones felt tired.

It hurt to think of Mikhail. My hand tightened on the bullwhip's handle, leather creaking under my fingers. The scar tingled again, a knot of corruption on the inside of my wrist.

Easy, milaya. *No use in making noise, eh? It is soft and quiet that catches mouse.* As if he was right next to me, barely mouthing the words, his gray eyes glittering winter-sharp under a shock of white hair. Hunters don't live to get too old, but Mikhail Ilych Tolstoi had been an exception in so many ways. I could almost see his ghost crouching silent next to me, peering at the alley over the bridge of his patrician nose.

Of course he wasn't there. He'd been cremated, just like he wanted. I'd held the torch myself, and the Weres had let me touch it to the wood before singing their own fire into being. A warrior's spirit rose in smoke, and wherever my teacher was, it wasn't here.

Which I found more comforting than you'd think, since if he'd come back I'd have to kill him. Just part of the job.

My fingers eased. I waited.

The smell of hellbreed and the brackish contamination of an *arkeus* lay over this alley. Some nasty things had been sidling out of this section of the city lately, nasty enough to give even a Hell-tainted hunter a run for her money. We have firepower and sorcery, we who police the nightside, but Traders and hellbreed are spooky-quick and capable of taking a hell of a lot of damage.

Get it? A Hell of a lot of damage? Arf arf.

Not to mention the scurf with their contagion, the adepts of the Middle Way with their goddamn Chaos, and the Sorrows worshipping the Elder Gods.

The thought of the Sorrows made rage rise under my breastbone, fresh and wine-dark. I inhaled smoothly, dispelling it. Clear, calm, and cold was the way to go about this.

Movement below. Quick and scuttling, like a rat skittering from one pile of garbage to the next. I didn't move, I didn't blink, I barely even *breathed*.

The *arkeus* took shape, rising like a fume from dry-scorched pavement, trash riffling as the wind of its coalescing touched ragged edges and putrid rotting things. Tall, hooded, translucent where moonlight struck it and smoky-solid elsewhere, one of Hell's roaming corruptors stretched its long clawed arms and slid fully into the world. It drew in a deep satisfied sigh, and I heard something else.

Footsteps.

Someone was coming to keep an appointment.

Isn't that a coincidence. So am I.

My heartbeat didn't quicken; it stayed soft, even, as almost-nonexistent as my breathing. It had taken me a long time to get my pulse mostly under control.

The next few moments were critical. You can't jump too soon on something like this. *Arkeus* aren't your garden-variety hellbreed. You have to wait until they solidify enough to talk to their victims—otherwise you'll be fighting empty air with sorcery, and that's no fun—and you have to know what a Trader is bargaining for before you go barging in to distribute justice or whup-ass. Usually both, liberally.

The carved chunk of ruby on its silver chain warmed, my tiger's-eye rosary warming too, the blessing on both items reacting with contamination rising from the *arkeus* and its lair.

A man edged down the alley, clutching something to his chest. The *arkeus* made a thin greedy sound, and my smart left eye—the blue one, the one that can look *below* the surface of the world—saw a sudden tensing of the strings of contamination following it. It was a hunched, thin figure that would have been taller than me except for the hump on its back; its spectral robes brushing dirt and refuse, taking strength from filth.

Bingo. The *arkeus* was now solid enough to hit.

The man halted. I couldn't see much beyond the fact that he was obviously human, his aura slightly tainted from his traffic with an escaped denizen of Hell.

It was official. The man was a Trader, bargaining with Hell. Whatever he was bargaining *for,* it wasn't going to do him any good.

Not with me around.

The *arkeus* spoke. *"You have brought it?"* A lipless cold voice, eager and thin, like a dying cricket. A razor-blade pressed against the wrist, a thin line of red on pale skin, the frozen-blue face of a suicide.

I moved. Boots soundless against the parapet, the carved chunk of ruby resting against the hollow of my throat, even my coat silent. The silver charms braided into my long dark hair didn't tinkle. The first thing a hunter's apprentice learns is to move quietly, to draw silence in tight like a cloak.

That is, if the apprentice wants to survive.

"I b-brought it." The man's speech was the slow slur of a dreamer who senses a cold-current nightmare. He was in deep, having already given the *arkeus* a foothold by making some agreement or another with it. "You'd better not—"

"Peace." The *arkeus*'s hiss froze me in place for a moment as the hump on its back twitched. *"You will have your desire, never fear. Give it to me."*

The man's arms relaxed, and a small sound lifted from the bundle he carried. My heart slammed into overtime against my ribs.

Every human being knows the sound of a baby's cry.

Bile filled my throat. My boots ground against the edge of the parapet as I launched out into space, the *arkeus* flinching and hissing as my aura suddenly flamed, tearing through the ether like a star. The silver in my hair shot sparks, and the ruby at my throat turned hot. The scar on my right wrist turned to lava, burrowing in toward the bone, my whip uncoiled and struck forward, its metal flechettes snapping at the speed of sound, cracking as I pulled on etheric force to add a psychic strike to the physical.

My boots hit slick refuse-grimed concrete and I pitched forward, the whip striking again across the *arkeus*'s face. The hell-thing howled, and my other hand was full of the Glock, the sharp stink of cordite blooming as silver-coated bullets chewed through the thing's physical shell. Hollowpoints do a lot of damage once a hellbreed's initial shell is breached.

It's a pity 'breed heal so quickly.

We don't know why silver works—something to do with the Moon, and how she controls the tides of sorcery and water. No hunter cares, either. It's enough that it levels the playing field a little.

The *arkeus* moved, scuttling to the side as the man screamed, a high whitenoise-burst of fear. The whip coiled, my hip moving first as usual—the hip leads with whip-work as well as stave fighting. My whip-work had suffered until Mikhail made me take bellydancing classes.

Don't think, Jill. Move. I flung out my arm, etheric force spilling through my fingers, and the whip slashed again, each flechette tearing through already-lacerated flesh. It howled again, and the copper bracelet broke, tinkled sweetly on the concrete as I pivoted, firing down into the hell-thing's face. It twitched, and I heard my own voice chanting in gutter Latin, a version of Saint Anthony's prayer Mikhail had made me learn.

Protect me from the hordes of Hell, O Lord, for I am pure of heart and trust Your mercy—and the bullets don't hurt, either.

The *arkeus* screamed, writhing, and cold air hit the

scar. I was too drenched with adrenaline to feel the usual curl of fire low in my belly, but the sudden sensitivity of my skin and hearing slammed into me. I dropped the whip and fired again with the gun in my left, then fell to my knees, driving down with psychic and physical force.

My fist met the hell-thing's lean malformed face, which exploded. It shredded, runnels of foulness bursting through its skin, and the sudden cloying reek would have torn my dinner loose from my stomach moorings if I'd eaten anything.

Christ, I wish it didn't stink so bad. But stink means dead, and if this thing's dead it's one less fucking problem for me to deal with.

No time. I gained my feet, shaking my right fist. Gobbets of preternatural flesh whipped loose, splatting dully against the brick walls. I uncoiled, leaping for the front of the alley.

The Trader was only human, and he hadn't made his big deal yet. He was tainted by the *arkeus*'s will, but he wasn't given superstrength or near-invulnerability yet.

The only enhanced human being left in the alley was me. Thank God.

I dug my fingers into his shoulder and set my feet, yanking him back. The baby howled, emptying its tiny lungs, and I caught it on its way down, my arm tightening maybe a little too much to yank it against my chest. I tried to avoid smacking it with a knife-hilt.

I backhanded the man with my hellbreed-strong right fist. *Goddamn it. What am I going to do now?*

The baby was too small, wrapped in a bulky blue blanket that smelled of cigarette smoke and grease. I held it awkwardly in one arm while I contemplated the sobbing heap of sorry manflesh crumpled against a pile of garbage.

I've cuffed plenty of Traders one-handed, but never while holding a squirming, bellowing bundle of little human that smelled not-too-fresh. Still, it was a cleaner reek than the *arkeus*'s rot. I tested the cuffs, yanked the man over, and checked his eyes. Yep. The flat shine of the dust glittered in his irises. He was a thin, dark-haired man with the ghost of childhood acne still hanging on his cheeks, saliva glittering wetly on his chin.

I found his ID in his wallet, awkwardly holding the tiny yelling thing in the crook of my arm. *Jesus. Mikhail never trained me for this.* "Andy Hughes. You are *under arrest.* You have the right to be exorcised. Anything you say will, of course, be ignored, since you've forfeited your rights to a trial of your peers by trafficking with Hell." I took a deep breath. "And you should thank your lucky stars I'm not in a mood to kill anyone else tonight. Who does the baby belong to?"

He was still gibbering with fear, and the baby howled. I could get nothing coherent out of either of them.

Then, to complete the deal, the pager went off against my hip, vibrating silently in its padded pocket.

Great.

2

Cities need people like us, those who go after things the cops can't catch and keep the streets from boiling over. We handle nonstandard exorcisms, Traders, hellbreed, rogue Weres, scurf, Sorrows, Middle Way adepts . . . all the fun the nightside can come up with. Normally a hunter's job is just to act as a liaison between the paranormal community and the regular police, make sure everything stays under control.

Or, if not *under control*, then at least *reasonably orderly*. Which, as a definition, allows for anything between "no bodies in the street" to "just short of actual chaos."

Hey, you've got to be flexible.

Sometimes—often enough—it's our job to find people that have been taken by the things that go bump in the night. When I say "find" I mean their bodies, because humans don't live too long on the nightside unless they're hunters. More often than not our mission is vengeance, to restore the unsteady balance between the denizens of the dark and regular oblivious people.

To make a statement and keep the things creeping in the dark just there—creeping, instead of swaggering.

And also more often than not, we lay someone's soul to rest if killing them is just the beginning.

We work pretty closely with the regular police, mostly because freelance hunters don't last long enough to have a career. Even the FBI has its Martindale Squad, hunters and Weres working on nightside fun and games at the national and cross-state level. It's whispered that the CIA and NSA have their own divisions of hunters too, but I don't know about that.

For a hunter like me, the support given by the regular cops and DA's office is critical. It is, after all, law enforcement we're doing. Even if it is a little unconventional.

Okay. A *lot* unconventional.

The baby I unloaded at Sisters of Mercy downtown, the granite Jesus on the roof still glaring at the financial district. The hospital would find out who it belonged to, if at all possible. Avery came down to take possession of the prisoner, who was sweat-drenched, moaning with fear, and had pissed his already-none-too-clean pants.

I must have been wearing my mad face.

"Jesus Christ. Don't you ever sleep?" Avery's handsome, mournful look under its mop of dark curly hair was sleepy and uninterested until he peered through the porthole in the door. He brightened a little, his breath making a brief circle of mist spring up on the reinforced glass.

"I try not to sleep. It disturbs the circles I'm growing under my eyes. This naughty little boy just brushed with an *arkeus,* didn't get much." I leaned against the wall in the institutional hallway, listening to the sound of the man's hoarse weeping on the other side of the steel observation door. Sisters of Mercy is an old Catholic hospital, and like most old Catholic hospitals it has a room even the most terrifying nun won't enter.

A hunter's room. Or more precisely, a room for the holding of people needing an exorcism until a hunter or a regular exorcist can get to them.

A lot of hunters have trouble with exorcisms. They're perfectly simple; the trouble comes from the psychological cost of ripping things *out* of people. Some hunters who won't blanch at murdering a half-dozen Traders at once quaver at the prospect of a simple tear-the-thing-out-and-dispel-it. Maybe it's the screaming or the bleeding, though God knows there's enough of that in our regular work.

Mikhail hadn't been a quavery one, and I guess neither am I. Exorcisms are straight simple work and usually end up with the victim alive. I call that an easy job.

"A standard half-rip, then. Not even worth getting out of bed for." Avery stuffed his hands in his pockets, rocking up on his toes again to peer in the thick-barred window. I'd kept the Trader cuffed and dumped him in the middle of a consecrated circle scored into the crumbling concrete floor. Etheric energy running through the deep carved lines sparked, responding to the taint of hellbreed on the man's aura.

"He was about to hand a baby over to a hellbreed. Don't be too gentle." I peeled myself upright, the silver charms tinkling in my hair. "I've got to get over to the precinct house, Montaigne just buzzed me. Maybe I'll bring in another one for you tonight."

Avery made a face, still peering in at the Trader.

"Jesus. A baby? And shouldn't you be going home? This is the fourth one you've brought in this week."

Who's keeping track? Traders *had* been cropping up with alarming regularity, though. I snorted, my fingers checking each knife-hilt. "Home? What's that? Duty calls."

"You gonna come out for a beer with me on Saturday?"

"You bet." I'd rescheduled twice with him so far, each time because of a Trader. People were making bargains with hellbreed left and right these days. "If I'm not hanging out on a rooftop waiting for a fucking *arkeus* to show up, I'll be there."

He came back down onto his heels, twitching his corduroy jacket a little to get it to hang straight over the bulge of his police-issue sidearm. "You should really slack off a bit, Kiss. You're beginning to look a little . . ."

Yeah. Slack off. Sure. "Be careful." I turned on my heel. "See you Saturday."

"I mean it, Kismet. You should get some rest."

If I took a piña colada by the pool, God knows what would boil up on the streets. "When the hellbreed slow down, so will I. Happy trails, Ave."

He mumbled a goodbye, bending to dig in the little black bag sitting obediently by his feet. He was the official police exorcist, handling most of the Traders I brought in unless there was something really unusual about them. He only really seemed to come alive during a difficult exorcism, the rest of the time moving sleepily through the world with a slow smile that got him a great deal of female attention. Despite that, not a lot of women stayed.

Probably because he worked the night shift tearing the bargains out of Traders or Possessors out of morbidly religious victims. Women don't like it when their man spends his nights somewhere else, even if it is with screaming Hell-tainted sickos instead of other women.

I hit the door at the end of the hall, allowing myself a single nosewrinkle at the stinging scent of disinfectant and human pain in the air. The scar burned, my ears cringing from the slightest noise and the fluorescent lights hurting my eyes. I needed to find a better way to cover it up, and quick.

It's not every hunter who has a hellbreed mark on her wrist, after all. A hard knotted scar, in the shape of a pair of lips puckered up and pressed against the underside of my right arm, into the softest part above the pulse.

Two days until my next scheduled visit. And there was the iron rack to think about, and the way Perry screamed when I started with the razors.

My mouth suddenly went dry and I put my head down, lengthening my stride. I'm not tall, but I have good long legs and I was used to trotting to keep up with Mikhail, who didn't seem to walk as much as glide between one fight and the next.

Stop thinking about Mikhail. I made it to the exit and plunged into the cold, weary night again, hunching my shoulders, the silver tinkling in my hair.

3

The precinct house on Alameda wasn't very active tonight. I nodded to the officer on duty, a tall rangy rookie who paled and looked down at his reports instead of nodding back. I placed his face with an absent mental effort—yes, he'd been in the last class I'd conducted. The one where I told each batch of shiny new faces about the nightside, and how and when to contact their local hunter.

Or as Detective Carper calls it, "Puking Your Guts Out While Kiss Talks." Each desk has a wastebasket sitting next to it during that class, and the janitor is busy those days. Still, few of the rookies leave the force after that little graduation ceremony. The nondisclosure clauses they sign are very rarely breached.

Most humans don't *want* to know about the nightside, and they unconsciously collude in making a hunter's secrecy easy.

I don't blame them. Some days even hunters don't want to think about what they do for a living.

Montaigne, his dark hair rumpled, was in a pair of blue-striped pajama pants. He wore a button-up and suit jacket over them, and palmed a handful of Tums as I came into his office, his bleary dark eyes rising to meet mine. He didn't flinch at my mismatched eyes—one blue, one brown—but I noticed he wore slippers instead of his usual polished wingtips. His ankles were bare.

Oh, God. I halted just inside his door, resting my right hand on the whip-handle. *This looks bad.* "Hi, Monty. Sorry I'm late, I had to drop off a Trader. What's up?"

"Jill." His cheeks were actually cheesy-pale. "There's something I need you to take a look at."

As usual, he sounded like he didn't quite believe he was asking a woman half his size for help. I barely come up to Monty's shoulder, but even if I gave him an Uzi and a little help he'd still be no match for me. Still, he'd never doubted my ability, once Mikhail introduced me as his apprentice.

We're back to Mischa again. Dammit, Jill, focus. "Animal, vegetable, mineral?"

"Homicide." Most of the time, that was the case. Monty ran his hand back through his hair again. It vigorously protested this treatment, becoming even more ruffled.

"How many bodies?" I was past uneasy and heading into full-blown disturbed. The charms in my hair tinkled, rubbing against each other. I realized I was slumping and snapped up to stand straight, dispelling the urge to yawn. I would be up to greet the dawn again and probably go all day, too. If I had to.

"Five."

A respectable number. But you're just calling me in now? "How fresh?"

"Two hours. I'm due at the morgue as soon as you show up, Stanton's going to do the dicing." Montaigne's jaw set. I began to get a bad feeling, hearing the way his heart was pounding, ticking off time. He reeked of fear, not just the usual uneasiness of facing me down and being reminded of the nightside. Monty had decided he didn't want to know about anything other than when to call me, which made him wiser than most.

"Come on, Monty. Drop the other shoe." I folded my arms. "Five bodies? *Found* two hours ago, or—"

"Killed two hours ago, Kiss. And they're all cops."

4

The morgue's chemical reek and fluorescent glare closed around me, and I was glad for the weight of my heavy leather coat. No matter how many autopsies I attend, the cold always seems to linger.

Still, I'll take an autopsy over a scene any day. The dispassionate light and medical terminology helps distance the ordinary horror of death a little bit. Just a little, just enough.

Sometimes.

Stanton was whey-faced too, wheezing asthmatically as he shuffled down the corridor behind us, his white coat flapping from his scarecrow-thin shoulders. His hair stuck up in birdlike tufts as well, and he was fighting a miserable cold. "It looks weird, Kismet." His nose was so stuffed the sentence came out mangled. *Ith lookth weird, Kithmet.*

"How weird?" *Am I going to have to kill them again? Please don't let it be scurf, or an Assyrian demon. I'm too tired for that shit.* "And if it looks this weird, why weren't the bodies left onsite for me? You all know the rules."

"They're *cops*." Montaigne hurried to keep up, his slippers shuffling. I kept lengthening my stride to keep him slightly behind me, just in case. "We couldn't leave 'em out there in the middle of the freeway."

"Freeway?" *This just keeps getting better and better.* "Take it from the top and give me a vowel, Montaigne."

The corridor was thankfully deserted, stretching through infinity to a pair of swinging doors at the end. Stanton's shoes squeaked against the flooring. He'd put on sneakers from two different pairs, as well as two different colors of socks—acid green and dark blue. Whatever had happened, both Monty and Stan had been dragged out of bed in a hell of a hurry.

Of course, matching his shoes wasn't really something Stan was too concerned about. Geniuses are like that.

"A pair of traffic cops reported something odd and called for backup at about 0200. The backup got there and reported seeing the first squad car sitting on the side of the road. After that, no communication. Dispatch kept trying to raise both of them, got no response. So another black and white goes out. By this time they called me, and I got in about 0300. The third fucking car had a rookie in it; for some reason the vet had the rookie stay in the car and went to go look for the others. Everyone was converging at that point, looked like a real cluster-fuck in progress." Montaigne stopped for a breath, his pulse thundering audibly, and dropped behind me. I slowed a little. "Four other cars got there at once and found the rookie bleeding quarts. Something had opened up the car like a soda can and dragged him out. He's at Luz General in trauma and last I heard it wasn't looking good. The other five—the first two teams and the vet—are all in picces."

Pieces? The scar was hard and throbbing against my skin, burrowing in. It never got any deeper, but the uncomfortable wondering of what it would be like if it ever *did* hit bone often showed up in the middle of long sleepless stakeouts, keeping me company along with Mikhail's ghost.

"Pieces?" I sounded only mildly curious. I couldn't make any sort of guess until I'd seen the evidence, and maybe not even then. A hunter is trained thoroughly not to make any conjectures in the initial stages. You can blind yourself pretty quickly by starting out with the wrong assumption.

A hunter blinded by assumption doesn't live long.

"Yeah, *pieces.* Whatever killed them tossed them out on the Drag like garbage. In pieces. Bleeding pieces." Montaigne's voice dropped.

We reached the swinging door, and I stopped short, forcing the other two to skid to a halt. "Before or after it carved the rookie up?"

An acrid stink of fear wafted out from Montaigne as he and Stan paused, following procedure now. They shouldn't have brought the bodies in until I'd been able to make sure they were truly dead and not just incubating something.

Monty reached across his wide chest, touched his sidearm, clasped in its holster under his armpit. "We don't know."

Jesus Christ. I took a deep breath, motioned them

both back. "All right, boys. Let big bad Kismet go in and see what the monster left us."

Montaigne actually flinched, but he understood. It sounds brutal and callous, but a hunter learns mighty quick to take the gallows humor where she finds it. Just like a cop.

It's the only way to keep from suicide or weeping, and sometimes it doesn't work. That's when you start drinking, or getting some random sex.

See what I mean?

I came through low and sweeping with both guns as the swinging doors banged against the walls on either side. Nothing but the glare and hard tiled floor of a ghastly-lit body bay, each table now full. It had been a busy night in Santa Luz. The five bags on the left-hand side were all shapeless, looking wrong even through heavy vinyl. The bodies on the right were bagged and normal, if there is any such thing as a *normal* dead body.

It used to bother me that each bag was a life, the sum of someone's breathing and walking around carrying a soul. Then the things that bothered me were details. Hair left crusted with blood, a missing earring, a bruise that had half-healed and would never fade now, or—worst of all—the smaller bags.

The ones for children.

I took a deep breath and smelled something I didn't expect—the sweet brackish rotting of hellbreed, added to another smell I hadn't expected. A dry smell, blazing with heat and spoiled musk, like matted fur and unhealthy dandruff-clotted skin. My nose wrinkled. I took another deep whiff, sniffing all the way down to the bottom of my lungs and examining the bags with both eyes. My smart eye, the blue one, saw no stirring or unevenness hovering in the ether over the bodies. My dumb eye, the brown one, ticked over their contours and returned a few impressions I wasn't sure I liked.

"Clear," I called, and holstered my guns. Montaigne's gusty sigh of relief preceded him through the door.

"Are you staying for the slicing, Jill?" Stan sniffed, and his bleary gaze skittered away from my breasts, roved over the five bodies on the right-hand side, and came back up to touch my face, uncertain.

Five autopsies take a lot of time. "I'll take a look, but I'll leave the deli work to you and Monty. I'll need the report. This is one of mine."

Stan's face fell. So did Monty's. They both looked sallow, and it wasn't just the fluorescents.

"Christ." Monty didn't quite reel, but he did take a step to one side, like a bull pawing the grass, uncertain what to charge. "What the fuck is it?"

"Don't know yet." That was the truth. "I'll go by the scene, see if I can pick up a trail. From what you're telling me, it either got what it wanted or was scared off by the black and whites. I'm guessing they didn't come in silently."

He rolled his eyes as Stan rocked back on his heels, stuffing his hands in his lab coat pockets and eyeing both of us. "Suppose you can't tell me anything useful."

Not yet. I haven't even looked at the bodies. "This is hunter's work, Monty. How much do you want me to tell you?"

Monty shook his head fiercely. If he could have clapped his hands over his ears like a five-year-old, he might have tried to do so.

Wise man.

"I'll take a look," I repeated, "and then I'll hit the street and try to find a trail. Nobody gets away with killing our brave blue boys in my city, gentlemen. Stan?"

He shrugged his thin shoulders, the pens in his breast pocket clicking against each other. "Be my guest."

He very pointedly didn't offer to unzip the bags for me, or caution me not to destroy any evidence. I couldn't even feel triumphant. Maybe it was just his cold.

I set my back teeth, the charms in my hair tinkling against each other, and paced cautiously up to the first body bag. Nothing stirred, and none of my senses quivered. I touched the zipper and let out a soft breath, glad the two men were behind me.

I pulled the zipper down. I have never figured out if it's easier to do it in one quick swipe, like tearing off a Band-Aid, or slowly, giving yourself time to adjust.

I usually go with the quick tear. Call it a personality quirk.

The body had been savaged, great chunks torn out. The face had been taken off, and his short cop-buzz haircut had beads of dried blood sticking to its bristly ends. The only thing left intact was the curve of a jaw, slightly fuzzed with stubble. He hadn't shaved, this man.

"That one's Sanders." Monty shifted his weight, his slippers squeaking a little against the tile. "About forty-five. Retiring next month, early."

A lifer. And before my time. Now he'd never retire. I drew the zipper down more, studying the mass of meat. His feet were stacked neatly between his knees, and his right arm was missing. The ribs were snapped, and the smell boiled up into my nose and down into my stomach, turning into sourness.

That's hellbreed, and something else. Something I should know. A reek like that is distinctive, and I should be up on it, dammit. Are we looking at a hellbreed working in concert with something else? They're not like that, most of them are jealous fucks. Still, it's possible. But nothing a hellbreed can control smells like this. The shudder bolted down my spine. I drew the zipper up, went to the next one.

"Kincaid," Monty supplied. "Twenty-eight. Good solid cop."

I nodded, pulled the zipper down in one swipe.

This one had a face. A round, blond, good-natured, blood-speckled face. I swallowed hard. The rags of his uniform couldn't hide the massive damage done to this body either—the purple of the torn esophagus, white bits of bone, a flicker of cervical vertebra peering up at me. His throat had been torn out and his viscera scattered. The bathroom stink of cut bowel flooded the chilly air. Both his femurs were snapped.

Marlow, the third, had been savaged. He'd been the driver in the first traffic unit, and whatever had attacked him had plenty of time to do its work. There was barely enough left to be recognizable as human.

The fourth—Anderson, Marlow's partner—was the worst. His arm had been torn off, something exerting terrific force to break the humerus just below the shoulder. The force had to have been applied at an angle for the bone to yield before the shoulder dislocated. His other limbs hung by strips of meat. *All* of them. And his head.

There wasn't enough of any of them left for an open-casket service.

As always, the shudder passed and the bodies became a puzzle. Where did this piece go, where did that piece go?

Then I would catch myself, horrified. These were *human beings.* Each one of them had gotten up out of bed this morning expecting to see sundown. Nobody is ever really *prepared* to die, no matter what you see in movies or read in fairytales.

My stomach churned, a hole of heat opening right behind my breastbone. Marty's Tums were starting to look pretty good. He bought them by the case, he wouldn't miss a few hundred.

I zipped Anderson's bag back up. Turned to find both Stan and Marty staring at me. "I'll drop in later for the files." My eyes burned, stinging, from disinfectant married to the smell of death. "What *exactly* did the first on-site traffic unit report?"

"Just 'something weird.' There wasn't a code for it." Monty's paleness had long since passed from cheese to paper. "Jill?"

"I don't know yet, Monty. Give me a little time to work this thing. Have traffic units take precautions; if it's weird and there's not a code, *don't stop.* Tell the beat cops too—they're vulnerable. If they see *anything* weird, they're to report so I can get a pattern of movement, but they are not to pursue. Got it?"

He nodded. "Do you have an idea, at least? I don't want to know," he added hurriedly. "But . . ."

But you feel better when the hunter at least has an idea. I know, Monty. I know. I could have given a comforting lie. "No." I looked at the bodies, lying slumped under their rubber blankets. All safe and snug, never having to worry about the job or the cold winter again.

Bile rose in my throat. "No. But I'm going to find out."

Because whatever this is smells like hellbreed and rips things up like no hellbreed should. The claw shape is strange. If I didn't know better I'd think it was a Were. But no Were, even a rogue, would go near anything hellbreed.

Great.

5

False dawn gathered gray in the east, veils of fog from the river reaching up like fat white fingers as I gunned the engine. I winced as my orange Impala's full-throated purr took on a subtle knocking. *Need to get that fixed. Should change the oil soon too.*

The interstate—or the Drag, if you're a local—comes up out of the well of the city in slight curves north through Ridgefield toward the capital, striking for the heart of desert and sagebrush once it's out of the low-lying area watered by the river. Coming down into the city it veers through suburbs, taking advantage of the high ground and flying over deep gullies and concrete washes built to siphon off flash floods. Once it hits the actual city limits it becomes three lanes in either direction, jammed during rush hour and perfect for illegal races once normal people are in bed.

Just south of downtown there's a stretch with hills on either side, thick with trees and trashwood, the green belt going up to chain-link fences facing the blank backs of businesses and warehouses. The scene was still crawling with forensic techs, and when I parked at the periphery a thin, nervous traffic cop came bustling up to tell me to move along—and retreated as I rose out of the Impala, meeting his eyes and keeping my silence. He recognized me, of course.

They all do.

I've heard they have a pool on where I'm going to show up and when, and the betting is fierce; there is a whole arcane system of verifying sightings left over from Mikhail's tenure. Hunter sightings are comforting for them; lets them know I'm still on the job.

It's when I disappear for a while that they get nervous.

Two lanes of southbound traffic were blocked off, and traffic was extremely light. Still, the infrequent cars were slowing down to gawk, and the scene was being trampled.

I couldn't blame them. Cops never like to lose one of their own. Most of them were observing a respectful silence. Quite a few of them looked like they'd been rousted from bed, too. I saw Sullivan, his red hair catching fire on top of his lanky frame as the sun began its work in earnest. His partner, a short motherly woman in a sweater-coat and knit leggings, stood beside him staring at one of the long garish streaks of wetness on the road. The streaks everyone was hypnotized by.

Blood doesn't dry as quickly as everyone thinks, even out here at the edge of the desert. It stays tacky-wet for a long time before it turns into a crust. A flat iron tang rose to my nose, like a banner through the stew of humans

milling around and the sharp dual stink of hellbreed and
something else, something I'd never smelled before.

*Mikhail would have mentioned something like this if
he'd ever come across it, wouldn't he?* I caught myself.
Concentrate on the job. Jesus, you're getting punchy.

Too bad I wasn't going to get any rest anytime soon.

I threaded my way through the milling crowd. As fast
as people arrived others left, to go back to work or home
after paying their respects. It was eerily quiet, and the
scar throbbed on my wrist, tension and frustration in the
air plucking at it. *Got to cover that goddamn thing up.*

Word of my appearance spread quickly, a murmur
through the crowd. Foster, his sleek dark hair pulled back
in a ponytail, was the only one brave enough to approach.
Of course, he was my Forensics liaison this month since
Pepper was out on maternity leave. He ducked carefully
under the yellow tape keeping everyone back—in this
crowd, there was no shoving. The mannerly silence was
almost as eerie as the palpable grief.

"Hey, Jill." Dark circles bloomed under Foster's blue
eyes, and the silver stud in his right ear glittered. "How
you?"

I don't often use the Forensics liaison; most hunters
don't. We work most closely with Homicide detectives
and next with Vice; they do the grunt work in getting
files ready. Most of the time a hunt goes so quickly we
don't have time for that type of legwork, and we don't
want the human law enforcement getting close to the
nightside anyway. They're our eyes and ears, since a
hunter can't be everywhere at once.

Nobody wants their eyes catching flak.

"Hi, Mike. Monty called me in." I pitched my voice

low, my hands thrust deep in my coat pockets. Leather creaked as I shifted. "What do we have?"

He was pale under the even caramel of his skin. "A total goddamn mess, that's what. Five goddamn bodies and that rookie bleeding all over everything. The main scene is up in the woods, there." He pointed to the ordered commotion on the hillside. "They didn't get more than twenty feet before something leapt on 'em. Just like shooting fish in a fucking barrel."

I winced at the mental image. And why would cops get out of their cars and pursue something up a hillside? "Any body parts you can't find?"

He shrugged. "Too soon to tell. Come up the hill. If Monty hadn't called you I would've. This is grade-A weirdness, just your type."

"I hate to be pigeonholed." I followed him, skirting the three traffic units parked in standard pattern on the shoulder, inside the cordon of yellow tape. Their lights still revolved, running off the batteries.

The last car in line had been shredded, its windshield broken and the roof ripped open, jagged metal edges exploding. Bits of broken colored plastic and glass from the lights were smashed to the side.

Christ. My blue eye didn't see any sparking and smoking of etheric energy, though the whole scene reeked of hellbreed. They are stronger and faster than humans, but a 'breed that could do something like this without sorcerous help . . .

What the hell is this?

The rapidly lightening sky triggered another idea. I glanced overhead. No circling copters yet. "The press?"

"Captain Bolton's putting together a release about

a car bomb or something. We've been able to keep the goddamn vultures quiet so far, but it's only a matter of time." Foster snorted, as if he wanted to spit but couldn't bring himself to do so. The two wide lanes of pavement were streaked and spattered with gore.

I was surprised the vultures hadn't scented it yet. *Last thing we need is footage of this getting out.* We crossed the ditch, me in a single leap and Mike over a piece of plywood someone had laid down, and plunged uphill into the bushes. The sharp smell of sage and pine stung my nose, mixed with the belching tang of death and that horrible stink of hellbreed and something else.

Dry fur. Dandruff clotted in drifts. Desiccated, exhaled sickness, as if a dog had crept into a hole to die.

What is that? I wished I could find something to cover the scar up. Preternaturally acute senses are useful, but it *stank.*

There was a clearing ringed with pine trees, their bark tinder-dry and needles crunching underfoot. Silence broken only by the shuffling of the techs' feet and occasional muttered directions. Flashes popped, taking merciless pictures, drenching the scene in brief shutter-clicks of light.

There was so much blood. I've seen plenty of butchery, but this was . . . The stench of a battlefield hung over the small clearing, cut bowel and wet red iron, as well as the heatless fume of violence. The smell of hellbreed and *something else* was so deep and thunderous my eyes watered.

The spindly tree trunks were shredded, and I stopped to examine the deep furrows carved in them. They were all vertical, and my eyes caught a thin reddish glint.

"What the hell?" I leaned closer, examining the long strands. Red-gold, and with a springy curl unlike anything I'd seen. It was all over, in the scratched furrows and rough bark. "Mike?"

"What, that shit? Hair. We don't know if it's human or animal yet."

"Where is it? All over?"

"All over. On the . . . the victims too." His voice didn't break, but it was close. "There's even some out on the road, in the blood. Patches of it."

Weird. "What about the scratches?"

"Just on the trees around this clearing."

"Huh." I thought about this, circling the clearing as Mike peeled off to exchange low words with a woman from the medical examiner's office, her dark hair pulled back in a sloppy ponytail. I took care not to disturb the techs at their work, and they took care not to get in my way. We're all happier that way.

You'd think a hunter wouldn't have to worry about evidentiary procedure and the like, but it always pays not to piss off the techs. And you never can tell when something small and insignificant they find is going to turn a whole case on its head, or spin it so you can see the pattern behind the events.

The stench was deep and dark enough I had trouble finding a trail. My nose stung and my eyes prickled with tears. One slid hot down my cheek and I palmed it away, silver chiming in my hair. The creaking of my boots and coat was very loud in the predawn hush.

I had unusual difficulty making a coherent pattern out of the scuffed and blood-soaked dirt. The chaos must have been intense at night with nothing but handheld flashlights—not even the current illumination of false dawn and the portable floodlights at the periphery of the clearing, mixing a throat-coating wash of diesel into the equation. I finally gave up on trying to reconstruct the fight. There simply wasn't enough on the hard-packed dirt scattered with pine needles.

For a moment I imagined being out here in the dark, something chasing me and nothing but a human's reflexes and one police-issue Glock to fight it off with, and my skin chilled.

I finally zeroed in on a usable trail, but it was a bust. The scent led away from the scene at a sharp angle, back down to the cars; I followed. Then I picked it up again at the edge of yellow tape down on the freeway, and pursued it across the open lane and the meridian before it vanished into thin air. One moment, nose-watering stink, the next, nothing but the smell of damp wiry grass in sandy soil and the scent of morning.

Dammit. If it's hellbreed it might be able to mask. A hellbreed and something working in concert? What would work with one of them? Even their own kind don't trust them.

Still, that's what the evidence points to. Hellbreed plus something else. In other words, a big fucking problem.

I let out a sharp frustrated breath. Traffic was beginning to pick up, and dawn was well under way. I heard the distinctive thrupping of a chopper and looked up. Channel Twelve had arrived.

Dammit.

6

My warehouse smelled like dust and there was nothing in the fridge except a takeout container of fuzzy green something that had once, I think, been chicken chow mein. I pushed the fridge door shut and leaned my forehead against its cool enamel for a moment, inhaling.

There was nothing I could do just now. When dusk hit I'd start canvassing the city. Anything that smelled that bad was leaving a trail, and that taint of hellbreed would give me a place to start. If any of Hell's citizens were developing a taste for cop, someone would know *something*. I had just the place to start, too.

You know what this means. You're going to have to visit him early.

I pushed the thought away. Hauled myself up and away from the fridge. Eating could wait. I opened up the cabinet over the dishwasher and got out the bottle, poured myself a stiff jigger of Scotch, and downed it. Poured another, tipped it down my throat, and relished the brief sting.

It helped, a little.

Mikhail had left me the warehouse. Its walls creaked, each sound echoing and bouncing. Nothing could sneak up on me here, between the acoustics and the wide-open spaces. My bed was set out in the middle of its own room, well away from the walls. The sparring-space was clean, swept regularly. A long spear-shape under amber silk hummed on one wall, beside the other weapons, all racked neatly.

Mikhail's sword hung in its sheath, its clawed finials and long hilt with the open gap in the pommel reflecting golden light. The sheath glowed—worn, mellow leather—the sword drawing strength from the square of sunlight resting over it, metal vibrating with its subliminal song. The skylight above had turned fierce, an open eye letting down a blade of light.

I shuffled out of the kitchen, swiping halfheartedly at the piled dust on the counter with one hand. Across the living room and down the short hall into the bedroom, my feet making little shushing noises against hardwood. My coat hung over the single chair, and my bed—two mattresses and a pile of messy blankets—beckoned.

Maybe just a short nap, so I'm fresh for tonight. The phone sat next to the bed, the answering machine blinking its deadly red eye.

I touched "Play" as I sank down on the bed, wriggling until knife-hilts didn't poke so badly, burying my face in the pillow.

"Jill? It's Galina. I have some more copper that might work for your wrist. Come by anytime."

Will do. My arms and legs were heavy. So heavy. Sunlight is a hunter's friend, it means rest and relaxation. Bad things generally don't come out during the day. They wait for cover of darkness to sneak around and cause trouble.

"Jill. It's Monty. I've buzzed you, something's up. Come by."

Already did, Monty. I'm on the job. I closed my eyes, breathing into my pillow. The smell of dust and my home gathered close and warm around me. I sighed.

"Kismet." A bland, blank voice. My breath caught. "It would profit you to visit me. Come tomorrow, after dark, and bring your whip." A soft gurgling laugh drew fingers of ice up my spine.

He said more, but I stopped listening, shivering as I burrowed into the bed, stopping my ears with the pillow. The sound of his voice faded.

Goddammit, Perry. Calling me wasn't part of the deal. But I was tired. So bloody tired. I decided to leave it for a few hours. I'd get worked up about it when I woke up.

I tipped over the edge into sleep, the answering machine saying something else to me in a low male tone. I didn't hear it, just slid under the edge of the world without a murmur as day walked the sky above.

Five months' worth of training ended up with me face-down on the floor again, aching all over, battered and bruised, sweat dripping from my split ends. The blond dye had begun to work its way out of my hair, the constant workouts made me scrawnier than ever no matter how much he fed me, and my heart pounded so hard I thought I was going to pass out.

"Get up, milaya." *Pitiless, the accent weighting his words. "Or I will hit you again."*

He meant it, I already knew him enough to know that. I gasped in deep heaving breaths, my chest afire, staring at his bare hairy feet against the canvas. My arms were bars of leaden pain, my legs wet noodles. Still, when a man told you to do something, you did it.

Didn't you? Obedience wasn't optional, either in the place I'd been raised or during the years hooking for Val. It was a survival mechanism. One I cursed even as it stubbornly forced me to do what Mikhail told me, one more time.

Hate you, I thought, and buried the words as soon as they drifted across my consciousness. God would surely strike me down if I ever allowed myself to truly think it, wouldn't He?

He was a man, too.

I pushed myself up. My left arm trembled, shivers spilling through the muscle meat, before it dumped me back facedown on the canvas-covered mat. I tried again. My arm refused to hold me, rebelling, so I pushed myself up with the other one.

"Get up." His cane clove air, a silken swish; I didn't flinch. I'd learned enough not to flinch, no matter what he did.

"How?" I wasn't being fresh—I honestly didn't know. When your body starts giving out on you, what do you do?

I was stupid, then. I didn't know it was the mind that rules the flesh. What you truly will, the body will do. But that's not the kind of truth you learn walking Lucado Street, you know.

CRACK.

Right across the lower back, gauging it perfectly, the thin bamboo cane would sting like hell and leave a bruise but not damage me. Unfortunately, my legs now refused to work, and I let out a dry barking sob. I wanted to do what he wanted. I needed to do what he told me to—this was my only chance, my only ticket out.

It was my road away from Lucado and my pimp's empty eyes as he slumped choking over a coffee table, a neat hole in his chest and blood trickling from the corner of his mouth, the clock ticking, ticking, ticking on the wall.

I didn't ever want to visit that room again. I would do anything I had to, to keep walking away, keep locking that door.

Mikhail said he would find me a job and a place, some therapy, something. But anywhere I went that room would be waiting. It was all I knew, and I'd be back on the street again sooner or later.

Probably sooner. I was a damned soul anyway. Who cared what I did?

Nobody. Nobody except the man in the long coat who had plucked me out of the snow as I lay bleeding, the .22 clutched in my scraped, bruised fist.

Mikhail didn't want to train me, he didn't need the trouble. But I wanted to do what he did.

I wanted to make him proud of me.

Mikhail sighed. "Get up, little snake. Don't crawl." Heavy, the words slid between my pounding ears. He sounded sad.

I tried again. Made it up to my knees. Red spots danced in front of my eyes, turned black. My feet hit the mat, I was upright without quite knowing how I'd gotten there. My left arm hung useless, the hand nervelessly clutching a knife, and he moved in on me again.

I threw my arm up just in time. Swallowed a harsh bark of pain as the cane clipped my elbow. The knife skittered away across the mats, and my eyes flew to his face, my right hand coming up instinctively, just the way he'd shown me and made me practice. Exhaustion sang in my ears and blurred my eyes, he shifted his weight and I responded, my knees flexing as I dropped into a crouch, knife lifted along my right forearm and a grimace of effort peeling my lips back.

I was too slow and too late, and I waited for the bamboo cane to descend again, braced myself for the pain. Blinked, gasping again as my lungs informed me they weren't taking any more of this shit. My arms and legs seconded that emotion, with my heart pounding out its own agreement.

It was official. My entire corpse was in rebellion.

"Very good."

For a moment my brain struggled with the words. I thought he'd spoken in Russian, it was so unexpected. Sunlight poured through the room, dusk coming on but the last half-hour of direct light working its way in through skylights, dust dancing in each golden column. Sweat dripped stinging into my eyes. I stared up at his beaky nose, the brackets around his thin-lipped mouth, Mikhail's pale hair turning to layers of ice.

"Very good, milaya. Come."

He bent down to take the knife from me, and I was so far gone I almost didn't let him have it, shifting my

*weight back, bicep and triceps tensing involuntarily,
preparing for the slash.*

*My teacher froze. Wariness crossed his blue eyes, and
the world stopped.*

*"I—" I'm sorry, I began to say. The magic words.
Sometimes they would stave off a beating if I said
them quickly enough. If I was placatory enough, pliant
enough.*

*"Very good." A broad smile turned up the corners of
his thin mouth and made him almost handsome, even if
he was too old. "I think, there is more to the little snake
than meets the eye, eh? Now hand me knife, milaya, and
we shall find arnica for bruises. I think we go out for
dinner tonight."*

*I stared blankly at him for a long moment. Did he
mean it, or was he going to punish me?*

*He made a quick movement with his blunt, callused
fingers. He never hit me unless we were sparring, and
he always tended the cuts and bruises gently. So far he
hadn't laid a hand on me except to correct me when I
was holding a weapon, or to point out some flaw in my
movements.*

*Or, of course, to beat my ass in sparring. But he was
capable of more, wasn't he? He was really able to put the
hurt on someone, you could tell by the way he moved.*

*He was playing nice with me. For now, the hard cold
survivor whispered in the back of my head. I tried to
ignore her. She wasn't a good girl.*

*I reversed the knife. Already the movement felt natu-
ral instead of awkward. Offered him the hilt, watching,
waiting.*

He took it, and the blade vanished into a sheath. He

stretched, muscle moving under his red T-shirt, and held out his hand.

"Are you deaf? Come, your teacher is hungry. Hard work, training little snakes."

My fingers closed on his, and Mikhail hauled me to my feet, then clapped me on the shoulder. I almost went down again, my legs weak as a newborn colt's.

"Go clean up. We go out for dinner." The kindness in the words was almost as foreign as his accent. "Good work, little snake. You are worth keeping, I think."

It was the first time anyone had ever thought so, and my heart swelled four big sizes. I made it about three steps before I passed out from the strain.

I spent two days in bed recovering, and when I got up again, my training started in earnest.

7

$\mathcal{N}$ight rose from the alleys and bars, spreading its cloak from the east and swirling in every corner. No matter how tired I am, dusk always wakes me up like six shots of espresso and a bullet whizzing past. It's a hunter thing, I suppose. If we aren't night owls when we begin, training and hunting make us so before long.

I surfaced from the velvet blankness between dreams, slowly. All was as it should be, the warehouse creaking and sighing as the wind came up from the river like it does every sunset, smelling of chemical-laden water and heat. My eyes drifted open, finding a familiar patch of blank wall. A knife-hilt dug into my ribs, hard. I blinked.

Then I rolled out of bed, catching myself on toes and palms, and did the pushups. Just like every time I woke up. Press against the wooden floor, bare toes cold, shoulders burning. Up. Up. Up.

Like a wooden plank. Nice and straight. Mikhail's voice again, so familiar I barely noticed it.

When I finished the second set, it was time for the

sit-ups. Then I padded, yawning and scratching, out into the practice room. Mikhail's sword glittered in one last random reflection, dying sunlight jetting through a skylight to touch the hole in the hilt. The glitter was gone as soon as it happened, I hung the harness that held my knives and guns up on its peg. Yawned one more time, the silver charms in my hair shifting, as I settled, my feet hip-width apart, and found my center.

The fighting art of hunters is a hodgepodge. Name any martial art, and we've kiped a move or two. Savate, kung fu, plenty of judo, we do a lot of wrestling on the floor, actually. Escrima, karate, good old streetfight fisticuffs—which is mostly common sense and retraining the flinches out of you than anything else—t'ai chi . . . really, the list is endless and a hunter is always picking new things up. There's even a style of fighting Weres train their young with, relying on quickness and evasion, that Mikhail thought was good for me. It's like a dance, and several hunters take ballet for flexibility and balance. Every hunter accumulates a set of favorite moves that work well, but you always have to revisit even the ones you don't like.

You never know what will save your ass.

After a half-hour of katas, I grabbed a pair of knives from the rack on the wall and really went to work. Knife fighting is close and dirty, and it's my forte. I'm smaller than the average hunter, and even before the scar on my wrist I had quicker reflexes than most.

Women usually do.

Mikhail had to train nastiness into me, though, and the ruthless willingness to hurt. Without it, even the quickest reflexes won't save you.

Mikhail.

Get up. My knives clove the air, whistling, spinning around my fingers, elbow-strikes, smashing the face with the knee. *Get up,* milaya. *Or I will hit you again. Get up!*

My own helpless sobs echoed in my ears, from years and miles away. My body moved easily now, gracefully, forms as strict as a dance become muscle memory, instinctive now. That wasn't always the case. I had been gawky and helpless when he'd found me, a teenage girl more used to streetwalking than lunge-kicks. The first year of my training had been hell in more ways than one.

Step, kick, turn, take out the knee, upward slash, break the neck with a quick twist, stamp and turn. The blades gleamed in the dimness as the last light of day leached out of the skylights. Metal sang as I flung both knives, the solid *tchuk* as they met the scarred block of wood set across the practice room reassuring. "Not so bad," I whispered, then it was time for the heavy bag.

I started out easy, double and triple punches, working myself into a rhythm. I have to be careful; if you've got a hellbreed-strong fist, you have to hold back even when your heavy bag is reinforced. Elbow strike, knee, the rapid tattoo mixing with exhaled breath at the end of each blow.

Sweat dripped stinging into my eyes. Not because of the effort, but because I'd been dreaming again. Memory rose like a riptide, swallowing me whole.

Snow. Shivering, the cold nipping at fingers and toes, exposed knobs of my knees raw and aching. Taste of iron and slick tears at the back of my throat. The place where he'd hit me throbbed, a swallowing brand of fire, and the gun was heavy in my hand.

I'd done it. I had committed murder, and I'd taken Val's gun. Still, the thing I worried about most was the money. The thought that he'd cut me, hurt me, maybe mark my face if he found me now, wasn't eased in the slightest by the fact that I'd shot the motherfucker.

The clock was still ticking inside my head. Tick tock, tick tock.

A white Oldsmobile eased by, its windows down even in the blinding cold, and a beer bottle smashed on the pavement. They yelled, and my dry eyes barely blinked. The gun was on my right side, hidden by my thin cotton dress.

I had already killed. I had already committed the greatest sin possible, to crown all my other sins.

If the car slowed down, if they stopped, it would be the last time. The last time.

Split lip. I'd had a split lip and a damn-near dislocated shoulder, and a busted-up spleen—and those were only the lightest injuries. Mikhail told me later it was a wonder I'd been walking, he could smell the blood and hurt on me even across the street.

Punch, bag shudders, follow it up with elbow, lift the knee, move in low, the force on a punch has to come from the hip just like whip-work or it's useless.

Useless. Like I used to be.

The purring of the Oldsmobile's engine returned, grow-ing louder. I stopped, head hanging, fingers tightening on the cold metal. Men. All of them, men. The same type of men I'd been so close to, so many times, swallowing if I had to, spitting when I could, letting my body do things while the real part of me retreated into a little box—a box that grew smaller and smaller each time.

When it finally became too small, would I vanish?

I had already sailed off the edge of the world. Now I just had to take as many of them with me as I could before I was finally put down. I turned, eyes wide, headlights blinding me, gun lifting—and warm fingers clamped around my wrist.

No, *the tall white-haired man had said, another lan-guage blurring through the words, a song of a foreign accent.* Not tonight, little one.

Kick. Kick. Stamp down, both fists smacking the heavy bag. Fists blurring, low sound of effort through clenched teeth.

I struggled, but he was too strong, and I squeezed the trigger as the car eased past. The sound of the .22 was lost under a blare of the horn and catcalls, and he twisted the gun out of my hand, ignoring the car. I tried to punch him, he didn't seem to move but the punch went wide, and I spun aside, falling. My arm stretched, my injured shoulder screaming. He let go, and I landed in snow, my skin burning. I coughed, and a bright jet of blood smashed out through my teeth.

The last thing I felt was gentle fingers in my ragged, strawlike dyed-blonde hair. I tried to curse at him, hooked my fingers and tried to take off some of his skin. My broken nails scratched only air. I tried to scream, choking on blood.

He had watched me for a few moments, weighing me.

My fists thudded into the bag. I stopped. My ribs flickered as I took in deep heaving breaths. How had he seen anything valuable in that broken girl in the snow? And the gun had vanished; he never mentioned it afterward.

Had he guessed how desperate I'd been, and what I'd done with the goddamn gun before he'd seen me? Did he care? Monty never mentioned my police record. Then again, my name was different by the time he met me. *I* was different, all the way down to the bone. Sometimes I wondered if my fingerprints had changed.

I gave the heavy bag one last punch, listening as it swayed on its chain. The creaking was familiar, and echoed through the warehouse. My breathing evened out, and my eyes tracked across the wall. A long slim shape under a fall of amber silk, the crossbow and hunting bow, the mace and the wooden spear with its tassels rusty and clumped together, its tip gummed with black residue.

And Mikhail's sword, a faint glow running through the clawed finials, the empty space in the hilt watching me.

The carved ruby in the hollow of my throat warmed, responding. Air brushed my skin, the scar twitching as I noticed it again, the preternatural acuity of my senses almost normal now that I'd spent a while with it uncovered. I would have to visit the Monde Nuit early, both to gather information about whatever hellbreed was killing cops, and also to express my displeasure to Perry. He shouldn't be calling me.

It wasn't part of the deal.

Not tonight, little one. I had not known my teacher's voice then. I hadn't known it was the voice of salvation.

As if I *deserved* salvation, deserved to be plucked from the snow and given a new life.

I don't want to think about this. "Mikhail," I whispered. The whisper bounced back, taunted me. He was dead, choked on his own blood, betrayed by a viper in woman's clothing, and I was still here. I hadn't been able to save him.

All the training, all the striving, all the pain—and I still had not been able to save *him*.

The heavy bag stilled, its chain making a slow sound of metal under tension. I wanted to kick it again, listen to the familiar creaking, but I didn't. Instead, I turned on my heel and stalked for the door, grabbing my harness from its peg.

I needed a shower.

One thing about being a hunter—sometimes your night doesn't work out exactly as planned. All I wanted was a few drinks to brace me before I had to go into the Monde, so I headed toward Micky's on Mayfair Hill, among the gay nightclubs and high-priced fetish boutiques. Micky's is a quiet place, an all-night restaurant where trouble never starts—because not only is it the place where the gay community comes to canoodle over blintzes, beer, and specialty pancakes, it's also staffed with Weres. Pretty much any night you can find a few nightsiders drinking, or stuffing themselves with human food, or just sitting and having a cup of coffee under the pictures of old film stars watching from the walls.

If you're on the nightside and you're legal, you're welcome in Micky's. Even if you're not-so-legal you're welcome, as long as you pay your tab and don't start any trouble.

I was heading up Bolivar Street to the foot of Mayfair when something brushed against my consciousness, and I put the Impala into a bootlegger's turn, headed back and around the corner onto Eighteenth. Tires smoked and screeched; a horn blared behind me, and I zagged the Impala into a halfass parking spot in an alley and was out of the car in a flash, my senses dilating.

The reek of the thing I was hunting smashed through my nose, and I felt more than heard its footsteps like a brush against a drum. Moving fast, and moving *away.*

I bolted out into the street, plunged into an alley on the other side, and scaled the side of the building by tearing my way up the outside of the fire escape. Vaulted over the side of the roof and began to *run,* my coat flapping behind me.

The baked smell of daylight still simmered up from pavement and rooftop, but the stink cut right through it with a harsh serrated edge. I leapt, etheric force pulled through the suddenly blazing scar, and hit a tenement rooftop going full speed, barely rolling to shed a little momentum, glad once again that I wear leather pants. Denim can get shredded when you're going this fast.

I don't wear leather because it makes my ass look cute, you know.

Fuck this thing's quick, watch it Jill, cross street coming up, you can head it off if it keeps going in a straight line—

But of course it couldn't be that easy. I landed *hard* in the middle of Twenty-Ninth Street, the shock slamming up through my hips and shoulders as I ended up on one knee, concrete smoking and puffing up dust under the strain of my sudden application of force. Air screamed away from my body, my coat snapping like a flag in a hard breeze. Two blocks down, an indistinct quadruped shape—the streetlight had burned out—squeezed down into the road itself.

Oh, shit. Please don't tell me it did what I think it just did. But I was already moving, and lo and behold things were about to get interesting.

The son of a bitch had just gone down through a manhole. The manhole cover lay off to one side, dents in its surface I didn't have time to examine. I *also* didn't have time to drag it back so a car wouldn't break an axle in the hole. No, I just breathed an imprecation and leapt, dropping down through the hole with arms and legs pulled close, bracing myself for whatever waited at the bottom.

And hoping I didn't hit anything on the way down.

The resulting thud had a splash attached, liquid splattering up to paint the crumbling concrete walls, and a new and interesting smell of waste threatened to knock me off my feet. Mixed with the gagging stench of the thing I chased, it was a heady bouquet.

Well, at least if it stinks that bad I can track it. No

ambush waited for me down below. I finished sliding a knife from its sheath and noticed something strange.

The smell of the thing was *different*. It didn't reek of hellbreed, just purely of sickness and fur. The silver in my hair and against my throat didn't start to burn; Mikhail's apprentice-ring on my third left finger didn't prickle with heat.

No time for questions. The water was knee-high and I splashed through, automatically noting how deep I was—it'd been a hell of a fall. *Christ. It couldn't fall into a nice clean department store, it had to pick a goddamn storm drain. Smells like something's dead down here too. Lovely.*

Running. Breath coming harsh and tearing, the knife held reversed along my forearm, my coat snapping and popping like a guitar riff, the liquid turning even soupier as tunnels began to branch off. I followed the worst smell, my gag reflex triggered—I didn't have *time* to throw up. *Jesus. This is foul. Why doesn't it smell like hellbreed? My coat is never going to be the same.*

Branching tunnels. A left, a right, a soft left in an intersection of four ways—did this thing know where it was going? Was it running blind or luring me into something?

I hate this sort of thing. The sludge started getting deeper, and the tunnel slanted downhill. *I really hate this sort of thing.*

Covered in guck, stinking to high heaven—there *was* something dead in the water—I reached a wide, deep chamber with a cleaner smell. A faint green glow bounced off the water's oily surface and dappled the walls. Above, pipes tangled, and several different round openings led off in different directions.

For the second time, maddeningly, the smell just *quit* between one step and the next. I skidded to a stop in thigh-high water, throwing up a sheet of it, and cast about frantically, trying to catch the thread again. A distant clang, like something sharply striking a pipe, tightened every nerve in my body.

To top it all off, the charms in my hair shifted, tinkling, and the silver chain at my throat began to burn. Mikhail's ring heated up, too. The knife blurred back into its sheath even as my blue eye scanned under the surface of the world and found nothing.

The smell was *gone*.

Goddammit, I REALLY HATE this sort of thing.

I backed up a step or two, and there it was again—but it was fading under the onslaught of fresh water lapping into the chamber, a cold current mouthing my thighs. Breaking a trail with running water, a trick so old even normal humans do it.

But the ability to mask a scent so thoroughly was pure hellbreed. I didn't know of anything else that could do that so cleanly, like a scalpel slicing off a nerve.

And hellbreed meant *possible nasty surprise* lurking somewhere.

This would be a really good time to get out of the water, Jill. Unfortunately, there was nowhere to go but one of the pipe openings, and God alone knew what was in those.

My guns cleared leather in both hands, and I turned in a full circle, my eyes—smart and dumb—traveling over every nook and cranny. No use. Whoever it was, they were gone.

The heat drained from my silver. The scar on my wrist prickled, working in toward the bone, unhealthy heat spilling up my arm, jolting in my shoulder as I pulled force through it, worked into taut humming readiness.

"God*dam*mit." The word couldn't carry the weight of my frustration. I searched for others. "*Shit*. Shit*fuck*. Mother*fucking*cock*sucking fuck* on a cheese-coated *stick!*" My voice bounced and rippled off the water.

A slight sound, behind me.

I spun, water tearing up in a sleek wave as etheric force swirled with me, both guns trained on one particular pipe, big enough for something very nasty to fit in. My pulse smoothed out, quit its hammering, and I tasted copper on my tongue through the reek of rot coating the back of my nose.

A glimmer, down low. Green-blue and flat, like an animal's eyes at night. My fingers tightened on the trigger even as I sensed another presence and half turned, one gun locking onto the first target, the other locking onto the second. *Come out and play, shitheels, whoever you are.*

The second one spoke. "Jill?" A female voice, low and husky with a touch of purr behind it. "Don't shoot. I'm coming out with my hands loose. Dominic's with me."

What the hell?

Memory placed the voice. One gun lowered slightly. "Harp?"

Harper Smith slid out of the second pipe. My pulse

thundered in my ears as I twitched, amped on adrenaline and oh so close to pulling the trigger.

She's tall—Weres usually are, even females. She moved with the fluidity and precision of a cat Were, all slinking graze and laziness. Long dark hair pulled back in two thick braids, wide liquid dark eyes, and a mouth that always seemed just short of merriment below an aristocratic nose and wide high cheekbones, she was beautiful in the negligent way almost all Weres are. She hung for a moment full-length from a slimmer iron pipe, then curved to land on a larger one, her booted feet placed for maximum effect. Her battered canvas jacket flapped briefly, showing her sidearm, and the feathers braided into her hair fluttered as she cocked her head, examining me.

Her mate, Dominic, peered out of the same pipe she'd been in. "Hey, Kismet." His voice was lower, a bass purr, and his sandy-blond hair was as long as Harp's but pulled back and bound in a club with leather thongs. His eyes glittered briefly too, and I caught a flash of the straight line of his mouth before he withdrew a little, into shadow. "Put the iron away, willya?"

The Terrible Two of the Martindale Squad. What the hell is the FBI doing out here? And two Weres without a hunter . . . that means a Were problem. I promptly turned my back on them, both guns pointed at the first pipe. "Hey, Dom. What are you guys doing out here?" My fingers tightened on the triggers. "And is that your fucking friend? If it is, you'd better speak up *now* before I ventilate him."

"Easy, hunter." The third voice was male, low with an

edge of vibrating bass like Dominic's. "Don't make me take that gun away from you."

Oh, you did not *just say that to me.* "Come and try it, cheesecake. Weres don't scare me. Who the fuck are *you?*"

"Calm down, both of you!" Harp sounded annoyed. "Jill, he's one of ours. He's a tracker from out on the Brightwater Reservation. Saul, come out and introduce yourself. This is Mikhail's student."

I kept the guns trained as the Were moved cautiously forward. He was a long rangy man, his dark hair shoulder-length and left loose, dark eyes flicking down my body to where the water lapped at my thighs and coming back up again. He had the classic Were face—high cheekbones, red-brown skin, thick eyelashes, chiseled mouth.

He looked Native American, like most American Weres. Native American on the cover of a romance novel, that is, a really bodice-ripping one. Jeans and a hip-length leather jacket, a black T-shirt stretching over his chest. The healthy clean scent of Were mixed with the stink, and I was abruptly conscious of being dipped in fetid goo and wet almost clear through.

"Saul." He gave his name grudgingly. "Saul Dust-circle."

"Jill Kismet." I lowered my guns, holstered them both. Measured him for a long moment. *I am not going to say it's a pleasure.* Then I rounded back on Harp. "What the fuck is the Martindale Squad doing down in the drains in *my* city, Harp? *Without* contacting me, I might add?"

"Left you a message yesterday." Dominic eased forward a little more, crouching with easy grace inside the pipe mouth. He reached up, scratched his cheek with blunt delicate fingertips. "You been busy?"

"That's the goddamn understatement of the year." *I should have listened to messages this morning; I knew there was something I'd missed last night.* I let out a long breath. "Five cops attacked out on the Drag last night. Montaigne called me in. Something that smells goddamn awful, and has a habit of cloaking itself. I repeat, *why are you in my city?*"

I should have been a bit more polite, but my nerves were a little thinner than I liked. This disturbed me badly. Something that smelled that terrible should *not* be able to disappear like a hellbreed could. Plus, I was covered in guck, and they looked cool and imperturbable like Weres always do.

To top it all off, I'd sensed hellbreed, I *knew* I had. It just kept getting better.

"Easy, Jill." Harp spoke up, soft and calm. "We just blew into town a couple days ago, and had to wait for Saul. We've been trying to reach you."

She took a deep breath, and her eyes met mine. The other male Were—Saul—made a slight scuffing sound as he moved, and I quelled the urge to twitch. He came goddamn close to getting silverjacket lead in his flesh.

I suddenly had a very bad feeling.

Then Harp went and said just about the worst thing she could have. "We have a rogue Were."

8

Some days the worst part of the job is cleaning up. I tossed the damp towel in the hamper, buckled my harness on, and stalked out of the bathroom. My coat was dripping in the utility room, having been hosed off thoroughly, and I suspected I was never going to be able to get my boots clean again. So I was barefoot, in a fresh pair of leather pants and a *Jonathan Strange* T-shirt, the weight of the harness comforting against my shoulders and back.

I heard voices as I padded up the hall.

"This place is a sty."

It seemed Mr. Dustcircle didn't think much of my housekeeping. Weres are inherently domestic, and my empty fridge was probably scandalous to the country boy. If he was fresh off the Rez, he probably hadn't had much contact with hunters, either. Most Rez Weres take a dim view of humans, and hunters are only tolerated because they're good backup when the scurf start infesting again.

I almost shuddered. At least I was fairly sure we weren't dealing with carnivorous bits of contagion. I've never faced a scurf infestation myself. God willing, I never will.

"Don't get snitty." There was the tinkle of glass—Harp was probably getting herself a drink. "She's a good hunter. Mikhail Tolstoi trained her."

My heart twisted with pain, kept on beating.

"She stinks of hellbreed." Dustcircle didn't sound mollified. "And she's not one of us."

It shouldn't have annoyed me, but it did. I stepped out of the hall, my fingers falling away from a knife-hilt. "Will you shut him up, Harp? That country shit is getting on my nerves."

Harp stood at my breakfast bar, and Dustcircle stood in the kitchen, his hands loose at his sides. The female Were kept pouring Jack Daniel's, steadily, into one of four chunky glasses. No Were strategy session is without munchies unless the situation's dire, and JD was as close to food as I possessed unless you wanted to count the science experiment in the fridge.

"Dominic went to get some takeout." Harp's dark eyes rested on the glasses. "I wanted to ask you, Jill, could you put Saul up while he stays in town? I would, but we're at the Carlton on expense account, and the pencil-pushers in Accounting don't look kindly on such things."

I leaned against the living-room wall, folding my arms. I couldn't see Dustcircle's face; the kitchen cabinets hanging over the breakfast bar blocked my view. "Why can't he stay in the barrio?"

It was rude of me, but he'd just called my house a sty.

Which it probably was, to a Were. But at least I scrub my own toilets, and there was nothing rotting in the kitchen.

Well, except for the science experiment in the fridge.

"Because," Harp said steadily, finishing her pouring, "he doesn't have kin in the barrio, and because I don't want to worry about you while this is going on. This neatly solves both my problems."

Worry about me? What do you think I've been doing out here, holding hands and having bake sales? "Heaven knows I live to solve your problems, Harp. Quit fucking around. I don't take in boarders, especially ones who can't even insult me to my face. Stash him with Galina, that's what a Sanctuary's for." I restrained the urge to rub at my right wrist, wishing I'd had time to drop by Galina's and take a look at the new copper cuffs. I could *smell* the alcohol in the glasses, and I badly wanted a jolt.

"What, and have a rogue battering at her front door? She won't thank me for that, and even if it doesn't matter to her it'll endanger everyone who pops by. Besides, I want this kept quiet, and everybody and their mother goes to Galina's. Come on, Jill. He'll behave, I promise." Harp scooped up two of the glasses, and stalked over the bare wooden floor to hand me one. Her skin was warm, a Were's higher metabolism bleeding heat into the air. "Let's sit down, shall we?"

"Help yourself." I indicated my ugly-as-sin second-hand orange Naugahyde couch. "Come on, Harp. Spill. Even if it is a rogue Were, what the hell is the FBI doing in on it? Rogue Weres are the responsibility of regional territory holders in conjunction with hunters. The Norte Luz pride should be in on this."

Harp settled herself on the couch. I downed the respectable dollop she'd poured me, felt it burn all the way down, and stamped over to the counter to snag the bottle. Dustcircle eased around the corner of the breakfast bar, eyeing me disdainfully. He smelled faintly of cherry tobacco and cigarette smoke, and he was much larger than me, being a Were. His gaze met mine, flicked down my body again.

I loudly ignored him.

"Well?" I prompted, when the silence stretched a little too far. "Come *on*, Harp."

"The rogue has crossed state lines." She was choosing her words with care. "And his kills are . . . disturbing. Very disturbing."

You know, when you say disturbing, *I bet it means something totally different than when* I *say it. And neither definition is very comforting.* I had a bad feeling about all this. "Would it have anything to do with the way the trail keeps vanishing? Or with the hellbreed I keep smelling?"

"You'd know all about that, wouldn't you?" Dustcircle's tone was tight and furious. He didn't like being dismissed.

"You going to muzzle him, Harp?" I settled down cross-legged on the floor near the couch. "I'm not as patient as Mikhail when it comes to dealing with little boys who bark too much."

To give her credit, she didn't roll her eyes. "Jill made a bargain with one of the resident powers in town," Harp said quietly. "With Mikhail's support and approval, I might add. She's a good hunter, Saul. Either be a polite little kitten or shut the fuck up, will you? I would hate to have to call your mother."

"I'm not a kit, Harp." Most of the growl left his voice. He picked up one of the drinks, paced smoothly across the room, and settled down on the floor about six feet from me, facing the couch. There was no other piece of furniture in the living room except the lamps, big antique iron things that had stood in Mikhail's bedroom, once upon a time. "I apologize, hunter. I haven't slept much, and I'm impolite."

By Were codes of etiquette, that was a bare-throat submission. I stared at him for a good thirty seconds. The mellow shine of electric light in his hair was tinted with red. "Forgotten," I said finally. "And forgiven. Nice to meet you."

Which, by Were codes, was a magnanimous refusal to prove my dominance.

That earned me a startled glance, but I turned my gaze back to Harp, who wore a wide white-toothed smile. I touched the back of my right wrist, scrubbed at it with my fingers. Touching the scar wasn't a good time, so when I had it uncovered for a while I rubbed at the back of my wrist, a nervous tic I was helpless to stop. "Fine. But one nasty comment and he's out the door. I haven't been half-drowned in storm-drain shit tonight to take lip from a Were you can't babysit. Now start talking."

The warehouse creaked as the side door opened. I smelled food, and Were. Dominic made no attempt to keep quiet. Wise of him.

Harp knocked back her drink in one smooth motion. I poured myself another.

"It started out in Massachusetts—this rogue is ranging further than any I've ever seen. The kills look strange, very strange. About three-quarters of the kills are a regular rogue's—tracked from a resting-site, muscle meat gone, a high level of violence, souvenirs taken. The other quarter are . . . well, too savage to be a Were, blood for the hell of it and no muscle meat taken." She took a deep breath as Dominic padded into the room.

"Your plates still in the same place, Jill?" He sounded unwontedly cheerful. "That Thai place on Seventy-second is still open. Go figure."

I didn't know there was a Thai place on Seventy-second. Trust a Were to know where all the munchies are. "Everything's where it should be," I told him, leaning back braced on my hands. "Drop the other shoe, Harp."

She did. "He's killed two hunters already. Devon Blue in Boston, and Jean-François Roche in Louisiana. Saul's sister was running backup for Jean-François. Our rogue killed her. It was a hell of a fight, from what we can tell."

My stomach turned over hard. "Holy *shit.*" My eyes jagged over to Dustcircle, who was staring into his drink. Killing another Were's sister is a big deal. The only thing bigger is killing another Were's mother. It's one of the few completely taboo things among them.

"I'm sorry." My voice dropped. No wonder he was in a bad mood.

And Boston and Louisiana were too far apart for a regular rogue. They tend to stay in familiar territory, which makes them easier to track. Rogues are normally completely predictable, behavior-wise, at the mercy of instinct run amok. To have a rogue acting *un*predictably was bad, bad news.

Or it wasn't a rogue at all. But if Harp said it was . . .

Saul glanced up, and I thought I saw surprise in his dark gaze before Dominic came out with plates and chopsticks, carrying two large plastic bags as well. He must have bought one of everything on the menu. "Chowtime, boys and girls. Kiss, you need to eat. You look like you're trying to diet yourself to death."

"Don't call me that." I wrinkled my nose as chili pepper and coconut crawled up into my sinuses and made themselves at home. "You got everything four-stars again, didn't you."

"Live it up, baby." Dominic handed me a plate and a pair of wooden chopsticks. "We've got the files, and you might as well take a look at them. You know the city better than we do, and we'll need to start checking everywhere a rogue might go to ground."

I caught the look he flashed to Harp, and was suddenly sure there was more. "If it's a rogue Were, why is it acting unpredictably, and why does it smell like hellbreed?" *But only sometimes. Still, even "sometimes" is enough to give me nightmares.*

God knows I don't get nightmares easy anymore. I just dream about Mikhail.

It's anyone's guess which was worse.

"We don't know." Harp sounded cautious again. "We were hoping maybe you'd have an idea. Operations suggested bringing you in, and when the trail veered this way we thought we'd pick you up."

Aha. Suddenly more about this makes sense. I tapped my chopsticks against my plate, meditatively.

Silence, broken only by the rustling of plastic. Dominic plopped down on the wooden floor between me and Saul, and Harp slithered off the couch to sit with us, folding her long legs up with inhuman grace. Warm air swirled, touching my cheek—their skins throwing out heat like sidewalks on a summer day.

Shit. Sometimes I wish I couldn't hear what people aren't *saying.* I set my plate down, my skin going briefly cold. Laid the chopsticks across them. *They want to talk to Perry.* "No way, Harp. He'll eat you alive."

"We just want to ask some questions." Her eyes met mine.

"Dinner first," Dominic said. "Eat, then argue. Come on, Kiss."

"Hellbreed *don't like* Weres. And this one's different, he's not your average shiny-eyed weirdo." The chopsticks rattled as I shifted, my knee brushing the plate. "Give me what you want to ask him about, I'll take it in. I've got to go in there anyway, I might as well."

And the more business I have to handle, the more I can put off going in there to make my monthly payment. My skin chilled afresh, gooseflesh prickling up hard all along my back.

"We're curious about this hellbreed, Jill. It's a golden opportunity for the Squad to find out what's going on inside his little domain. We have half a dozen cases he might have his fingers in, and nobody can get close enough to even snap a picture of him."

No doubt. "That should tell you something." I poured another healthy cupful of JD, set the bottle down, and tossed the whole glass back. "Jesus Christ, Harp. Don't push this one. You know better, Mikhail would tell you the same thing. *Did* tell you the same goddamn thing."

Harp decided to push it. But carefully, her voice soft and uncertain. "Not even a meeting in a neutral place?"

Perry doesn't do neutral, sweetcheeks. "*No,* Harper. Not a chance." I shifted restlessly, and Dustcircle twitched. Dominic, a takeout container in his hand, studied me with lambent eyes. Brown feathers in Harp's hair stirred, and the warehouse echoed, little chuckles and sighs as my voice bounced back to me.

"I had to ask. Operations feels it's a priority." She dropped her eyes, looking at her plate.

Two submissions from as many Weres in under ten minutes. It was a record of sorts, but one I didn't feel good about setting. "You can tell that snake to slither back into his hole, I'm not taking you to see Perry. I can barely keep my own skin whole around him, and looking out for you is a distraction I *don't* need. You *know* how hellbreed feel about Weres." I poured myself another healthy dose of amber alcohol, knocked it back, and set the glass down with a small, precise click. Decided it was time for a subject change. "So we have a rogue ranging out of accustomed territories, a quarter of the kills not following a rogue's standard pattern, and the stink of hellbreed. A hellbreed manipulating a rogue Were, maybe?"

Dominic busied himself with dishing up the food. Harp settled into her seated posture, rubbing at her eyes as if tired. She looked so lovely and languid, it was hard to believe she could shift and tear an ordinary human to shreds in less than fifteen seconds.

Dustcircle piped up. "A rogue Were is hard to control."

Bingo. "Easier than a Were with his wits about him." I stared at my empty plate, the white circle with the cheap chopsticks bisecting it. "You said something about files, Harp?"

"Yeah." She accepted a filled plate from Dominic with a nod of thanks, one blonde braid dipping forward over her shoulder. The feathers were brown and stippled, hawk from the look of it; her tribe was allied with the Washington D.C. hawkflight. "But not until after we eat."

Good idea. My stomach rolled uneasily, but I put a bright face on it. "The night's young. I'll peek at the files and then you can start canvassing the barrio while I go through the hellbreed clubs. I want to find out what hellbreed's tangled up in this, or we're just shooting in the dark."

"A rogue should be predictable," Dustcircle muttered, as Dominic glorped some pad Thai onto his plate. "We've missed something. But regardless, we should hunt him first."

My temper all but snapped. "You've done a bang-up job of catching this *predictable* guy so far. And for your information, *Were,* I am the resident expert when it comes to hunting hellbreed."

"Is that why you smell like one?" Dustcircle nodded his thanks to Dominic, not bothering to glance at me.

Harp already gave you my bona fides, country boy. I counted to ten. It didn't work, so I counted again. Harp's hand paused halfway to her mouth, as if she wanted to clap it over her lips but couldn't quite make it there. Dominic, his chopsticks in midair, sighed wearily. Being mated to Harp must mean a whole lot of uncomfortable moments, and he was a smooth-it-over type of guy.

To top the whole damn unsatisfactory conversation, my pager buzzed against my hip, clipped to my belt. The damn thing was waterproof, which I alternately vilified and blessed. I unclipped and glanced at it, barely seeing the number. *Perfect. Just what I need.*

I got to my feet slowly, the floor creaking underneath me. "Duty calls." My voice sounded unnatural even to myself. "Harp?"

She made a small noise, as if the breath had been knocked out of her. "Jill."

"While I'm gone, will you teach the country boy some manners? My job is hard enough without assholes complicating it. I presume you have a copy of whatever file you want me to face Perry down with. Leave it here, lock up when you're done."

I turned on my heel and stalked away, the warehouse echoing and my teeth clenched so tight my jaw ached. They were silent. I was hungry. And my coat was still sopping-wet.

Great.

9

Avery clasped the bag of ice to his face. "Don't say a word," he groaned, leaning back in his chair. "Not one single fucking word, Kiss. I'm warning you."

I hunched my aching shoulders, bracing my elbows on my knees as I inhaled, exhaled, dangling the bottle of beer in my right hand. "I'm not saying anything, Avery." My wrist burned, I'd pulled a hell of a lot of etheric force through the scar. "I'm not even thinking it."

"Liar." His leg was tightly bandaged, his throat bruised, and the tiled hall echoed as he let out a gusty sigh. Here at the downtown jail, below the five stories that held the normal criminals overnight or during trials, this corridor terminated in three rooms, each with a circle scribed on the floor. Sometimes they were empty for two or three days at a time.

Then there were nights like tonight. Two exorcisms referred in by the two Catholic parishes, one by the local Methodist church, and another three dragged in by Eva and Benito, two-thirds of the regular exorcists in town responsible for doing straight rip-and-stuffs. Wallace was visiting his mother in Idaho, and on a busy night like this I could have strangled him, though he needed the vacation.

Regular exorcists shouldn't do more than two a night. It's draining psychic and physical work, and for anything out of the ordinary they were supposed to call me in. Avery had tried to take on his third exorcism of the night by himself, and I'd arrived just as the possessed— a meek little morbidly religious shut-in on Benton Avenue who was even now unconscious inside one of the holding cells for the night—did her level best to tear his eyes out after chewing his leg open and throttling him. She was lucky to still be alive, as I'd had to tear the Possessor out of her in a hell of a hurry and drag both her and Avery downtown for some medical attention.

Possessors are nasty little things, and once an exorcism gets referred it's almost a given that they've wormed their way into someone with weeks of effort, driving them crazy a little bit at a time. Most of the possessed have no memory of the whole time—big chunks of their life gone—maybe an unconscious reflex, the psyche shutting away the trauma of having a parasitical psychic rider. It's one of the biggest violations imaginable, your mind and soul not your own—and the fact that Possessors, the little worms, tend to prey on the religious and naive, not to mention the middle to upper-middle class, isn't much of a comfort. For once the poor aren't targeted by a species of hellbreed, but that was small reassurance at best.

Plus, Possessors find it easier to slide in while the ambient psychic temperature is fermenting-hot. Like right after one hunter passes away and a new one takes his place. All in all, big fun.

I took a long drag off the beer. It was ice-cold, filched from the small fridge under Avery's desk, the same desk I leaned my knee against as I eyed him. Technically you're not supposed to have alcohol anywhere near you on duty, but exceptions were sometimes made for exorcists.

You don't last long without a drink or two—or six—in this line of work.

Wrestling on the floor with a woman who was no doubt very nice and sweet when she didn't have a Possessor inside her just made a cold beer go down that much better. My shoulders ached, and she'd gotten her teeth in my throat, worrying at the band of the sterno-cleidomastoid muscle. If she'd been true hellbreed or even Trader, that might have given me a problem. But Possessors are the low end of the hell pool, I could handle five or six of them on a given night without getting tired like a regular exorcist. Still, more than one or two a night wasn't good for anyone involved.

"How you doing?" Avery's good eye blinked furiously, tears running down his scraped cheek from the stinging of ice against swelling tissue. "You look pissed."

No, what I am is tired. Though I just had a snotty-ass Were country boy run his mouth off about hellbreed at me. "New case."

"Heard about that." Avery shifted a little in his chair. The entire jail above us seemed to hold its breath. I cocked my head and took another long draft of cold beer.

"News travels fast."

"Five cops."

"Yeah." I sighed. *I don't even know if that rookie survived the night. No matter, if he wakes up and he's coherent Montaigne will buzz me.* "Christ, Avery. Jesus Christ."

"You'll get whoever it is." He lowered the ice, the plastic chair creaking as he shifted. "If something ever happened to me, you'd kill the bastard that did it."

You're right, Ave. I am the avenger, it's my job. But Jesus. "Let's hope that never happens. I'd hate to have to train your replacement just when I've gotten used to your silly punk ass."

He shrugged, one corner of his mouth lifting painfully. He would be bruised all up that side of his face tomorrow. "Hand me a beer, willya? And tell me what's really bothering you." A flash of his pale chest showed through his torn shirt, and the St. Anthony's medal glittered briefly on its silver chain. I opened the small fridge and passed over a fresh cold bottle, his skin briefly touching mine. The scar on my wrist throbbed. I heard moans and shuffles overhead in the holding cells, and a subliminal thrill ran under my skin.

Dawn. A hunter always feels it, the sun rising and the city settling into daytime geography.

Yet another night spent on the run. I opened my mouth, but my pager buzzed again. "Jesus *Christ*." I sighed, knocked back the rest of the bottle in a few long swallows. Avery let out a sharp little adrenaline-jag laugh, his dark hair sticking sweat-damp to his forehead. He smelled like a good hard workout on a clean human male, no taint of hell. No exotic corrupt smell of hellbreed.

Not like me.

"Why don't you get a cell phone?" He clasped the ice to his eye again, hissing out between his teeth. His other hand was occupied with the beer.

"As many times as I get dumped in water? Or shot? Or hit with levinbolts?" I shook my head. "Can't afford it. Pager works fine, and the buzz won't give me away when I'm playing snake-under-the-rock." I unclipped the pager, setting the empty bottle down. Avery's desk always looked about to disappear under a mound of paper, and he'd stuck slim candles into the bottle mouths, some burned down and others pristine.

Well, an exorcist usually ends up eccentric. It's the nature of the job. Eva paints and gilds hollowed-out chicken eggs. Benito likes hanging upside-down in a gravity rack, says it helps him sleep. And Wallace likes going out into the desert for jaunts with only a loincloth and a canteen for company.

The number on the pager blurred as I blinked at it. Then I let out a soft breath, my ribs squeezing down, and the sound caught in my throat became a low reedy whistle, as if I'd been punched hard and had to suck the air back in.

When I could talk again, I said, "Fuck."

"What's up?" Avery didn't sound very interested. He leaned back, his good eye closed, the ice clasped to his face.

"Got to go. It's past dawn, you should be all right for a while. Call if you need me." *Shut up, Jill. You had to go see him anyway.*

But he shouldn't be calling me, dammit. Christ. Why am I so upset?

It wasn't just the prospect of going into the Monde Nuit. I did that every month.

She stinks of hellbreed.

That was it. I smelled like hellbreed. Like the very things I fought. Usually I ignored the point successfully enough to function.

Thanks to a stinking country-boy Were, I now had to think about it.

I stood up. Avery waved his beer bottle, languidly. "Another parade of heart-stopping excitement, brought to you by the Santa Luz Exorcist Squad." The ice crackled as he shifted it against his face. "I'm going to go see Galina, have her fix this eye. Don't forget about Saturday."

"I'll see if I can squeeze it in," I tossed over my shoulder, settling my coat with a quick shrug. The whip brushed my thigh as I strode away, and the ruby warmed in the hollow of my throat.

I was grateful for that warmth. It crawled down inside me, and as I hit the stairs at the end of the hall—one exit and entry for any exorcist's lair, it works out better that way—I looked down at my left hand. The ring was there, silver still bound tight around my third finger. Mikhail's promise, Mikhail's mark, given to me before I even knew Perry existed.

I blew out between my lips as I swung up the stairs, my shoulders coming up and a welcome heat beginning behind my breastbone. It was anger, and I fed it with every last scrap of energy as I blew down another long hall and out the back door of the administrative section of the jail, into the cold, clear light of dawn.

10

I knelt in a back pew at Mary of the Immaculate Conception, my forehead against the hard wood of the seat in front of me. Candles flickered dimly, and despite the simmering heat of midmorning outside it was cool and quiet in here. My pager had stopped buzzing.

Get it together, Jill.

There was only one thing to do, and I was putting it off. I swallowed dryly, heard my throat click.

"Thou Who," I began, and heard Mikhail's voice next to mine as he taught me the prayer. "Thou Who hast . . ."

I couldn't say them, so the words unreeled in my head as I forced my shaking hands together in tight fists.

Thou Who hast given me to fight evil, protect me; keep me from harm. Grant me strength in battle, honor in living, and a swift clean death when my time comes. Cover me with Thy shield, and with my sword may Thy righteousness be brought to earth, to keep Thy children safe.

A tall order, even for God. In a fight between God and hellbreed, I would rather have a good stock of ammunition on my side.

That's blasphemy, Jill, no matter how much it helps. But you're damned anyway, aren't you. What does it matter?

I lifted my face. The crucifix over the altar was a gentle one, not like the twisted screaming monstrosities I've seen in some churches. This Christ looked almost tranquil, as if there had been no pain at all, as if death was a balm and not something to fight tooth and nail against.

Maybe that's what Mikhail saw in me. Fighting tooth and nail. Like a Were, tooth and nail. So I stink of hellbreed, do I? Well, it keeps the innocent safe. Or safer, at least.

That was the trouble with the prayer, Mikhail told me. Even if you only mouthed it, you ended up doing it. *Believing* in it.

Stupid, he would snort after a few shots of vodka. *They call us heroes. Idiots.*

But I didn't want to think about that. If I started brooding about how much I missed Mikhail, I might inadvertently give Perry an opening. And nobody wanted that except Perry himself.

I started again. "Thou Who," I whispered, my lips numb. "Thou Who . . ."

I could not frame the middle part of the prayer. There was only one part that mattered, anyway. I whispered it into my sweating hands, clasped together in prayer. "O my Lord God, do not forsake me when I face Hell's legions."

I've had enough of being forsaken, God. You think

you could cut me a little slack? Run, running, my brain like a rat in a cage.

You're not too tightly bolted right now, Jill. Maybe you should do something to take the edge off. But what?

I dropped my forehead down again and breathed in, smelling incense and wood and candle smoke, the particular mix that means *Catholic*. Get out your guilt and your rulers and your smell of wax and wine, and you had my childhood. Or at least the part of it that gave me the reflex of prayer.

As a hunter, I was barred from both Confession and Communion for the sin of murder repeated every night, not to mention trafficking with Hell's minions. But I could still pray, and I would, by special dispensation, be buried in hallowed ground if there was enough of me left to bury.

Unless I died contaminated. Or unless, like Mikhail, I wanted to go into Valhalla with flame licking my bones. *Mikhail.* The anger rose again, tattered and thread-bare, and I petted it, coaxed it, mulled over it to give myself strength. Rage was my best friend, for all I kept it a banked fire most of the time. You cannot fight effectively if your head's full of anger. You have to think *past* the rage, let it fill you and see the world in front of you as action and reaction, with your own path laid clear and shining in front of you, whether through a fight or to the door of a hellbreed nightclub.

Oh, fuck. Get going, Jill. You have shit to do and a rogue Were to catch. Get out there and kick some ass. You've done it every month since you made the bargain, sometimes twice, and you're still here. You smell of hell-breed and you're tired and your temper's a little frayed, but you're still here, goddammit. Now get up, and go twist Perry's arm until he gives up what you want.

And teach him to stop fucking with you. Be unpredictable.

I licked dry lips and pushed myself up. The hard wooden back of the pew slipped under my slick palms. My voice was a bare whisper, but it came. "O my Lord God, do not forsake me when I face Hell's legions. In Thy name and with Thy blessing, I go forth to cleanse the night."

Though it's more like midmorning. My bootheels clicked as I reached the end of the pew, genuflected, and turned my back on the altar. I dipped both hands in the holy water, lifted its coolness to my face, hissing out slightly as a thin tendril of it rolled over the scar with a tracer of acid fire. I wiped the holy water in my hair, smeared it over my shoulders, and took a deep breath.

Then I got going.

The Monde Nuit is a long low building, and it sits in a bruised depression of etheric energy. The silver on me warmed, responding to the contamination of hell-breed in the air. The parking lot was mostly paved, but the far edges were gravel, and a spindly, thorny edge of greenbelt looked sucked-dry, clinging to the edge of contagion. I left my Impala parked in the fire zone and headed for the door, eyeing the bouncer. This early in the day, there were only six cars in the lot, not counting mine. One was a low black limousine, its windows blind with privacy tinting, pristine despite the dust and haze of the day.

My coat flared on the edges of a hot afternoon wind. This close to the desert, up on the fringes of the valley the Rio Luz kept watered and kind-of-green, everything smelled of sand and heat. The whip tapped against my thigh and I kept my hands loose and easy. Touching a knife now would show nervousness. Weakness.

You *never* show a hellbreed any weakness. It's a cardinal law, not to be bent or broken like so many other laws.

The bouncer didn't stop me, though his was a face I hadn't seen before. He was a massive slab of muscle with a flat sheen to his eyes, and he didn't quite meet my gaze. His submachine gun, slung on a leather strap, was a flagrant violation.

Goddammit, Perry. You son of a bitch.

My heart stopped pounding by the time I palmed the doors open and saw the Monde's interior, vast and cavernous during the day, no shaft of sunlight piercing its gloom. Nightclubs always look saddest during the day, and even though the Monde pulsed with the glamour of Hell, it was still a broken sight at this particular hour, dappled bits of light sliding over the deserted dance floor, the tables all empty, and the electric lights on overhead. Two janitors—ancient, decrepit, broken things that might once have been Traders—shuffled aimlessly, pushing brooms.

The massive bar was off to the left, and as usual Riverson was there, his blind filmy eyes widening as he took me in. "Kismet." His tone was flat, and he reached behind himself for the bottle of vodka. "You're here."

Score one for you, blind man, stating the goddamn obvious. I kept the words behind my teeth.

Mikhail had brought me in here to meet Riverson, who for a human with no taint of Hell was extremely knowledgeable about Hell's citizens, not to mention still alive to be questioned—both incredible achievements. The blind man hadn't been blind back when Mikhail first met him, but by the time I saw him he was a scarecrow with a shock of white hair and those filmed, useless orbs that seemed nevertheless to notice a good deal more than most of the sighted ever would.

And the first time I'd come here, Perry had shown up at the end of the bar, looking *very* interested. Mikhail had almost drawn on him, but Perry made an offer . . . and a few months later, I'd sat in a chair with Perry circling me, negotiating the bargain that made me able to do what I do so well.

Murder, chaos, and screaming, that is. Hey, when a girl's got talents . . .

I shoved the memories back down into their little black box, took the shot Riverson poured, tossed it back, and slammed the shot glass down on the bar. The sound was a rifle crack in the hush. "I'm early." My voice was flat, uninflected. "I'm here on business. Put it on the tab."

"You can wait up in his office. They're finishing the meeting—Kismet! For God's sake, *don't!*"

The old man actually sounded concerned. *A meeting, eh? Wait in the office? I don't think so. Perry, your meeting's about to be adjourned.*

And by making a statement here I could probably find out something useful. I bit back an iron-edged laugh and stalked through the open maw of the building, skirting the dance floor and aiming to the left of the stage. The painted-black door opened smoothly, and I found myself in a back hall lit with red neon tubes along the ceiling. The light tinted everything bloody, and I strode down the linoleum, my heels clicking even more sharply and the charms in my hair chiming sweet and soft.

Perry, you have been a very bad boy.

The scar prickled, a fiery loathsome tendril of pleasure twining up my arm. I'd had it uncovered for so long it almost felt normal.

Almost.

The door I wanted was at the end of the hall, and as I approached it I heard the mutter, like flies magnified by the space inside a stripped-out skull. It was Helletöng, the language of the damned, and my heart gave a smothered leap and settled back into its regular pace.

Do it quick, Jill. Just like ripping a Band-Aid off. Do it hard and quick.

The door—blank steel, no knob on my side—was maybe three yards away. I gathered myself and skipped forward two long strides, kicking it inward and adding a generous portion of etheric force pulled through the scar on my wrist turned hard and hurtful, a bruised swelling. The steel crumpled, smashing inward, and I rode the motion down as the door crashed into the floor.

Two of them, one on either side. I took the first with a quick upward strike, smashing him across the face with a hellbreed-strong fist braced by the handle of my whip. The gun was in my other hand, speaking for me, smashing the shell of the hellbreed on my left. The whip struck, its thundercrack lost under the noise of the gun, and I uncoiled in a flung-wide kick, both boots smashing hellbreed flesh, one on either side. They folded down, both of them stinking now that I'd shattered their shells and dosed them with silver, and the whip coiled itself as I landed, both feet striking the battered curve of the door again.

As entrances go, it wasn't bad.

There was a long table polished to a mirror-shine, and tasteful sconces along the wall with yet more red neon, dyeing the air with crimson. Candles hissed in branched iron candelabra, their warm glow somehow bleached.

At the end of the table, a pair of blue eyes met mine. Perry sat in a high-backed iron chair, the red velvet of its cushions contrasting with the pale linen of his suit. His face under the expensive sandy-blond haircut was bland and interested, but I thought I caught a steely glint far back in his pupils. His fingers were tented together, and he didn't look surprised to see me at all.

Then again, he never did.

Gathered on either side of the table were other hell-breed, none as bland or unsurprised as him. The damned are always beautiful, and these were no exception—black leather, exquisite silk, frayed lace, glittering liquid eyes and sculpted lips, four or five had leapt to their feet on seeing me. The table was full, except for the seat directly to Perry's left.

And there was another surprise, oh friends and neighbors. Most of the damned in the room were instantly recognizable. The movers and shakers of the entire hellbreed population of Santa Luz, the maggots every smaller hellbreed answered to in their network of feudal obligation. There was the tall, sloe-eyed female who owned the Kat Klub downtown; the broker who ran the influence net out in the financial district; the short tense male in the black cloth half-veil that did assassinations for one faction or another, according to who hired him first or paid him most.

A meeting, and the resident hunter wasn't invited. Why am I not surprised?

My boots grated against the door, I took another two steps and leapt, landing catlike at the foot of the table, the whip coiled neatly in my hand. The gun tracked onto the nearest 'breed—a slim dark male with a leather vest over his hard narrow chest. I suspected him behind a large chunk of the cocaine trade that had recently soaked the poorer quarters with a wave of overdoses from whatever the supplier had cut it with. The current bet over in Vice was twelve to eight in favor of simple Drano, but Forensics hadn't come up with a verdict yet.

Jesus, with a submachine gun and some heavy-duty sorcery I could make the world a much better place in about ten minutes.

The trouble was, there were always more. If I erased this batch others would move in, and I'd have to threaten them into behaving all over again. Talk about your futile efforts.

Still. . . . My finger tightened on the trigger. "So many scumbags, and all in one room. Fish in a barrel." My lips peeled back from my teeth. "Feels just like Christmas."

The silence crackled, and leather made a slight sound in my right hand as my fingers bore down on the handle of the whip. The candleflames hissed. *Jesus. I should have thought about this before I kicked the door in. Good one, Kismet. Get out of this alive.*

But still, for what I wanted, this wasn't a bad situation. Odds were they knew about a hellbreed misbehaving in my town, and by getting a little nasty in here I might be able to avoid nastiness later.

The silver chain at my throat burned fiercely, and Mikhail's ring scorched. The charms in my hair shifted and jingled sweetly. I took another few steps down the table, bracing myself, as my eyes came up and met Perry's.

He finally spoke, his words a mere murmur. "So good of you to join us, Kismet."

It was like a slap of cold water across a dreamer's face. The other hellbreed blinked, shuffled, one of the females baring her teeth at me and hissing. I stilled, looking down at her. The Kat Klub figured in one or two cold cases I wanted to get to the bottom of as well, though its owner usually followed the rules.

Do we need another example here? Because I'm just aching to teach you motherfuckers the rules of operating in my goddamn town. The table resounded like a drum under my soles. I locked gazes with the hellbreed female. "You want to repeat yourself a little louder, bitch?"

"There's no need to be rude." Perry hadn't moved. His eyes had turned a little darker, that was all. Indigo spread through his irises, but his whites were still clear. My mouth had gone dry, and the scar on my wrist sent a jolt of heat up the bones of my arm to my shoulder socket. "You were, after all, invited to this meeting."

Invited? Fuck that. "I must have missed the engraved invitation." My lip lifted, in an almost-snarl. Our eyes locked, two magnets pushing against each other with invisible force. Pure repulsion.

Or so I hoped.

"We called this meeting today to address . . . extraordinary circumstances." He pressed his fingers together, his mouth making a little *moue* of distaste at my obtuseness.

I beat him to the punch. *Keep it business, Jill. You might just get out of here without having to spend more time with him than necessary.* "Five cops, out on the Drag. Dead. The scene stank of the damned. Hand over the 'breed responsible, and we'll all get along just fine."

The wet, icy silence that fell warned me. One corner of Perry's mouth lifted, and a chill worked its way all the way down to my bones. Except for the scar. The mark of his lips on my skin warmed obscenely, burrowing in toward the bone.

I suddenly wished I'd been able to get out to Galina's and get another copper cuff. Without the bar of blessed copper between the scar and the outside air, I was wide-open to him fiddling with it.

"You are all dismissed." His voice made the candle flames twist. "Spread out through the city. Find the one we seek."

Wait just a goddamn minute. I thumbed the hammer back, the small click loud in the dim-lit silence. "I didn't give any of you permission to move, Pericles." My soft killing tone couldn't rival his, but it was pretty good anyway. Too bad my lips were numb. My heart began to pound, and that was very bad. They could all hear my pulse, just as I could hear the subliminal rumble of Hell-etöng warping the walls and the strings of energy below the surface of the world.

The other corner of Perry's mouth lifted, a small smile running steel ice along my skin. "We are already

apprised of a hellbreed causing trouble with the police.
We are seeking her even now."

"Her?" My right eyebrow raised. I noticed with a thin
thread of gratification that none of them had moved a
muscle. The dusty, exotic, corrupt smell of them filled
my nose, coated the back of my dry throat.

Perry's smile was full-fledged now. He wasn't hurtfully beautiful like the other hellbreed, which made
him—once you thought about it—even scarier. *Much*
scarier. "Her name is Cenci." His tented fingers relaxed
a fraction. "I will tell you all we know, my dear Kiss.
After you have paid me my due." He now looked ex-
traordinarily happy, and my heart sank, turning to heavy
steel inside my chest.

Oh, fuck. I suddenly, frantically wished I'd thought to
stop by the warehouse and pick up the FBI files. They
would make an excellent excuse for keeping this meeting all business.

*Like he's going to be fobbed off. You just cost him
some face in front of his little lieutenants.*

Then, wonder of wonders, my pager buzzed. I swallowed bile as other hellbreed rose to their feet from
the small iron chairs; the ones already standing merely
waited. They shuffled out, avoiding the dead bodies at
the door, the masked one watching me with eyes blank
from lid to lid, black as the devouring darkness between
stars. I ignored it.

If one of them moved on me now, it would give me
cause to get the hell out of here without spending quality
time with Perry.

I wasn't as comforted as I could be by the thought.

As soon as the last one had left the room, I lowered

my whip. The gun swung around, fixed on Perry while I dug in the padded pocket. The number displayed on the pager's display couldn't have been more welcome.

Montaigne. Which meant there was another body. Or three.

Which *also* meant Perry would have to wait. Guilt curled hot and acid under a bald edge of relief. What did that say about me, that I was glad about someone's murder because it would get me the hell out of here?

I looked up from the pager, trying not to let the relief show. It was useless, he saw it anyway and his smile broadened, cold sweat bathing my back.

"It's the police." I had to work for an even tone. "I'm on the job, Perry. You're going to tell me what you know now, and I'll come in to pay you when this is over."

He didn't move, but his eyes darkened slightly. "I have waited an entire month for the pleasure of your company, and I don't intend to deny myself that pleasure any longer."

Oh, Christ. God help me now. "Tough." The gun settled, pointed right between his eyes. He wasn't a low-level grunt like the 'breed at the door. If I popped him in the head, it might just make him angry. "Bodies in the street take precedence over our bargain, Pericles. You know that. Start talking."

"I could talk to you for hours, dear one." His tone had turned silky, and the scar throbbed. The heat in my lower belly dipped down, and I had to choke back a sharp inhaled breath. He was doing it again, using the scar to fiddle with my internal thermostat and mimicking the physical aspects of desire.

It had to be a mimicry. *Whore,* the voice in my head snarled. *Just like a goddamn whore.*

God help me, but it felt familiar. Did he guess that was where I was weak? How much did he know about me? About my past?

Stop it. Mikhail made you stronger than this. Don't let Perry get to you.

I set my jaw. He liked playing with the scar while I was near him. Each time I visited it was the same—him messing with my pulse and my nerves, trying to make me respond.

At least I wouldn't have to use the flechettes this time. Or my whip.

Most of the time, he liked to be strapped down, and he liked to be cut while he bled the blackish ichor of hellbreed. Sometimes he would even talk while he made me cut him, and that was the worst. The closest he came to worming inside my head was while I was frantic with loathing at what he told me to do, cursing myself for ever making the goddamn bargain despite anything Mikhail ever said.

Oh, God. Come on. Get me out of here. "Stick to the *point,* Perry, or I'll track it down from the other end. That'll mean I won't come in when it's done, since you've refused to help."

"When have I ever refused you anything, Kiss? I could give you so much more than you've ever dreamed." His voice dropped, and the lights dimmed, candleflames twisting and hissing, sputtering as darkness spilled through the air. Silver shifted and chimed in my hair. The chain holding the ruby was a thin thread of fire, the ruby's setting hot against the hollow of my throat. It had never singed me yet, but each time I wondered.

My legs were shaking. I braced my knees. "Cut the crap. Give me what you have on this hellbreed. That's my final word, Pericles."

"You're no fun." He sounded genuinely regretful, but that smile was like sharp rocks under icy water, just waiting for naked feet. "All we have is her name and her general description. Fair, but with dark eyes, and for some reason, allied with a Were. Surprising, no? She is far from her master and should be returned. Which we have undertaken to do. We cannot, after all, have our vassals going about with animals. It destroys the general sense of order so necessary for a smoothly running society."

"Why is she hanging around with a Were?" *And a rogue one, to boot.* My mouth was parched, the fumes of the Jack Daniel's I'd taken down reaching my head. I hadn't eaten; my body was starting to get that funny shaky feeling it usually did just before Perry ordered me to strap him into the frame and start.

I knew that shaky feeling. It's the same thing as when your body rebels and tries to collapse on you, but your mind won't let it.

Sometimes he wanted the knives. Most of the time it was the flechettes, razor-sharp and silver-plated. On a few very bad nights he made me use my fists until his preternatural skin broke and bled, and the only sounds would be my sharp exhales of effort and his low, bubbling breath right before he gurgled *More.*

Just the single word. Each and every time.

I'd given up wondering why he wanted me to hurt

him. Maybe it was just another move in the game he played, trying to get inside my head. Maybe he couldn't get it anywhere else. Still, my mouth tasted sour and my hand felt like it was shaking, though the gun was steady.

"If we knew, Kismet, I would not be allowing this show of defiance from you, however charming I find your homicidal little displays." He finally moved, waving one elegant finger at me. "When I receive more information, I shall bring it to you." A meaningful pause. "Personally."

That's mighty nice of you, Perry. Not like you to be so accommodating. "Who's her master, then?"

"A certain gentleman in New York. One who is most displeased with her disobedience, and intends to teach her a lesson as soon as she is returned to him." Perry's smile broadened. "See what a very *good* boy I am being, my dear? And all for your sake." Two of the candle-flames died under the weight of his voice, and his hands came down, curled over the ends of the chair arms. He pushed himself up to his feet, very slowly, his eyes on mine the entire while.

New York? Jesus. The master of the Big Apple's hellbreed was so old and frightening I'd heard even the city's contingent of hunters steered clear of him. I hoped the one looking for this hellbreed was just a smaller fry from that pool. "Fine. Thanks for the information." Slowly, so slowly, my thumb came up and uncocked the gun. It took all my fading courage to holster it. "If this pans out I'll have the mayor give you a medal."

"Stay with me for ten minutes, Kismet." His tone had turned soft as velvet, cajoling, and the stretched-wide smile was gone, replaced by a look of utter seriousness that might have been almost human except for the indigo staining the whites of his eyes. "Only ten minutes. I will forgive your visit this month and wait until the next if you stay with me for that short while."

Shock threatened to nail me in place. This was something new, and my busy little brain started worrying at it, trying to decipher his angle. "You'd give up this month's visit for ten minutes now?"

He stood at the end of the table, looking up at me. Two more candles snuffed, then another two. The light darkened, even more bloody now. I should have felt a little better, having the physical high ground here.

I didn't.

"Ten minutes now, and I will forgive your payment on our bargain this month. My word on it, Kiss."

I wish he'd stop calling me that. I licked my lips, wished I hadn't when his eyes fastened on my mouth. "I don't suppose you'd forgive next month's too."

That earned me a sardonic look. He said nothing, merely stood there, and just that much was enough to make a shallow trickle of sweat trace its way down the channel of my spine.

"Fine. Starting from when I came in the door." I backed up, hopped off the table without looking, and breathed out through my mouth. The two 'breed I'd killed stank.

He didn't even quibble. It was a bad sign. "Come here." He indicated the seat on his left, the one that had been empty. "Sit . . . there."

I walked slowly down the table, my coat rustling and creaking. Here in the meeting room the floor was mellow hardwood, not linoleum. More candles snuffed, and my breath came short and sharp. I looked at the chair, tested it with one finger, and sank down in it.

The iron was hard, and cold. Velvet and horsehair pillows did nothing to stop the chill from biting immediately through the layers of my coat and leather pants. The ruby at my throat sparked, a single bloody point of light in the charged silence.

"Good," Perry murmured. He lowered himself down in the tall chair. "Put your hands flat on the table."

I swallowed. Did it, the mirrorshine surface cold and slick under my sweating palms. The last of the candles died. I was alone in the neon-lit dark with Perry and two rotting hellbreed corpses by the door.

God, do not forsake me now. Then I quit praying. God was fine, but He was often busy. It was up to a hunter to pick up the slack.

Perry exhaled, a soft sound of satisfaction like a sheet drawn up over a cold dead face.

What is he going to do? Best not to guess. Best just to wait and see.

It was, after all, bound to be unpleasant.

When his hand came down over my right wrist I started nervously. "Shhh." He made a low cold hissing noise, maybe meant to be soothing. "Be still."

His skin was warm, and felt human except for its supple invulnerability, like metal made flesh. The shell of a hellbreed, hard to breach without a lot of luck and firepower.

Silver. Lots of silver, and lots of luck. I swallowed again, pressed my hands into the table. *If I killed him, would his mark fade? Do I chance it? If Mikhail was here . . .*

But Mikhail, like God, wasn't here. I was on my own.

"Have you visited your teacher's grave?" Perry's voice was so soft I almost didn't catch the words, my every nerve strung tight.

What the hell? Mikhail's grave, where his ashes were buried in consecrated ground, its headstone with curved Cyrillic script scored deep into granite, hoping to last a little longer than other, more perishable things. Like flesh. Or memory.

Bile rose in my throat again. I made no reply. It was all part of Perry's game, trying to worm his way into my head. Less than ten fucking minutes, and I'd be free for another month.

"Answer me, Kiss. Have you?"

My mouth was so dry I had trouble with the word. "Yes."

His thumb moved a little, a slight flexible movement. The mark jolted another wire of unhealthy heat through me, my ears suddenly picking up sounds from the rest of the building. Creaks. The rumble of Helletöng. Running water from the bar. If I looked down with my smart eye I would see the mark flushing with power, swelling with corruption.

"And?"

"And what?" *Don't, Perry. Keep your fucking mouth off Mikhail's name.* But I wouldn't say it. That would be like blood in the water.

"Did his ghost rise to comfort you?"

"No." *I poured out a bottle of vodka, though. Wher-*

ever he is, he's sleeping sound. I drew my breath in, shut my eyes. Exhaled.

"You need some small comfort." His thumb moved again. "You allow me so little. I could help you so much more."

If this is a sample of your help I'll go my own way, thank you. I bit back the words. He hadn't asked me a direct question, I could get away with silence. It was the safest course.

Perry made a small annoyed sound, his fingers suddenly biting down. Small bones in my wrist creaked and crackled. The pain was almost a balm.

"Why do you make this so hard?"

I found my voice. "Make *what* so hard?" *I don't need to make this hard. You do that very well, thank you.*

Besides, the harder Perry found this game, the better I liked it. It gave me an edge.

He tried again. "Think of what it could be like." His tone had dropped to a murmur. "If you sat here, with me at your right hand. Imagine what I could do with you to direct me. There's nothing I wouldn't do for your asking, my dear."

I had to swallow a braying, hysterical laugh. "You're *hellbreed.*" It was all I needed to say. If I bit into the apple of that offer, the snake wouldn't be far behind. It was the same old song. Take a little, then a little more, and before you knew it you were up to your eyeballs in filth—your own, and a good deal more.

What makes you different, Jill?

I knew what. Mikhail had made me different. And as long as I was true to him and what he taught me, I was on the side of the angels.

Figuratively, of course. God needs killers as much as Hell does, I guess.

Maybe more.

"What kind of hellbreed?" Perry sounded only mildly interested.

I had to admit it. "I don't know."

"Ah." Now there was amusement, the lazy grin of a shark evident in his voice. "All I ask is that you turn a very little, Kiss. Just a very, very little."

It was a jolt of cold water. He could fiddle with the scar and try to worm his way in all he wanted, but Perry was just too fucking impatient to crack me. And I wasn't a stupid teenager anymore, ready to believe anything a man told me.

Just a little bit. I've heard that line before. Just do something small for me, and I'll give you everything you ever wanted. How stupid do you think I am, Perry? I set my boots against the floor, tensing in every muscle. "We have our bargain. You won't get anything else from me."

As soon as I said it I knew it was a mistake. My wrist ached as Perry squeezed, a fraction of a hellbreed's strength enough to make sweat break out along the curve of my lower back.

"I have enough time. I've broken stronger Traders than you."

So I've heard. Since I'd already pissed him off, I might as well go with it. "I'm not a Trader." *I'm a hunter, and one day I'm going to kill you too. When I do, Perry, I'm going to throw a party afterward. Hell, I'll have it catered and bring out the barbeque. It'll be a red-letter day.*

His fingers eased up on my wrist, caressed the back of my hand, and finally slid between mine. How could such a small touch feel like such a violation?

I flinched, yanking my hand back, but those gentle fingers turned to steel again and pain tore through the hard knot of the scar as he pulled my hand up, turning the palm toward the ceiling and baring the pale glimmer of my wrist under the pushed-back cuff of my coat.

"Naughty, naughty," he murmured, as if I was a puppy. An edge of delight coiled under the words. He'd made me react.

Good for him.

His mouth met the scar, something cat-rasping against my skin, a brief caress.

I set my jaw, my neck aching with tension. Perry chuckled, a low satisfied sound, his breath oven-hot and swamp-wet against my skin as I went rigid in the chair, an invisible knife twisting in the scar, tangling and ripping at nerve-strings. Great pearly drops of water stood out on my forehead, my neck, the curve of my lower back, the backs of my knees.

At least it was pain this time, and not the sick gasping-sweet heat of the first time his lips pressed into my flesh, his aura injecting a nugget of corruption into mine. Pain can be controlled, even if it's your skin being torn off one millimeter at a time. Even if it's the nerves themselves turning traitor and running with hot acid.

Even if it went on until I made a small betraying sound in the back of my throat, instantly swallowing it. It was a half-broken, hurt little cry, as if I'd been punched.

Immediately, he let go, his head coming up, his fingers sliding free of mine. My hand fell limply to the table and I slumped, the sudden relief almost enough to wring another sound out of me.

Perry let out a long breath, jagged, as if he had just finished spending himself. It was an intimate sound, and I cringed away from it. A filthy feeling circled my skin, as if I'd pressed my naked body against a cold grimy windowpane.

Silence returned, neon buzzing finally intruding on my ears like a bee caught on a dead dry windowsill.

I was shaking. I pressed my hands into the table's slick glassy surface and wished I could kill him. The need to get up, to empty a clip into his body, to flick the whip forward and listen to him scream like an *arkeus*—the temptation shook me. Like a dog shakes a toy in its sharp teeth.

"You may go." Dark amusement burbled under his light even tenor. "Unless you want to stay, my dear. I'd like that."

"Fuck you." It managed to come out steady. I pushed myself up to my feet, managed to stand. Sweat cooled icy on my forehead. The charms in my hair tinkled. "I won't be back until next month."

The urge to kill him shook me even harder. A physical need, like the need to eat or empty my bladder or even the need to *breathe*.

Kill him, one part of me whispered. *You can do it. It might not be easy but you can do it.*

The rest of me dug in heels and resisted. If I killed him now, I'd be violating the bargain. And I knew what that would make me in my own eyes.

Just as bad as the things I hunted, that's what.

The amusement intensified. Perry sounded almost

goddamn *gleeful*. "You'll see me before that. Tell your friends from the government I'm hunting their little problem, too. We'll be quite a cozy little bunch, won't we. Like *family*."

I could have replied, but I didn't. I hit the broken door at a run, his laughter rising behind me, and got the hell out of there.

11

I ducked under the yellow tape and breathed out through my mouth. Foster hopped down from a Forensics van and hurried over, his dark-blue windbreaker glaring wetly under the afternoon's heat haze.

I still felt cold, and more shaky than I liked to admit. Especially since I'd gotten off easy. Way too easy for Perry. He usually liked to mess with me more.

I had the sick unsteady feeling that he probably would before this was over.

Don't think about that. I blinked the thought back and met Foster's eyes. "What do we have?"

The gully at the edge of Percoa Park was stony and full of trash, and I smelled the thunderous odor of the thing I was chasing, but with no exotic taint of hellbreed. My hair was dry from the heat in the Impala, both windows rolled down, but salt still filmed my skin. I hadn't even managed to stop for a burrito. My stomach was unhappy, and the rest of me wasn't too prancing-pony either.

Still, I was free until next month. I'd make it. Piece of cake.

"Three, we think. Maybe more." Foster was pale, his sleek dark hair slightly mussed. "The Feebs are looking at it."

I shook my head. "Is Juan with them?" Juan Rujillo was the local FBI liaison, and a good one. Not like the last asshole.

"No, he's on vacation." Mike gave me an odd look. It wasn't like me to forget that kind of detail. "You look like shit, Jill."

"Thanks." *I just played patty-cake with a nightmare.* "How many feds?" *I hope the country boy stayed at home.*

"Two. Man and woman. She's a looker."

"Hands off if you know what's good for you. I'll just follow my nose." Since I hadn't covered the scar yet, I could smell it all—reek of rotting trash, anemic out here in the dryness, the gassy ripe smell of human death, and the smell of a rogue Were.

Well, at least it was cleaner than the stench of dead hellbreed. And at least now I knew what a rogue smelled like.

Good. Keep thinking about that, Jill. Don't think about Perry. You've put it off until next month. Clever girl, aren't you?

I walked down the gully, the sides rising above me, fringed with succulents and other scrub. This was still part of the river-fed, low-lying cup most of the city rested in, the closest park to my house. Still, the gully at the back showed traces of desert, especially since it wasn't watered until the flash floods came along in fall—an event that wasn't too far away, this being the beginning of September. Percoa was just a slim wedge of a park anyway, a piece of land nobody wanted because it was a buffer between an industrial zone and a patch of suburbs undergoing urban renewal and becoming higher-class every year.

Guess which side my warehouse sat on. Still on the wrong side of the tracks, even after all these years.

Around the bend, a sudden knot of activity swallowed me. More forensic techs, snapping pictures, triangulating. Montaigne, in a gray suit and a brown tie I knew his wife hadn't picked—it was far too ugly—stood sourly to one side, his hands dangling by his sides. He saw me, and I watched as if from behind myself the curious relief, then even more curious flash of dread cross his haggard face. "Jill!" He almost slipped on a loose patch of gravel, his wingtips not meant for grubbing out here in the brush. "You look—" He pulled himself up short, and I felt a click in my head, a door shutting away the feel of Perry's lips on my skin and the shaking temptation to just start killing until there was nothing left that could hurt me.

It was a good thing, that click. I felt cleaner, though I knew I would strip down and scrub myself raw as soon as I could get home. It took a lot of harsh scrubbing and the water turning pink-red as it went down the drain before I *ever* felt clean after a visit to the Monde.

I don't keep a wire brush in the house because I'd be too tempted to use it.

"Hi, Monty." I squinted against the hot oven glare of sunlight, shifted inside my coat. When I lifted my left hand to push a strand of hair weighted by a silver horseshoe back, the charm glittered in my peripheral vision. Like a mirage. "Just tired. What do we have? Foster said three, maybe more."

I spotted Harp up further on one side of the gully, bending down to examine something, her braids fastened back. Dominic stood next to her, his hair bound and his shoulders straight.

"It's over there." He pointed at the beehive of orderly activity. Half-moons of sweat darkened his suit under his arms. "Jesus. Do you have anything yet, Jill? Anything at all?"

I nodded. "Some things." *Not nearly enough. A runaway hellbreed and a rogue Were. If ever there was an unlikely combination, that's one.* "How's your man? The rookie?"

"Still in critical." Monty sighed. It was a weary sound. "Jesus fucking Christ. Sullivan and the Badger are next up, do you want them on this?"

I shook my head. The last thing I wanted was a homicide detective or two dealing with a rogue Were. "The feds over there are my people, I don't want any more of yours getting killed."

He took it better than I thought he would. He only paled more, and shivered despite the heat. Indian summer had struck with a vengeance this year. "It's bad, then."

Worse than you can probably imagine, cheesecake. "I'll go take a look." I wanted to touch him—clap him on the shoulder, maybe. Offer some comfort. But if I did, he'd just flinch away from my essential difference.

My essential taint.

She stinks of hellbreed. It hadn't been so much the

words as the tone in which they were delivered. What should I care what a country-boy Were thought of me?

Because of the other voice whispering in my head, bland and weighted with terrible finality, as if he considered the deal already struck—a newer deal, one Mikhail hadn't approved. *I've broken stronger Traders than you.*

It wasn't so much that he said it. It was that I suspected, deep down, that he might be right. Without the steady compass and experience of my teacher, things were getting more precarious by the day.

I was getting more precarious every day. Out on the edge with nowhere else to go.

I flinched inwardly as I inserted myself into the dance of gathering evidence. A few of the techs looked a little green.

The bodies were tangled together in a messy heap under torn-down branches that had wilted in the heat. I saw a long scarf of brown hair crusted with sand, and thought maybe that one was female. But they were such a mess I couldn't tell for certain. Some of the bigger bones—femur, humerus—had been gnawed, sharp splinters worried up. The faces were marred with deep claw marks.

I looked again at the brush cover. The techs were photographing, picking up, and bagging each torn branch. The ends were ripped, not broken with leverage but torn straight out from the tree or bush that had hosted them. The tougher ones—juniper, sage, pine from the park, probably—were still springy and sap-full.

They were fresh.

So were the bodies. *Really* fresh, even though they stank in the heat.

Had the rogue just blown into town, killed a few cops, and started on an orgy of murder? It was a distinct possibility. The usual rogue Were rules—a kill every few days, mostly for food, a pattern of familiar places—wasn't holding true. What other rules was this case going to break?

A prickle touched the back of my neck, cold even under the sun's assault. Was it just nervousness from dealing with Perry, or was it intuition? As raw as my nerves were, I couldn't tell.

That's bad. You've got to take the edge off or you aren't going to be good for anything. I looked up, shading my eyes, as one of the techs, a slim Asian woman with her hair cut in a sleek bob, approached me.

"Can we move the bodies?" She didn't look me in the eye, rubbing her fingers together against the latex gloves. Latex was miserable in this weather, with the sweat and cornstarch. "Or at least start to? The Feebs said to wait for you."

I should have been looking at the bodies, marking each one and swearing to avenge them. I should have looked to see what had mangled them so badly, what had stripped the face off each one.

A rogue Were kill, dehumanizing the victims? That *was* standard behavior for them, but the shape of the marks on the faces were wrong somehow. Another click sounded at the very bottom of my head.

Why would a rogue Were kill cops? But some of them are Were kills, I recognized that claw shape on the others. And look at the bodies, those are Were claws. Why the different marks on the faces? Dammit. This isn't making sense, and there's a hellbreed in it somewhere.

The prickling at my nape slid down my back, gooseflesh rising hard. The mark on my wrist was a mass of tiny hair-fine needles, responding to the uneasy swirl of my aura as my senses dilated to take everything in.

Something about to happen, Jill. Look around. Be aware.

I looked up. Harp had come to her feet, immobile, even the feathers braided in her hair motionless despite the soft breeze. Her lovely face was set, color draining away and turning her ash-pale. Dominic unfolded slowly, like a cat will rise quietly from its haunches when it sees prey. My blue eye, hot and dry, saw the deep thrumming swirling through both of them.

"Hey." The tech was still trying to get my attention. "Can we move the bod—"

I was already moving, extending in a leap over the pile of bodies, touching down, and bolting for the end of the gully. A few pebbles drifted down, and the slim shape silhouetted against the sky vanished hastily with a flutter of pale hair. I heard scrabbling behind me, and a scream. Didn't care. My skin came alive, flush with heat, leather coat flapping as I sank one hand into the scree of the slope and made it up the hill, throwing up a chunk of gravel as I catapulted over the edge, recklessly pulling etheric energy through the scar.

I'd just paid Perry, I was going to use it.

The whip uncoiled, each individual flechette burning itself into my retinas as metal flashed, the small sonic booms of the crack like a tattoo against my hellbreed-sharp ears.

Improbable became flat-out impossible, gravel shifted under my boots, and I *missed.*

It was a woman with the full-lipped beauty of the damned, wide liquid dark eyes and a cloud of platinum hair. Her eyes were rimmed in red and her skin flushed from the anathema of the sun, and she wore long sleeves and jeans, the sunglasses she'd been peering through knocked off her face as she scrabbled away.

She skittered back, showing white teeth in a snarl, and spun, her heels digging in as Harp rocketed past me, driving her shoulder into the other woman's midriff. I heard the coughing roar of a panther behind me, and Dominic thundered past me too, engaging with the hell-breed. He had *shifted,* the sunlight gilding his dark hide as he leapt, with all the grace and authority of a Were. They are a little bigger than humans in human form, and a little bigger than normal in their animal forms, and when a Were shifts quickly like that he means business.

"No!" I yelled over the noise, yanking the whip back. *"She's hellbreed goddammit stop it!"*

It was too late. Blood exploded and a high cat-whine screeched across my senses. I was still moving forward, dropping the whip, my fingers closing around knife-hilts, metal singing free of the sheath as I uncoiled in a kick, my boot thudding solidly into Dominic's side. The panther curled away, snarling, and I promptly forgot about him, twisting in midair to collide with the spitting growling mass that was Harp and the hellbreed.

Who was out here in full sunlight, in the middle of the *day,* at the site of a rogue Were kill.

Or something that had been made to look like a rogue Were kill. Something that had been *altered.*

I took a hit low on the side, pain spiking up my ribs like oil against the skin, and heard something snap. Harp was flung away, and I drove the knife in my left hand forward, a flickering slash meant to come under the ribs and open up the hellbreed's abdominal cavity.

She twisted, snarling, and the world turned over, the side of my head ringing with pain. Gravel boiled up and I made it to my knees, panting, scooped up my left-hand knife. No blood or ichor on it. Warm wetness spilled into my eyes, ran down my neck. I blinked it away, irritably.

I'd missed again. The sun beat mercilessly down, and I heard the retreating drumbeat of the hellbreed's footsteps. Filled my lungs with the spoiled, delicious, unique smell of a hellbreed, let the smell sink below the conscious level. Without the other reek of death and Were, it was easier.

I could track her now, if I could get close enough to break through whatever masking-sorcery she was using to cover her scent. My head felt light, strange, stuffed with cotton.

A low whining sound of pain intruded. I gained my feet, shaking gravel out of my hair, heard shouts and scrabbling below. Harp was bleeding badly, and Dominic had shifted back, rumbling the low throbbing distressed note of a cat Were whose mate was injured.

Goddamit. Fucking around with a hellbreed can get a Were killed. I decided now was not the time to tell him so.

They were scrabbling up the slope behind us. Dominic glanced up, the lambent glow in his gaze warning me. I could either pursue the hellbreed, who was too far away and probably had enough breath to cloak herself now, or I could defuse Dominic and keep the humans away from him. He might not hurt anyone, but he'd make them awful uncomfortable, and forensic techs don't deal well with that kind of discomfort. They like more conventional uncertainties, probabilities, percentages.

Not the crazy logic of the nightside when it erupts in daytime. Most human brains stall when presented with something like that.

I blinked away more wetness, heard liquid pattering on dry dusty ground, and ignored it. The copper reek of blood boiled up.

I swore viciously, shook more gravel out of my coat, and edged past him, not turning my back. Harp would be all right, she'd already stopped bleeding but lay pale and gasping-still. Weres don't often come away breathing from tangling with hellbreed.

Especially hellbreed who don't need night's cover to come out and cause havoc. That meant she was high up the chain of Hell's citizens, capable of doing a lot of damage and possibly unfettered by feudal obligation. Was a hellbreed looking to horn in on Perry's territory?

You know, I almost wouldn't mind that. Even if he is the devil I know.

I almost didn't see it. A thin glint caught my eye, and I bent down, picking out a long platinum strand. It twisted around a red-gold curling hair, twined tight, and curled in on itself even as I watched, the hairs tangling together.

More wetness fell in my eyes, and I couldn't seem to take a deep breath.

Curiouser and curiouser. Nothing about this is making sense.

Blood sliding out from the ragged claw gashes along my ribs pattered on dry dusty ground in an almost-painless gout. The world turned over, and I pitched head-first off the drop and into the converging cops.

12

Mikhail's hand spread against my belly, calluses scraping. The carved chunk of ruby at his throat glimmered with its own secret life, and sweat dried on his forehead. "What is best way to kill utt'huruk, you think?" He hadn't smoked a cigarette yet, so the day's lessons weren't over.

I lay on my back, looking up at the skylight full of afternoon gold. A hard nugget of silver pressed into the back of my head; I shifted so the charm wasn't digging in. Mikhail had started giving me the charms one by one, mostly when I'd performed well, and I'd taken to tying them in my hair with red thread, just like he did.

Hey, anything helps.

"Holy water? After you've punctured the shell?" I thought about it some more as his fingers tapped my belly idly, obviously unsatisfied with my answer. Of course. I'd been caught assuming again; assuming Assyrian bird-demons had a shell, like hellbreed. You can't *ever assume, so I asked the question I should have asked straight-up. "What's the weakness in their anatomy?"*

He shifted a little under the covers. The air conditioning was on, but even so sweat cooled on my skin and my body sparked pleasantly. Four years ago I'd've called Mikhail an easy dime—street lingo for a john who wants vanilla, straight-up, and doesn't get nasty with you. They're also called milks—as in, you milk them and go home.

He was my teacher, not a john, and falling into bed with him felt more than natural. Here was no sparring and no hurt. Here, in this queen-sized, hip-high monstrosity covered in threadbare red velvet, with the iron lamps standing guard on either side, was the place where I became more and more thoroughly what Mikhail made me.

To hear Mikhail talk, it was normal for two reasonably heterosexual people so close in such extreme circumstances to end up in bed. It was even to be encouraged, the sex made the bond between teacher and student stronger and balanced out the harshness of training.

I didn't care. I just liked that . . . well . . .

Me. Of all people. He'd chosen me.

"There is seam that runs through their heads." His fingers left off my belly, touched my forehead and ran down my nose. "Like so. Hit them there, and head explodes. Very dramatic."

I laughed, pushed my hair back with my right hand. Mikhail caught my wrist and turned it, looking at the bracelet of pale skin. I'd taken to wearing a copper cuff over the mark.

The lip-print was a bruised purple now, the color

slowly leaching away, but thankfully not into the sur-rounding flesh. I held very still, watching the skylight. Golden sunshine filled my eyes, safe warm light.

"Does it hurt?"

"Burns sometimes." I settled my naked hips, my salt-touched shoulders. "But it's okay. It just looks funny." And I had to be careful, having a hellbreed-strong fist was . . . interesting, to say the least. I was still getting used to it.

"Eh." He let go of my wrist, one finger at a time, and settled down next to me. Then came my favorite part, his arm over me, and we cuddled together. The feeling of safety returned, palpable enough to set a lump in my throat. "Woman always has edge in bargain like this, lit-tle snake. You remember that when old Mischa is gone."

The lump got bigger. "You're not going anywhere, Mik. You're too nasty."

He pinched my arm, but gently, and I giggled. It was a little-girl sound, a laugh I only heard here in the bed-room with the silkscreened Japanese scrolls on the walls. Only in Mikhail's arms.

"Someday, milaya. *It comes for us all. But we have a choice of how to meet it."*

This one I knew. "Head high," I said.

"Guns out," he answered. "Good, little snake. Now rest. Night soon, time to work."

It came sooner than either of us thought, but after that day we never spoke of it again. I fell asleep easily in his arms, but I don't know if Mikhail slept. I rarely saw him relax, and he was always awake when I dropped off, and awake again when I surfaced.

Of all the men I ever knew, all the men whose bodies

pressed over or into mine, he was the only one I ever felt
safe with. He was also the only one who held me in the
middle of the day when I woke crying from nightmares I
remembered all too clearly.

More and more, the longer I go without him, the more
I wish I could have seen him sleeping.

Of all the things I expected to smell, frying bacon was
the very last.

My head boiled with pain. I groaned, turned over, and
buried my face in my pillow, which smelled different.
Like . . . fabric softener?

It *was* fabric softener. I didn't use frocking fabric
softener. I had a hard enough time running the damn
washing machine without frou-frous like that.

What the hell? I lay very still, my awareness suddenly
dilating. The last thing I remembered was falling head-
long off the high drop into the crush of people struggling
to find some way up the almost-vertical slope. I dimly
remembered Montaigne yelling, and Harp's voice, thin
but determined.

Sleep beckoned, warm and wide and full of welcome
oblivion.

It was no use. I couldn't crawl back into unconsciousness. I had too much to do.

I rolled slowly, lethargically, onto my back. Blinked
at the angle of sunlight. It was all wrong—low and gray,
with the peculiar translucence that meant morning. How
long had I been out?

What had happened out there on the streets while I'd
been out? How was Harp?

I pushed myself painfully up to my elbows. My belly was tender, as if I'd taken one hell of a sucker punch. My scalp itched and smarted too. But that wasn't what surprised me the most.

I was on my mattress in the middle of my bedroom, but the sheets were on the bed instead of tangled and wrecked, clean and smelling freshly washed. The messy pile of blankets had been washed too and the bed, despite my usual thrashing, had obviously been neatly made. The blinds had been dusted, and the hardwood floor looked suspiciously shiny. On top of that, the maddening smell of bacon in the air was joined by the smell of coffee brewing.

What the flying fuck?

I was in a battered extra-large Santa Luz Warriors T-shirt, again, not usual. There was no knife under my pillow, but one of my guns lay on the milk crate next to my bed, which now sported a red bandanna as covering and a lamp I'd been meaning to fix.

I grabbed the gun, then touched the lamp. It flicked on, warm electric light flooding my suddenly strange bedroom.

It looked like the floor had been *waxed* or something, for God's sake.

Hello, Toto? Are we still in Kansas?

I slid my feet out of my warm nest. They met cold hardwood, I rocked up to my feet—and collapsed back down again, my head pounding and my muscles rebelling. I'd run myself into the ground. I'd need food to get back up, something to digest so I could fuel my body's now-unnatural ability to heal.

I heard footsteps, deliberately loud, and raised the

gun. It pays to be cautious. The warehouse echoed, and my heart thudded in my ears. Copper lay against my palate, the taste of fear.

Saul Dustcircle appeared in my bedroom door. He was barefoot, in jeans and the same black T-shirt. His hair was pulled back from his face with two small braids on either side, the rest of it loose against his shoulders. His dark eyes passed over me once, not pausing at the gun.

He carried, of all things, a plastic tray I used for holding bullets while I refilled clips, so they didn't roll around. Steam rose from it, and I smelled coffee and maple syrup.

If that wasn't enough, the first thing he said was utterly confusing, too.

"Breakfast." His voice was neutral enough. "And an apology."

I'll admit it. I goggled at him, my jaw dropping but the gun remaining steady.

"I was rude to you. I shouldn't have been; my mother raised me better. I was just tired and frustrated. We've been chasing this bastard a long time, and he keeps slipping through my fingers." His mouth turned down at both corners, bitterly, but his eyes still held mine. "You're a hunter, and a good friend to Weres. I apologize."

I still stared, my jaw suspiciously loose. Of all the things I've heard in my life, a Were apology is high on the "real seldom" list. They don't often say the words out loud.

But when they do, they mean them.

He watched me for another few moments before one corner of his mouth quirked. His eyebrow raised.

"Truce?" He indicated the tray, lifting it slightly, and I set the gun down on the milk crate with a click, suddenly ashamed of myself.

"Jesus." My voice cracked. "How long have I been out? How's Harp?"

"Thirty-six hours or so. Harp's fine, she and Dominic just left to meet with some of the Norte Luz lionesses. Captain Montaigne called to make sure you were all right, and some guy named Avery called twice and left messages for you. Something about missing a beer date." He approached with the tray. "You need to eat first. You passed out from blood loss and exhaustion, and you look like you've been pushing yourself lately. If you go killcrazy it won't help us."

Only Weres go killcrazy. On us hunters it's called suicidal. I swallowed the words. Harp was okay. Thank God.

The tray held a plate of buckwheat pancakes, buttered and drenched in syrup, toast with strawberry jam, a mound of scrambled eggs, and six strips of bacon. There was a huge glass of orange juice, and a coffee cup that smelled absurdly good. Not to mention the mint sprig to garnish everything, and the decoratively cut strawberry fanned out in thin slices.

"Holy *Christ*." I managed to sound horrified. "Where did you—"

"Harp and I went shopping. You had nothing but ketchup and some green lump I think was achieving sentience in your fridge. I figured the least I could do was clean up a bit around here and make you something to eat—I don't know how you like your eggs, so

I scrambled them. Come on, it won't stay hot forever. Scoot back."

He even fluffed the goddamn pillows and settled the tray across my knees. Then he turned around, without so much as another word, and left the room with a long loping stride.

I stared down at the food. *Wow.* Most Weres, especially the males, are pretty domestic. It was a peace offering instead of a violation for him to clean up my house, since he wouldn't understand much about personal property—again, being Were. And the food . . . if I didn't trust the verbal apology, the food would have convinced me.

It looked ridiculously good, and I started in. It tasted even better than it looked, and I was munching on nice crispy bacon and feeling my blood sugar level rise slowly but surely when he came back, carrying a coffee cup and something that looked suspiciously like a stack of files. "When you're done." He laid them at the end of the bed just past my toes and settled down, cross-legged, on the floor a respectable distance away. His dark eyes half-lidded, and he relaxed abruptly into the peculiar lazy alertness of a Were.

I took a gulp of the coffee and almost closed my eyes. *Goddamn.* Finished swallowing, and examined his face. "I'm sorry." The tray balanced itself on my knees, I cut myself another bite of pancake. "I wasn't very polite either. Guess I'm strung a little tight. It's been a bad year out here."

He nodded. "Harp told me. About your teacher."

The sharp pain in my chest was expected and natural now. I swallowed hard against it and took another bite.

I chewed, and decided he had a nice face. Most Weres are handsome, at least, but he actually looked approachable. Like Theron at Micky's, who's a goddamn headache to have on a hunt but who manages to be good backup anyway. "Yeah? What else did she tell you?"

"Not much." He grinned, acknowledging the uselessness of the words. "Just to keep your skin whole. Can't stand to lose another good hunter."

So you've decided I'm worthy of being called "hunter" instead of "hellbreed trash." My eyebrows rose. "Harp told you that?"

He nodded, took another sip of coffee. His hair had reddish highlights, and his aura—plainly visible to my blue eye—swirled a little, different from a hellbreed's brackish stain. He was most likely a cat Were, he had that grace.

I decided it was time to ask a few questions, or hopefully just get the conversation off the subject of me. "So where are you from?"

"South Dakota way, 'round the Black Hills. I'm 'cougar."

I would have guessed it anyway, from the tawny immobility of him. His face was a little broader than a panther Were's, but not as broad as a lion's, and his dark eyes held a gold tint that made me think of dappled shade along a muscular cat's side. He smelled healthy, a little like Dominic but muskier, with the edge of dry maleness boy Weres give off. Human testosterone smells slightly oilier than theirs, especially to my sensitive nose.

"You're a ways from home."

"Promised myself I'd get the rogue that did in my

sister." His face changed a little. "She and Jean-François were friends, too."

"I'm sorry." *If it makes you feel any better, we'll get him. Nobody kills cops in my town and gets away with it.*

He shrugged, a fluid movement. "How are the eggs?"

In other words, time for a subject change. "Good. I don't cook much." *At all.* "Don't have time."

"I guessed as much." Silence fell, his eyes hooding and the staticky sound of a not-quite purr rumbling out from him. I finished most of everything, took a long draft of orange juice, and found my hands had stopped shaking.

He got up to take the tray, and when he loped out of the room I scrambled from under the covers to get to the bathroom. I had to pee like nobody's business, and I wanted to get some clothes on. Just wearing a T-shirt was bad for my image, even if he was a Were.

13

"A New York hellbreed, connected to the rogue?" Harp chewed at her lower lip gently for a moment. "How far can you trust the information, Jill?"

Sunlight fell in through the skylights, but the warehouse was cool, air conditioning and a small beneficial sorcery adding up to ward off the heat outside. I stretched, my back crackling as I reached for the sky. Then I leaned forward, my legs out to either side, almost touching the floor. It wasn't a perfect split but close enough, and I needed the stretch. The stack of files stood just beyond my fingertips as I exhaled, letting my neck relax. I spoke into the floor, shutting my eyes. "He doesn't give me information unless it's true. That's the agreement. If he lies to me, we renegotiate and I get the upper hand. He doesn't want that." My toes pointed, I shuddered, relaxing into the stretch again. "I'm beginning to think there's more to this story, though."

"How so?" Dominic lay on the couch, one arm flung over his eyes. He didn't look good, dark circles under his eyes and his face hollowed out. It was probably Harp getting hit that did it.

Weres are serious about their mates. They have no conception of civil or religious marriage; they simply pick their mates and settle down. I've never seen a Were mating that isn't happy. Like so many other things, they do it in a way far more humane and relaxed than humans have ever learned to.

"I looked through your files. There's a pattern. First there's the rogue kill, then there are these other bodies—but the other bodies only show up with someone disturbing the Were. We have a rogue, killing for meat in an irregular cycle, and someone else killing whenever someone disturbs him." I exhaled again, then inhaled, bringing myself up and bending over my right knee, the leather of my pants creaking slightly against the floor. My forehead touched my knee. "The bodies we just found were a regular rogue kill. Four bodies, muscle meat gone, faces missing—but the faces weren't Were work, those were hellbreed claws—and bones chewed. The cops were *mostly* rogue kills—except the rookie. He's an exception, not only because he's still alive. A rogue won't tear off the top of a car to get at prey; it'll take opportune bits of meat."

"Humans," Harp corrected softly. Dishes clinked in the kitchen—Dustcircle was washing up, or cooking something.

Nice of him.

"Humans," I agreed. "The point is, something peeled open that car and slashed at him to kill him quick and messy. It's a hellbreed kill."

Dominic perked up. "The hellbreed's covering a rogue's tracks?"

"Or trying to." I straightened, my eyes still closed, and bent over my left leg. My *Dies Irae* T-shirt rode up, a finger of coolness along my lower back, my breasts pressed against my thigh. A knife-hilt jabbed into my ribs again. "And this hellbreed—Cenci—is desperate enough to come out during the day and tangle with a hunter and two Weres."

"Suicidal," Dominic muttered.

I pushed myself up and brought my bare soles together, then leaned down, feeling the stretch in the insides of my thighs. "Not necessarily. Who expects a hellbreed to attack during the day? If indeed she intended to attack, which I'm not convinced of."

That got Dominic's attention. "You're right. She was hanging out up there like she wanted to stay hidden."

I shrugged. "She almost made chow mein out of Harp, and if I'd been down with the bodies and tangled up trying to keep the humans out of her way she'd have gotten away scot-free, maybe with both of you dead."

Dustcircle came around the breakfast bar, wiping his hands on a towel. "Tell me this one again, where Harp gets bitch-smacked by a hellgirl." He was trying for levity, but it didn't go well with his deadly set face. "Because, you know, that never gets old."

Harper stuck her tongue out at him, a thrumming growl rattling the air. But it was a playful sound, and she went back to looking at the stack of files with a line between her eyebrows. That thoughtful look, when she seemed distracted, was when she was most dangerous.

"Shut up." Dominic sighed, sinking into the couch. "I'd have been mincemeat too, if it wasn't for Jill. Christ."

"Glad to be of service. Besides, I'd hate to break in a

new set of Feebs." I sighed, leaned forward again, pressing my knees down. The stretch filled my hamstrings with prickles and I had to remind myself to breathe out and relax my lower back. "So, boys and girl, we have our work cut out for us."

"Well, we've been chasing this asshole across the goddamn country, I'm ready for a change." Harp yawned. "I'm *hungry*." She actually sounded plaintive.

"Working on it," Dustcircle replied, easily. "So what is the plan, then?"

I was hoping you'd ask. The warehouse echoed and rang around us, its midday song of a building ticking and expanding under the sun's weight. "I put in a call to the hunters up in New York and ask them to dig, tell 'em it's urgent. Set them to finding out exactly why this Cenci left and what her story is, and why a high-up hellbreed out there is so all-fired set on getting her back—because something about that smells, there's a piece we're missing. You three go down in the barrio and rouse every Were you can, get them spreading through the city to flush the rogue out."

"Wait a second—" Harp tried to dive in. If I was a Were I might have let her have the floor.

But I'm not, so I rode right over the top of her. "Meanwhile, I start burning hellbreed holes out here until someone comes forward. She can't hide in my city without *someone* knowing about it, and I'm going to find out." I straightened and stretched my legs out, sighing. I was already beginning to feel more like myself. I didn't have to see Perry for another month.

Small favors, but I'd take it.

"Saul goes with you." Harp said it like it meant something. "It's a rogue Were, and you're not going to handle one of those on your own. We leave the hellbreed to you, you leave the rogue to Saul."

"I don't need a babysitter." I rose to my feet in a smooth wave, charms tinkling and shifting in my hair. "And where I'm going tonight, Weres aren't welcome."

"So he'll wait outside in the car like a good little boy." Harp folded her arms and glared at me. "Don't make me sit on you, Jill. This is serious."

"You think I don't know that? You got eviscerated, I got clipped, and we lost thirty-six hours because of it. Someone else could be dead right now, or dying. Or *several* someones." My voice rose a little, I took a deep breath and contained myself. "I might have to move quickly tonight, Harp. He won't be able to—"

The country Were in question decided to pipe up. "I can keep up," Dustcircle said dryly. "Believe me, I don't want to tangle with any hellbreed. I'll leave them strictly to you, and stay out of your way. Now if you'll excuse me, I think the pot roast needs attending."

Pot roast? Just what did they put in my fridge? I folded my arms and glared back at Harp. But she had a point. Hellbreed I could handle—hopefully. A berserker Were gone over the edge and looking for meat I might not be able to take without losing some serious blood. If I ran across them both together a little backup might be nice.

I *really* wanted to leave the country boy at home. But part of being a hunter is being allied with Weres, and the idiot had apologized. I'd be rude and stupid if I kept this up, and while I don't mind being the first, the second can get you killed.

"Fine." I gave in. "You're right. Backup's far from

the worst idea when it comes to something like this. But still, it bothers me. Why would a hellbreed be cleaning up after a rogue? It just doesn't make *sense*."

"Unless she's not cleaning up, she's somehow directing him." Harp leaned back on her hands, looking relieved. Dominic let out another gusty sigh and began to purr, the throaty rumble shaking dust out of the couch. He was relaxing.

I restrained the urge to pat his belly like a cat's, touched a knife-hilt instead. "If she was directing him, she'd have picked better targets. Killing cops in a hunter's town is just *asking* for trouble, and none of the victims have any nightside ties at all."

"There is that." Dominic sighed.

The phone shrilled, and I let out a curse, striding into my bedroom to pick it up. "'Lo." I stared at the fall of sunshine through a skylight, my abdominal muscles tightening as if expecting a punch. I was still sore as hell. The scar's channeling of etheric energy meant I healed a lot faster then even the ordinary hunter, but I never felt quite right while my body was knitting itself back together. The food helped, but the sheer animal part of the body doesn't bounce back so easily from a wound that could have been mortal.

Each time you get close to death the body gets a little nervous.

"Jill." It was Monty, again, and my back went cold and prickling with gooseflesh. But he had good news— sort of—for once. "Saddle up. The rookie's awake. You want to talk to him?"

14

Luz General rose like a brooding anthill. It isn't a Catholic hospital like Sisters of Mercy, but it's still an old building, and the ER doctors there know me. Eva and Benito usually brought their exorcism cases here to be checked out afterward, but they were probably in bed at this hour.

"You scared the shit out of Forensics." Monty didn't mince words, running his hands back through his thinning hair. The bags under his eyes could give mine a run for their money. "You were bleeding pretty bad. What the fuck happened?"

You're better off not knowing, Monty. "Do you really want me to tell you?" I matched his stride as we set off down the corridor. Harp and Dominic would finish dinner and head out into the barrio once dark fell, to gather the Weres and start hunting.

Behind me, Dustcircle's footsteps were almost soundless. Whatever Monty thought of a big man in a brown leather jacket who looked like Crazy Horse in whiteman drag shadowing li'l ol' me, he didn't say a word. I was oddly, pointlessly grateful. It's good to work with normal people who might not understand but don't actively fear you.

It reminds you of what you're fighting and bleeding for every night on the streets.

Monty sniffed. "Guess not. The Psych Department is earning its cookies on this one, that's for damn sure. I had to send four of the techs in for trauma counseling."

"Seeing the unexpected does tend to knock the wind out of them. Sorry."

"It wasn't you. It was the goddamn werewolves."

"Cat Weres, Monty. Your pop culture is showing." My trench coat made a slight whooshing sound as we turned a corner. Fluorescent light coated the walls and linoleum floor. It was unforgiving glare, harsh and institutional. Or maybe the smell of Lysol and suffering in the air made it that way.

"Fuck you." He said it a little louder than he'd intended to, as we passed a bustling nurse in the hall. The heavyset woman gave him a glance of disapproval, her graying hair cut short in a cap of curls. I smelled disinfectant, pain, and the smell of filth that always lurks under the bald edge of sanitation in a hospital. "I never get used to that," he muttered. "How do you stand it?"

"A finely developed sense of the bizarre. Plus a good bottle of booze every now and again." *The human mind is amazingly adaptable, Monty. You'd be surprised at what you can live with once you see it often enough.*

"Christ, it's that easy?" Monty pointed, and we went through the glass doors to the ICU.

Immediately the air turned thick with tension, and I

felt Dustcircle draw a little closer to me. It was, dare I say it, almost comforting. "It's not that easy. But the booze and random sex help a lot." I heard my own tone, hard and falsely bright. "What's our lucky boy's name?" I should have asked before now, but Monty didn't even shoot me a disapproving glance.

"Cheung. Jimmy Cheung." Montaigne had gone pasty-pale. He pointed again, with a nicotine-stained finger. He'd smoked cigars for years before his wife made him give it up, but old habits and addictions die hard and he still chomped a Cuban or two when the going got really rough. "He knows you're coming. Down there, in room 4."

No shit, Monty. The only room with a couple of uniforms guarding it. "He's coherent?"

Monty's shrug was a marvel of ambiguity. "In spates, I guess. He's pretty well sedated. The doc says not to agitate him, but . . ."

"But we need whatever I can get out of him. I'll be gentle." *A regular angel of mercy, that's Jill Kismet.* "He's one of mine, Monty. I'll be *very* gentle."

"Good." Monty folded his arms. "I'll be down in the caff if you want me. Gonna get some fucking coffee." His eyes flicked past me, the question implicit.

"He'll come with me. Backup." I watched Monty's eyes widen and the blood drain from his face again. He really did go alarmingly pale sometimes, for such a big tough slouching bear of a man. "I don't expect any trouble. But better to be safe, right?"

"You got it. Just don't shoot up the fucking hospital, I don't need the paperwork." He turned on his heel and left me there, and Dustcircle moved a little closer.

Right into my personal space, as a matter of fact.

I took a deep breath, controlling my twitch. Weres don't have the same concept of space humans do, and most every hunter gets itchy when someone else gets too close. When a Were moves in like that, it means they're offering support. Cat and canine Weres are very touchy-feely, and bird Weres have a whole elaborate protocol for brush and flutter. Snake Weres like to get right up into your aura and breathe in your face, all but rubbing noses like Eskimos.

And let's not even talk about Werespiders. I shivered, the hair on my nape rising briefly. Decided to let him know I didn't feel too chummy, despite his offer of comfort. "Any reason why you're in my personal space, Dustcircle?"

"Just being friendly." He didn't retreat, setting off down the hall with me, matching me step for step. "He's a friend of yours?"

"Monty? Yeah, he's a good guy." We were approaching the uniformed officers, standing to attention at either side of room 4's door, which was slightly ajar. I could almost feel Dustcircle breathing on my hair. *Even for a Were, this is too close. Get him away.*

I didn't have time. I nodded to the uniforms—Tom Scarper, a good cop, and his partner Ramon, both guys I remembered from their rookie class with me—and accepted their quiet murmurs of welcome. Even foul-mouthed Fuckitall-Ramon looked serious, his dark eyebrows drawn together.

Then I was through the door, the Were right behind me, and in a hospital room full of tubes, soft sterile light, and the sound of machines beeping softly, monitoring heartbeat and respiration, standing their ceaseless watch.

"Jesus," I whispered. The thing on the bed looked vaguely human, but it was bandaged to within an inch of its life.

Get it? Within an inch of his life? Ha ha, Jill. Very funny. I swallowed with an effort, moved up to the side of the bed. Half of Jimmy Cheung's skull had been shaved, and a wet glaring line of unbandaged stitches showed where his scalp had been opened up. I calculated the angle of the scar and felt my heart thump sickly inside my chest.

Not Were claws. Those are likely hellbreed marks, if I spread my fingers just so and had curved claws the marks would look similar. So it was probably our girl Cenci who opened up the car like a tin can and reached in for this kid.

One liquid brown eye was open. He was awake. His breath hissed in, hissed out without the aid of a ventilator, at least he was breathing on his own. An oxygen tube lay under the bandages that covered his ruined nose.

I found my voice. "Officer Cheung." My tone was soft, respectful, and Dustcircle bumped into me from behind. I shoved back, subtly, pushing him away with my hip. "It's Jill. Jill Kismet."

The eye widened. Blinked. His other eye was lost under a sheeting of gauze. I wondered if I wanted to see the damage, decided I didn't. The rhythm of his breathing didn't change, and his heartbeat didn't waver. It was uncanny, seeing the EKG spikes match the pulse my preternaturally sensitive hearing was picking up.

The Were moved closer, bumped me again. I suffered it, my eyes on the bandaged face resting against the pillow's whiteness. The blankets were pulled up on his chest, and I smelled the sharpness of urine. He had to have a catheter; no way he could make the bathroom in this condition.

God. Tangle with the nightside and this is what you get. Even if you're innocent. Do your job, Jill.

"I'm going to take down whoever did this to you," I promised the slack face on the pillow. "But I need you to tell me anything you can about the attack. If you can't, just shake your head. Or blink, or something." I kept my tone very soft, conciliatory. "But if you can, it would help me. A lot."

When he spoke, I was surprised. His voice was strong but reedy, and his lips weren't bandaged. They were bloodless, and a thin crust hung at their corners, the effluvia of sickness. "It was a woman." He exhaled, took a gasping breath, and I smelled the peculiar sick burning scent of the human body struggling to cope with damage. "They radioed, said they'd seen something by the side of the road—a dog, or something. Coyote. But *wrong*. By the time we got there . . ." A slight cough, and I eyed his IVs. He was on morphine, which explained the dreamy tone and his lack of affect. "She came right through the windshield. Tore . . . the top of the car open. So quick. And quiet, nothing but the metal screaming . . ."

"What did she look like?" I pitched my voice low, respectful.

"Blonde. Pretty. Red eyes." His own eye closed briefly. Opened wide. "She was going to kill me, but it scrambled over the hood. She went after it."

My breath caught. "It?" *Coyote? Dog? A canine Were,*

stuck between human and animal form? Likely, but don't make assumptions, Jill. This is tenuous enough.

But there was no more. His eye drifted closed again, and the rhythm of beeping from the machines smoothed out. Gone into the dark depths, just like a submarine sinking.

Blonde. Pretty. Red eyes. The glow of a maddened hellbreed? It meant she wasn't a Trader, their eyes didn't change, just acquired the flat dusty shine.

Besides, no Trader could have fought off both me and Harp. It wasn't possible. Still, I felt a thin thread of unease, and was glad I'd received at least one hard piece of information to hang *that* assumption on.

I reached down. Mikhail's ring glinted on my left hand. My middle two fingers touched the rough gauze over his hand, then the very edge of one knuckle showing through the swathed white and the bumps of the IV. His skin was cold, inert.

"I promise," I whispered. "I'm on the job. Rest easy."

There was no reply. I took my hand back, straightening, and bumped into Dustcircle again, acutely aware of how much taller he was. *Dammit. What's he doing?* I half-turned, pushing past him and heading for the door; I had to damn near ooze around him, he stood so still. My heart lodged in my throat as he turned to follow me, each move as graceful as a dance.

Outside, the Were left the door ajar again, fluorescent light glowing in his dark hair. I nodded at Ramon, the obstruction in my throat turning dry and massive.

Scarper's cheeks flushed under his stubble. "Hell of a thing," he said, the words falling dead in the corridor.

"Yeah. Hell of a thing." My voice didn't seem to want to work quite properly either.

"Gonna fuckin' get 'em, Jill?" This from Ramon, whose dark eyes were bright with unspecified emotion.

I met his gaze, and for once someone didn't flinch when I looked at them. "Of course I am. Nobody fucks with cops in my town and gets away with it, gentlemen." I turned on my heel and stalked away, almost tripping as Dustcircle moved in close again.

I waited until we reached the end of the hall to bring it up. "What the hell are you *doing?*"

"Just being friendly," he repeated, his steps matching mine. "You take this seriously, don't you."

You have got *to be kidding.* "Is there any other way to take it? I'm a hunter, this is my town. Aren't Were-cougars territorial?" *And what the fuck do you care anyway, country boy?*

"About some things." He was still too close, his warmth brushing my coat.

I rubbed at my right wrist, delicately avoiding the scar's pucker. It throbbed uneasily, reacting to the spill of pain and grief in the air. *Give him something a Were would understand.* "They're my people. Nobody messes with them and gets away with it."

He eased off a bit, giving me a few inches of space that felt damn wide by then. "What's next?"

My lungs filled, a deep breath like a sigh mixing his smell and my own, plus the comforting, ever-present aroma of leather from my coat. "Next I drop by the ware-house and our local Sanctuary to pick some things up, and as soon as dusk hits I go out to torch a few holes."

"Sounds like fun." Was that amusement in his voice?

It felt like he was getting really personal, but it just could have been some Rez Were custom I didn't know about.

"Lots of blood and screaming, severed limbs—the usual." I sighed, and moved away as he homed in on my personal space again. It took a half-skipping motion that looked awkward, my coat swirling, but he quit trying to plaster himself to me. "Lucky you. You get to wait in the car. Now quit rubbing on me."

15

*G*alina held up a handful of thin silver bracelets, her soft green cat-tilted eyes troubled under dark bangs. She looked like a thirties film star, between her paleness and the marcel waves in her sleek hair. "You want to try these, Jill?"

I swept four hinged copper cuffs off the counter and into my largest pocket, laying down a fifty-dollar bill. Eyed the chiming bracelets speculatively. They were blessed, I could see the clean blue glow running just under the surface of the silver, spilling out into the ether. "You think they might hold up better? The copper's taking a chunk out of both of us."

Westering sunlight fell through the high windows of the small shop. Galina lived up on the second floor, and very rarely left these four walls. Sanctuaries are tied to their particular houses; it's the bargain they make. They finish their training, settle, and drive roots in deep; a Sanctuary's house is well-nigh invulnerable. If they're caught out in the open, several nightside species consider them a tasty snack.

For all that, the local Sanctuary is where hunters, Weres, and other nightsiders go for supplies—silver, icons, bullets, other things—and gossip. Name it, and your local Sanc can get it for you. If your credit's good, that is—and if you haven't been too irritating lately. And lots of Weres or hunters will smack you down hard if you're caught messing with a Sanc.

Sancs have a lot of discretion once the Order finishes training them, and if you start trouble inside one of their houses you'll be on your ass in seconds flat. The sorcery they use is weak out in the world, but inside the confines of their own Houses, a Sanctuary's will is law.

Sancs most often die old in bed after a few hundred years. Hunters don't.

Galina shrugged, her smile flashing for a moment as the sun picked out highlights in her hair. Saul had busied himself in the corner, playing with the Were toys—drums, claw-shaped knives, feathers and other bits for making amulets and fetishes.

"If it'll help you with that thing, I'll import it until the cows come home. But I get these—" The silver chimed in her hand, responding as the walls of her house creaked a little, fluxing in answer to her smile. "—from Mexico; they're cheap and readily available. I can even *make* them, if I have to. They might corrode less easily, too."

The glassed-in counter between us was full of little trinkets: Saint medals—Anthony, Jude, and Andrew, as well as George and Catherine—all specially blessed by Father Guillermo over at Sacred Grace, who had a dispensation from the Vatican to use some of the . . . ah, *older* blessings. Small stuffed alligators yawned, and a collection of rock-crystal scrying orbs glittered under the golden light.

Galina is slim and even smaller than me, her short stature belied by the shifting cloak of red-gold energy that is a Sanctuary's trademark. She wore the traditional gray, a tunic-top and a pair of bleached jeans, but was as usual barefoot. A silver pendant with the mark of the Order—a quartered circle inside a serpent's curve—winked at her throat.

I took one of the thin hinged bracelets. *If I wear more than one to cover the scar, it'll make a hell of a lot of noise when they tap together. But if it works, I might have her make me a cuff.* "Well, let's see." I snapped it shut over my wrist, held my hand out, and shook it a little to make the bracelet fall against the scar's ridged pucker.

An amazing jolt of pain leveled me to my knees, Galina's short blurt of surprise echoing uneasily against the walls. The defenses on the building sprang into humming alertness, but I couldn't have cared less, my arm was on *fire,* as if I'd just stuck it in an oven and the flesh was crisping all the way down to the bone. I fell over, scrabbling at the bracelet with my other hand, but the hinge had locked, silver ground against the scar and I let out a sharp cry as the pain spilled down my chest, reaching for my heart with clumsy clawed fingers.

Abruptly the pain receded, hot thick tears squirting out of my eyes. I exhaled, blinked, and found myself flat on the floor, Saul Dustcircle crouching next to me. His fingers locked around my wrist, the silver bracelet—

curled like paper in a hot fire—was busted open in his other hand.

"Jesus," I whispered.

His eyes were very dark, and they held mine for a moment. He didn't ask a single question, just turned my wrist up and looked at the scar, his eyebrows drawing together.

Shame boiled up inside me, hot and vicious. Galina arrived, having vaulted the counter; she slid her arm under my shoulders and helped me sit up. "Christ, Jill, I'm sorry, I'm so sorry, my God, are you all right?" The defenses settled back into their humming, and I was grateful for that. Triggering Sanctuary defenses would make the pain from my arm seem like a cakewalk.

"F-fine." I tried to yank my wrist out of Saul's hand. His fingers bit down, a Were reflex, but I tore free, dispelling the urge to examine my arm and make sure I wasn't burned. My nerves twitched and screamed. "That was interesting." The words rode a breathy scree of air.

"Are you okay? Do you need to sit down, a glass of water, anything?" Galina was close to tears, her eyes glimmering and pale now. "I didn't think it would do that. Honest, I didn't."

Jesus, Galina, I know. "No worries." I sounded shaky even to myself, took a deep breath. "At least now we know silver won't work to cover it up. What'd you do to that batch?"

"I blessed it using a Greek invocation to Persephone. An old one I dug up out of some of Hutch's books." She was even paler than usual, helping to haul me to my feet and trying ineffectually to dust me off. "Are you really all right?"

Saul rose gracefully, holding the bracelet. It had twisted into a tight little corkscrew and sang a thin little note of stress before it stopped quivering. I didn't blame it, I felt the same way.

Goddamn. Well, let's call that an experiment and chalk it up to experience. All hail Jill Kismet the scientist.

I shook my hands out. The pain had vanished, leaving me weak-kneed and a little sweaty. "Fine. It was just a jolt, that's all." *And I hope nobody finds out about this, because having someone do that to me for torture would be unpleasant at best.* "I'll stick with the copper for now. We'll think of something."

"I'm sorry." She really was contrite. Galina was a gentle soul, when all was said and done. It was why she was a Sanctuary. The Order is concerned with preservation and peace; it's a pity so few pass the entrance tests. Human nature, I guess.

"Don't worry." A sudden idea struck me. "Can you bless all the silver for my bullets like that? It's heap powerful mojo."

Her sleek hair brushed forward over her shoulders as she nodded. "I can do that. How much do you need?" She didn't mention what any fool could see: I was wearing my ammo belt and bandolier, preparing for serious trouble tonight.

If she'd seen the trunk of my Impala, she might have been even more worried. I thought about it for a second. Took a shaky breath in, my heartbeat finally smoothing out. "Enough to refill my ammo belt. I'll stop by tomorrow if I have time." Translation: *if I'm not getting shot at, or dealing with another crisis.* I gauged the fall of sunlight. Near dusk. In another forty-five minutes it would be night.

The thin taste of copper laid itself over my palate again, my body reacting both to the pain and to trouble coming. I was going to throw myself into something dangerous and potentially deadly tonight, and my animal instinct was having a difficult time with the thought. Dumb idiot body, getting all worked up before the fun started.

Going out to torch hellbreed holes is just *asking* for trouble. But sometimes asking for trouble heads off even deeper trouble up the road.

"All right." Her eyes moved past me, to Saul. "Anything you need, sir?" Her tone was polite, and I thought I caught a twinkle in her eyes. Theron and some of the others from the barrio were regular visitors; the Order and the Weres are old friends. Back when the churches both Catholic and Protestant used to hunt the furkind—not to mention the feathered and scaled—the Order was doing its best to protect them. European Weres had caught the worst of it, but those in the New World have suffered enough to remember in different ways.

On other continents Weres had—and have—different problems.

"Leather. A strip this long—" His hands shaped the air. "And these." He laid a handful of stuff on the counter. Probably meant for amulets, and Galina nodded, patting my shoulder.

"I'll ring you up in a moment. Are you sure you're okay, Jill?"

Don't sound so worried, kiddo. I do this for a living, remember? I've been trained. "Peachy keen." I tried not to sound sarcastic, turned away. When she got this soft and worried I felt an acutely uncomfortable need to reassure her, and always ended up sounding like an idiot. Safer just to change the subject. "I'll wait out in the car."

"Be safe," Galina called after me. I made a noise of assent—what *can* you say, to something like that? I couldn't be safe if I tried.

I didn't even know if I wanted to. I was, in my own special way, as much an adrenaline junkie as Avery. Or even more. Hard not to crave the jolt of staring down death or the feeling of skating the edge of terror and coming out on top, once you've tasted it.

The bell on the door's crossbar tinkled as I stepped outside the safety of her shop, taking in the street with a quick glance. My Impala sat at the curb obediently, her orange paint gleaming. My baby.

Dustcircle came out a few minutes later, carrying a small bag. He settled into the passenger's seat as I roused the engine. "Nice lady."

"Just don't start any trouble around her, and she stays that way." I shifted into first and pulled away from the curb. "Find everything you needed?"

"Yup." He paused as I accelerated, heading up Fairville. I'd catch Fifteenth and drop down toward Plaskény Square.

My first stop of the night. My heart thudded once under my ribs, settled back into its regular rhythm.

"Mind if I smoke?" He dug in his pocket and came up with a pack of Charvils. The smell of cherry tobacco reached my nose. It was oddly pleasant, especially since he'd stopped looming over me.

"Knock yourself out. Just roll down the window." *I redid the upholstery in here, I don't want it reeking.*

"Can I ask you something?"

Depends on what you ask, furboy. "Ask." I hit my turn signal, eased us around a corner.

"What happened to your teacher—Tolstoi, right? He was famous."

"Harp didn't tell you?" My heart leapt up into my throat, my palms suddenly slick. "He fell in love and she killed him." *He fell in love with a Sorrow, she stole his amulet and tore his throat open. If I ever get the chance, I'm going to kill her.* "The Weres gave him a pyre. He deserved it."

The pause was uncomfortable. I shifted, ramming the clutch, and opened my mouth again. "He was the only man who ever thought I was worth a damn."

Shut up, Jill. He doesn't need to hear that. He's just a visiting Were. Stop it. I reached forward, twisted the radio knob angrily, and got lucky. They were playing Jimi Hendrix, and I turned it up, accelerating, the sound of music and wind through the windows sweet enough to drown the lump in my throat.

Mostly.

The Diablo was a hellbreed hole on Plaskény, a long, low vaulted basement at the bottom of a flight of dusty, narrow, filth-drifted stairs. I poured a thin tidal wave of vodka on the bar before smashing the bottle, a nice theatrical touch. The screaming had stopped, but there were still moans and little clicking sounds from the *arkeus* I'd just finished mostly dismembering. The clicks dissolved into a gurgle, and a titanic stink rose.

One more hell-thing dead, more or less.

Most of them were dead, draped over chairs, dissolving on top of tables. The dance floor was chaos, and my shoulders hurt. So did my face, I'd taken a shot right on the cheek that could have broken a human hunter's neck. My shirt was torn, and my long leather trench had ragged claw marks in it. It was just one rip short of the dustheap.

Burning a hellbreed hole is never easy, especially for just one hunter. The only good thing about it was I didn't have to watch where my shots went, eventually they'd hit someone who deserved it. When I used to do backup with Mikhail we'd have to be careful not to clip each other—but working with your teacher is like working with a telepath who *anticipates,* and if you're a good student you get to the point where you can anticipate too.

Or at least stay the hell out of the way.

I held the gun steady on the bartender, a thin ragged hellbreed with a shock of piebald hair and a twisted upper lip. Despite that, he was attractive, in a worn sneering way, with that aura of the exotic 'breed carry. He eyed the gun and opened his mouth to say something—

—and I half-turned, lashing out *behind* me, the whip flicking, striking with a crackle across the face of a slick little female 'breed sneaking up on me through the wreckage. She collapsed, screaming, holding her face. If she lived she'd be scarred by the silver.

Hot nasty satisfaction spilled through my veins like wine-fumes. I was grinning madly, blue sparks crackling over the blessed silver tied in my hair, charms chiming a sweet counterpoint to the violence.

"Spread the word." I turned back to the bartender. The gun didn't waver. I used to use baby Glocks, being cursed with smaller wrists than a man. No more. I like the big ones, my bones can handle recoil a lot better now. "Whoever's hiding this New York chippie 'breed is on a one-way track back to Hell. I want her, and I want her *yesterday*. Got it?"

He made a thin whining sound as the whip returned, wrapping itself neatly in my fist. My fingertips tingled. I ached to pull the trigger—someone had hit me with a chair, crunching my leg and almost cutting my throat with a broken bottle. Most of the hellbreed in here I'd just wounded and put down to bleed out, but that one I'd killed.

The hammer rose back as I squeezed the trigger, delicately, gently. It clicked into the up position. "I am not going to tell you again." My voice was deadly soft. My ribs ached—having a couple 'breed pummel you will do that. It had taken a ridiculous amount of ammo, but I'd wanted the first one messy enough to make a statement. Enough of them had escaped to spread the word that I was on the warpath.

It had certainly *been* messy enough to satisfy. A chaos of blood and screaming, the music pounding through it all until a stray shot had thankfully knocked out a vital connection in the DJ's booth. Then just screams and shouting, and hellbreed cries.

And death.

The bartender scrambled away and fled toward the shattered front door. I hadn't been particularly subtle.

Red and purple light flickered, random reflections cast by the blastball hovering over the dance floor. The rest of the place was wreckage.

It had taken me only fourteen and a half minutes. Give or take. There's something about working overtime and double semiautomatics that makes a girl capable of kicking serious ass.

I filled my lungs. My fingers prickled, the heat becoming uncomfortable. The scar pulsed wetly, thrumming with the force I'd pulled through it. Hey, I could afford it; I was paid up through the month.

Don't think about that, Jill. I flicked my fingers.

Vodka on the bar ignited with a *wump!*

A thin pale-blue flame smeared like oil. Banefire. It would spread to thin flammable hellbreed blood and more spilled liquor, and this place was a firetrap anyway. I spent a few moments examining the shell of etheric energy on the concrete walls—the concrete would keep the fire from spreading, but this flame would consume every trace of hellbreed, cleansing the entire interior and leaving a thin coating of inimical-to-hellspawn blessing behind.

Thank you, God. I did *not* want to burn down more than I needed to.

I turned on my heel, the ragged strips of my coat fluttering. Under its protection, I was mostly whole. I hadn't lost much blood tonight.

Yet. This is only your first stop. Don't get cocky.

The place began to smoke and flame in earnest. I strode up out of the fire, up the steps past the subterranean iron door hanging by one hinge, stepping over the pool of ick that used to be a burly hellbreed grunt

bouncer, finally out into the night's cool sweetness. The
bartender had fled, and I faintly caught the echo of his
running feet, heading north and veering to the west.

*Probably heading for the Monde. Happy birthday,
Perry.* I sighed, rolling my shoulders in their sockets, as
something detonated behind me and the flames started to
lick and sizzle in earnest. Banefire doesn't sound like real
flame. It sounds like whispery, papery voices screaming
behind you, like a cold sweat in the middle of the night.
It is a flame of cleansing, not like the black twisting fire
a hunter can call upon to fashion levinbolts.

And definitely not like hellfire.

The scar throbbed aching tension against my wrist.
Mikhail's ruby warmed the hollow of my throat. I
crossed the street, heels clicking, since I didn't have to
be quiet at all tonight.

Dustcircle leaned against the hood, smoking one of
his cherry cigarettes. He smelled of tension, musk, and
sleek electric fur on end. Seeing the bartender blunder
up out of the hole and into the night must have been
worrisome.

His eyes flicked past me to the doorway. My back
prickled. If any 'breed came out now they'd be angry but
wounded, and not much of a threat.

*That's pride talking, Jill. Even a half-dead 'breed is
dangerous. Do not get cocky.*

"How many were down there?" He asked it so calmly
I almost didn't believe the tense thrumming coming out
of him, the Were version of a fidget. Not quite a growl,
but certainly more than a purr.

"I stopped counting at twenty." I fished my pager
out and checked it. No calls, and it was early still. "I've

got lots to do tonight, Dustcircle. You want to get in the car?"

He remained where he was, staring across the street. I restrained the urge to look back over my shoulder.

He took his sweet time examining the twisting blue shadows of banefire. Finally, he spoke. "Were you kind to them?"

I almost went slackjawed in amazement. Kind to them? They were *hellbreed*. Spoilers and corruptors, sorcerous maggots, predators.

After a moment, I understood. When Weres kill, they do it swiftly. They don't play with their prey.

Unless they're rogue, gone berserk and violating the oldest of Were taboos.

Thou shalt not eat people.

It irked me that he'd even asked. What did he think I was? "I've killed more 'breed than you can possibly imagine," I told him, flatly. "Not a single one of them was ever what I'd call happy, and I put them down as quick and clean as I can. You can call that kindness if you want. I like to think I'm being kind to the innocents they prey on. Get in the *car*."

He did.

16

Two holes and a short streetside gunfight to mop up later, I was tired more than physically. I braked to a stop down the street from the Random, a step above the norm.

Most 'breed like their holes underground, with one entrance. It just shows the burrowing instinct in them. The holes are womblike and thump with music during the night, and any human dumb enough to wander or be lured inside is lucky to escape with only psychic damage.

The Random, however, was a Trader club. If hellbreed came here, they were actively looking to make a deal. Any humans that showed up were the same.

It was a ramshackle building, its windows painted black and its door guarded by two beefy Traders with glittering dusted eyes. I watched through the windshield and let out a soft breath, the scar throbbing. It was time to open up the trunk.

Unfortunately, Dustcircle picked that moment to open his mouth.

"What exactly is this supposed to accomplish?" He sounded uneasy.

You idiot. What do you think I'm doing, having Captain Kangaroo *sing-alongs and eating caramel corn?* I had to work for an even, nonsarcastic tone, and suspected I failed. "The 'breed community functions on profit and loss. If it becomes too expensive for them to hide this Cenci, they'll police themselves and turn in any information they have. Besides, I'm a new hunter, kind of, I've only been knocking around on my own for half a year. If Mikhail was alive we wouldn't have to do this; he'd visit a few of his sources and we'd track her down that way. They'd *know* not to mess with him. Me, I'm still teaching the bitches who's boss."

"Proving you're alpha?" He sounded dubious. "Do we have time for this?"

"It's the quickest way to get what I want, which is no more bodies in the street." I felt the shiver even as I said it. It wasn't the whole reason I was clearing out these places. Every 'breed I killed tonight was a slap directly to Perry's bland blond face.

Fuck around with my head, will you? Just see how easy it would be for me to fuck right back. I pushed the flare of murderous rage down. *Save it for the Random, Jill. Do it just like you were trained to.*

Make Mikhail proud.

"All right." He sniffed, inhaling deeply and tasting the air. "This smells different."

Sure it does. "It's a Trader club. General rule, above ground it's Traders, below it's pure 'breed." *Though there are exceptions. Like Perry's place, which switches back and forth according to some weird rule I haven't figured out yet.* I eased my hands off the wheel. "This one might take me a while."

"I can come with you." He didn't ask, he just *said* it, and tossed the remains of his most recent cigarette out the half-open window. "I'll leave the 'breed to you and stay out of your way. Watch your back."

It wasn't a half-bad idea, except I'd never worked with him before. This wasn't a place for amateurs. "Probably not a good idea," I said, diplomatically enough. "Harp wants—" *Harp wants her deposit back on you,* was what I intended to say.

"Harp wants me to keep your skin whole, hunter. I can handle Traders." He rolled up the window, his profile austere in the wash of orange lights from streetlamps. The twin braids on either side of his face moved with him; he opened the car door and stepped out.

I weighed the situation for a few moments, opened my own door. Cool air touched my skin, and dried sweat crackled as I moved. I'd had to scrub the blood off my face more than once tonight.

He stopped at the rear of the car, much bigger than me and wider in the shoulders. He loomed over me with very little trouble, but I had the scar and enough experience to give him a serious run for it. The thought passed through my head, circled, came back, and was gone again.

You can't shut off that part of your brain when you're a hunter—the part that jots everyone down in columns according to how easy or difficult they'd be to kill. The part that doesn't really care *why,* the part that just wants to survive, by hook or by crook. That cold, calculating, utterly amoral part you have to harness, use—but never let completely free.

I was suddenly very aware that I smelled like death and hellbreed blood, as well as sweat and effort. Dustcircle, of course, looked immaculate and smelled of clean male Were.

He won't be pretty for long if he goes in there. Apparently it was my night for not-very-nice satisfaction. I felt a quick burst of shame, discarded it as useless.

"All right." I popped the trunk and started exchanging spent ammo clips for fresh ones, tucking them into my belt and bandolier. "Pop quiz. A Trader comes at you with his eyes glowing red. What do you do?"

"Get out of the fucking way and let you handle it. Trader eyes don't glow." He folded his arms, his leather jacket creaking a little. One eyebrow raised briefly, and his lip almost curled.

So he's not a complete novice. "What do you do if a hellbreed has me down on the floor with her hands around my windpipe?"

"Stay out of the way and let you handle it. If a 'breed's that close to you it's stupid, doesn't deserve to live." His eyes glowed, a flat green-blue sheen covering them for a moment as the streetlamp overhead reflected against a nonhuman pupil. Just like a cat's eyes, when the light hits them right. "I'm not a complete idiot, Kismet."

So I'm Kismet now, not "hunter" or "hellbreed-smelling bitch." I've been upgraded. "Good to know. Last question." I reached down, picked up the slim length of Mikhail's sword, its clawed finials capped with leather and its blade wrapped in a soft sheath. "We walk in the door and immediately a Trader jumps you. What do you do?"

"Rip its heart out, break its neck." He didn't even

blink as I ducked through the strap, settling it diagonally across my body so the sword rode my back. The snaps on the soft sheath clinked a little; if I reached up for the sword a quick sideways jerk would free it, since it was too long to really draw or hang at my side like a rapier. "That's a big chunk of metal, kitten. You know how to use it?"

Kitten? If I didn't know better I'd think you just called me a little kid. The smile that rose to my face wasn't pleasant at all. I made sure all my guns had a full clip and one in the chamber. "That's the advantage of having a hellbreed scar on my wrist, furboy. I get to play with all *sorts* of toys that are too big for me." I slammed the trunk and turned. "You can come and play. Stay low, stay away from the 'breed, and try not to get clipped. Harp would kill me if I let something happen to you."

"I'll do my best." He sounded sardonic. When I glanced at him, he wore a slight smile, a feral light shining through his dark eyes. He looked ready to cause trouble, with the edgy good humor of a Were about to explode with frustration. "If I'm a very good little boy will you stop fussing at me?"

Fussing at him? I was so irritated I almost forgot how tired I was, and how I did *not* want to be doing this. "I don't *fuss.* Now shut up—I've got work to do."

"Sure."

I darted another quick glance at him as we stepped out into the street. He stared straight ahead, toward the Random's neon signs and the huddled mass of people lining up at the front door, threads of contamination swirling through the ether around them.

Nobody paid us any mind. We hopped on the sidewalk, and I plunged into an alley slicing off to the side.

"Back door?" Was that grudging admiration in his tone? That rubbed me raw too. What did he think I was, a dolt or a novice? Both? Plus a hellbreed-smelling almost-traitor to the good guys?

"Of course." I tried not to sound too sarcastic. "I wouldn't be much of a hunter if I didn't know where the back doors are."

"Guess not." Grudging, barely giving an inch. I supposed it would kill him if he admitted I knew how to do my goddamn job.

I wondered what he'd say when I told him the back door was on the roof.

We dropped down into a bath of crimson light and a dancing mass of Traders. I landed hard, the dance floor cracking in a radial pattern as the force of my breaking a law of physics crackled out in random spiderweb spokes. My aura flamed, visible suddenly in the inky etheric contamination, a sea urchin made of light. Then I came up all the way from the floor with a punch that sent one Trader flying, blood from his smashed face hanging in the air for a moment before splashing out. The knives left their sheaths, and I started weeding through them in earnest.

Twenty seconds later, I forgot about Dustcircle. It was apparent he could take care of himself—except for when one Trader leapt for his back, and the knife left my hand with a glitter, a short wordless cry like a hunting falcon's escaping my lips. Just afterward I took a shot right in the gut from a squat bearded Trader who gibbered when I snarled at him, the silver in my hair burning and the ruby sparking at my throat, and I brought up the Glock in my free hand. The whip uncoiled, and I was just about to leap down from the dance floor into the club proper through strings of swaying glass beads when something smashed into me from the side.

I went flying and twisted, getting my feet under me and skidding across the bar, bootsoles smoking as I *kicked*, another Trader going flying. Then it came after me again, so fast it almost blurred, and I recognized the veiled 'breed who did assassinations.

Oh, fuck. I dropped to the side, firing with both hands now, trained reflex tracking the 'breed as he leapt above the bar and sank his fingers into the concrete wall, hissing at me with bared teeth I could see through his fluttering veil.

He was unholy quick, but I'd been trained by the best and aimed *before* him, knowing he would twist in mid-air to get leverage so he could bring his claws to bear on me. Silver-loaded bullets punched through his shell, black ichor flying, then I *rolled,* gaining my feet with a convulsive movement most people don't think a woman is capable of using—knees drawn in before feet flung out, back curving, feet coming under to catch, I spun in a tight half-circle and caught the next hellbreed—a female with flying black-ink hair—as she was at the apex of an arcing leap down on me. Silverjacket lead flew, the nightclub suddenly a roil of screaming chaos, and I heard the deep coughing roar of a Were in a rage.

Hope he's all right. I was too busy to worry about him, I had troubles of my own. My eyes found the whip again, but it was too far away and the veiled 'breed thrummed in Helletöng, the curse flashing past me and slicing through a pair of Traders who had been looking to leap on my back.

Thank God I brought it. My right hand flashed up, closed around the hilt, and I gave the sharp sideways jerk that burst the snaps on the sheath. Leather parted and the ruby at my throat flamed into bright bloody light.

Okay, you sonofabitch. Let's tango.

I actually had time to let go of the hilt, flip my hand while the sword was in midair, and close my fingers on it again before the veiled 'breed crashed into me yet once more. The shock tore something in my side, and my scream rose with his growl, an inhuman sound that caused no few of the Traders to drop to the floor, clapping their hands over their ears—but my aura flamed again, blocking the force of his cry, and all I heard was the horrible choking of a gallows-dropped man whose neck has not kindly snapped. I got my feet underneath me and dug my heels in, the bright blade coming up as my other hand closed on the hilt.

Orange flame burst along the sword's long straight line. It was a two-handed broadsword, with its point on the floor the finials reached my ribs and the blade was as wide as my hand at the base. The hilt's metal claws sparked, flexing down to feed power into the blade, and a crimson gleam showed in the empty place in the hilt, echoed by the bloody gem at my throat.

You can't use a sunsword without a key, after all.

Fighting with a broadsword isn't like knifework. It's a matter of hack and slash, and the speed that gives me such an edge when it comes to knifing is handicapped by the sheer weight of the blade and the pommel, still too absurdly big for my fragile-seeming hands. Still, the ruthlessness trained into me comes in handy. I don't hesitate to hack *or* slash.

And once all that mass gets moving, the momentum gets easier to control. My speed kicks back in, becoming an asset once more.

The sword coughed, reacting to the contamination of Hell's citizens in the air. Then it burst into its true flame, golden like the noon sun dawning from hilt to tapered point.

Howls. Screams. The veiled 'breed ran right into the slash as I stamped, driving forward with the long muscles in my legs. Preternatural flesh parted, and the 'breed gave a deathly scream, spiraling up into a falsetto squeal. I half-turned again, continuing the motion and sweeping the sword up, meeting the second wounded 'breed. *What do you say, God, let there just be two of them, please, what do you say, give me a break*—The thought was gone in an instant as ichor sizzled on hot steel, and another squeal tore the space inside the Random. Flame dripped, and the flooring smoked. It was only a matter of time before the place started to burn with sunfire.

My side healed in a brief burst of agonizing pain as I *pulled* on etheric force, sweat dripping down my back. The scar on my wrist screamed with agony, but the ruby pulsed reassuringly. The sword still recognized me, and *didn't* burn me to a crisp. That, at least, was comforting.

Then the world exploded into chaos. I heard Dust-circle's short yell of warning and whirled, only getting halfway before an amazing, terrific weight smashed into me from behind.

I *flew*. Good thing I wore leather, my skin would have been erased as I landed, fetching up against the floor and skidding into a pile of rotting Trader bodies. It was on me again, fingers sinking into my hair and yanking my head up, before I shook the dazed noise out of my head and found myself still holding the burning sword. A pile of decomposing Traders was beginning to smoke, waves of heat spreading out in concentric shimmering-air rings.

My hellbreed-strong right arm came up, and I used the clawed pommel to smash the side of the thing's head in.

It tore away from me, and cloth ignited with a low hissing sound. I staggered to my feet, bracing both hands around the hilt, and got a good look at him.

He was slim and dressed in black, with dusty black eyes. When I say black eyes I mean the iris and pupil were so dark as to be indistinguishable yawning holes in his face, and that blackness spread through the whites, staining them with rage. He wore, of all things, a nice pair of Tony Lamas in plain black, and his hair was scorched on one side but appeared black and curly, his coppery skin and hooked nose giving him a vaguely Italian cast.

The world fell away. Etheric force hummed through the scar, cycling up as his aura tightened, a black hole of swirling force.

Oh, shit.

The sunsword hissed, coming up and dappling the air with heat. It blocked the force of the hellbreed's eyes, and I tilted the blade, deflecting the second curse he rumbled at me in Helletöng. Still, I felt it pass me like a train rumbling past at midnight, and my knees almost buckled.

This wasn't just a hellbreed.

It was a monstrously powerful hellbreed, and I'd just pissed it off big-time.

I dug my feet into the floor, filled my lungs, and got ready for a fight I would almost certainly not win even with the sunsword's help.

17

*S*tasis. The world slowing down, stopping, as the hellbreed stared at me, force crackling over him in an egg-shaped shield. Everything hung in the air—drops of blood, shattered bits, a Trader falling from the roof where he had tried to get some height to leap down on Saul Dustcircle, who had finished rolling aside and was ready for him, a Bowie knife somehow appearing in his hand, a random dart of light jetting from the blade.

Goddamn Weres and their damn little camouflage tricks.

The 'breed's eyes met mine. He was old, and I bet he'd produce hellfire in at least the green spectrum. Anything above red is seriously bad news, and anything above yellow means kiss-your-ass-goodbye-hunter-it's-time-to-die.

Unless you have a share of hellbreed strength yourself. I drew in an endless breath, the tatters of my coat brushing out on a breeze coming from nowhere, my own aura extending, spiking with a random pattern of brightness. A hunter's aura: disciplined by the training and each exorcism I've performed, a hard shell of etheric energy that makes sure I stay in me—and *nothing* else gets in.

The sunsword roared with flame, more than I'd ever seen, a tail of orange and yellow like the sun's corona spiking up to touch the ceiling, heat shimmering.

I dared him, silently, and knew that he read it in my eyes, in the slight lift of my chin and the way my fingers grew almost soft on the hilt. You never, ever clutch a sword, it makes the strike inaccurate.

His answer was just as slight—a shifting of weight, an infinitely small smile lifting the corners of his sculpted lips. I realized he was grinning under his thatch of wet-dark hair, and I saw again, *noticed* again, his eyes were almost completely black. Infinitely black, with a pale shimmer like disoriented oil floating on the top of a deep sucking tarn. Those eyes were deadly, threatening to suck me in and drown me.

Riptide. Grabbing, whirling, sinking, arms and legs weighted with lead, even my eyelids suddenly drowsy, heavy as a guilty conscience and just as deadening.

Why are his eyes so deep? The thought glittered like a flung knife, like one of my knives, flying true, its load of silver along the flat of the blade—where it couldn't be sharpened off—hissing with white flame as it streaked under the 'breed's uplifted arm and socked home in his ribs. The sound, a heavy solid thunk like an axe driven into dry wood, smashed through my head as the sunsword swept down, painting a fiery streak after its edge.

The clash—sunsword versus hellbreed—was like Mack trucks colliding. The shockwave threw me back, clutching at the hilt, feet scraping in debris shaken down from the roof. The collision blew every bit of glass in the place, including the lightbulbs and the bottles over the bar. The 'breed screeched, no murmuring rush of Helletöng now but a wounded scream, and there was a rushing confusion.

The sword dimmed. Darkness closed almost-absolute around me, light filtering down through the shattered roof as I gasped, my eardrums rattling and a hot wet trickle of blood sliding down from my nose, matching the hot trickles dripping out of my eyes. I collapsed to my knees, only vaguely aware of Saul Dustcircle's arm under my shoulders as I bowed over backward, fingers still loose around the pommel but other muscles tightening up, convulsing. The scar prickled, wetly, a satisfied little lick that sent revulsion spinning down through my stomach.

Don't throw up, Jill. You're alive, you survived, don't puke. Not in front of the Were.

"What the *fuck* was that?" He sounded a little less than calm. A lot less. It was the first time I've ever heard a Were actually sound *frantic*.

Don't worry, country boy. Everything's under control. I wanted to reassure him, but my mouth for once didn't obey my brain.

"You threw my knife," I whispered.

Then I passed out.

It was only a brief second of unconsciousness. I came to right afterward, the sunsword quenched and weighing down my hand. I heard footsteps crunching through smashed and shattered bits. The reek of dead hellbreed and crisped Trader was incredible.

A slight sound to my left brought me fully back into myself. The scar ran with wet heat, as if hot, inhuman breath was touching the ridged skin.

"Look at this mess." Perry finished lighting a cigarette, flame caressing his face with gold for a moment before he clicked the lighter shut. My eyes stung, then adjusted. We'd caused a hell of a lot of damage. "I am going to be hard-pressed to make amends for this, Kiss. You really do know how to complicate matters."

Oh, Christ. Not now. I coughed and choked on the reek, wetness smearing my cheeks. Blood or tears, I couldn't tell. The sunsword keened a little, metal vibrating as it cooled. The red glimmer in its hilt didn't quite go out, but I could tell it would need several hours of direct sun to recharge it. Time to use Galina's greenhouse again.

Am I still alive? A mental inventory returned the verdict that I was, indeed, still alive. And conscious. Plus possessing all my usual bits and pieces.

Hallelujah.

"Who the fuck is that?" Dustcircle jerked me upright, rising to his feet with one fluid motion and dragging me with him by default.

"Friendly," I managed, between whooping retches. I bent over, and my stomach did its level best to rebel against the rest of me. It was declaring its own country and seceding from my union, so to speak.

"Doesn't smell friendly," the Were muttered. "Are you all right?"

He doesn't smell friendly because he isn't, but if you

jump him it's going to get real ugly in here real quick. I got in enough air for a word. "Fine."

"You'd better put a leash on that Were of yours," Perry remarked. He stood in a fall of orange citylight creeping through the shattered ceiling. The fires, all of them, were snuffed. And it was *cold.* My breath made little icy puffs as I gasped. The red eye of Perry's cigarette winked as he inhaled, the smell of burning tobacco and another darker perfume cutting through the death-reek for a moment. "Do you know what you just did?"

Miracle of miracles, the amount of breath I could get in doubled. Enough for two words. "Fuck . . . you."

"Charming. Do you think we should? It would certainly put a whole new shine on our relationship. I repeat, my dearest, do you know what you just did?"

I just cleared out the Random and almost got hooked like a fish by a 'breed with dark eyes and probably an accent. You know how I am for those tall dark and gruesome boys. I couldn't get in enough oxygen to say it, settled for glaring at him between retches. Silver in my hair chimed, and Saul rubbed at my back over the shredded rags of my trench coat.

I didn't have the heart to tell him to stop.

"Take it easy," he murmured. "You looked dazed."

No shit I looked dazed, it almost had my guts for garters. "C-compulsion." My teeth chattered over the word. *"Christ."*

Never. My brain shuddered, came back to itself. *Never met anything like that before. Jesus Christ. Mikhail, why didn't you tell me about this? I could handle everything a lot better if you were here.*

The heaves stopped, and Saul steadied me until I

could stand again. "Made a hell of a mess." His voice was back to calm and even, maybe even a little disdainful. "Nice trick, with the sword."

Nice trick, hell. You saved me by throwing my own knife. Is it the one I tossed at the Trader who almost jumped you? There were more pressing questions. I held the ember-dim sunsword away from both of us, awkwardly, and shook him off. Faced Perry over the heave-cracked floor of what had been, a very short time ago, a thumping, jiving Trader nightclub.

I sure know how to throw a party, don't I. "What the fuck are *you* doing here, Perry?" It came out hoarse, and my throat burned with bile even though I was forcing my stomach to stay with the program.

"Saving your delicate skin from being peeled off in strips. Do you know who that was?" The hellbreed cocked his head. He was pristine in a pale suit, as always, and the lamps of his eyes scored a hole in the darkness. They weren't deepening to indigo yet, which was a good thing. If Perry got seriously pissed off, I was in no condition to handle it right now.

"Some jackshit little hellbreed with a nice pair of eyes." I waved my left hand, dismissive. My apprentice-ring ran with blue threads of light, not breaking the surface of the silver yet but close. "I repeat, Pericles, what the everloving *fuck* are you doing here?"

"I told you, saving you. You just committed violence against Navoshtay Niv Arkady." The faint orange light caressed his pale hair, sliding over its smoothness.

I froze. Passing out again began to sound like a really good idea.

"Who?" Saul didn't sound impressed.

My lips were numb, so Perry answered for me.

"The head hellbreed of New York and the accompanying territories, Were. Our little Kiss just clocked the highest-ranking 'breed on the East Coast—here on diplomatic business, I might add—over the head and gave him a sunburn. And *you* tossed a knife into his ribs." Perry actually, damn his eyes, sounded pleased as punch at the thought. "Oh, Jill, my pretty little Jillian, do you have any *idea* what you are going to owe me when this is all over?"

18

I held up the coat.

My hands were still shaking.

Blood dripped from its tattered leather edges—my claret, and the thin black fluid that passes for hellbreed blood. My head felt a little too big for my neck, and the ringing in my ears wasn't doing me much good either. Hunger crawled under my ribs along with a sickish feeling. The battered, comfortable knee-length Santa Luz Warriors T-shirt didn't help, nor did the idea that I wasn't alone in the warehouse.

My washing machine finished filling and started agitating. Through the glass door, I saw the suds were deep pink. I'd been bleeding a lot lately, and most of the clothes I was bothering to wash were useless rags now. I was going to have to get another two or three *Dies Irae* T-shirts. A one-woman support for cottage industry, that's me.

You just committed violence against Navoshtay Niv Arkady.

Perry had hied himself off to do whatever it was hell-breed do when they aren't fucking with me. He was also going to go and do his diplomatic best with the head of New York's nightside.

I wished him luck. *Lots* of luck. Of course, Perry thought I was still useful for his purposes, so he didn't want Arkady to kill me. On that count, at least, I was in total agreement, even if Perry was a hellbreed.

My hands lowered, so did my head. Silver in my hair chimed. I'd fastened a copper cuff over my wrist, and the resultant blunting of preternatural acuity was both welcome and frightening. I could smell onions sauté-ing—Saul was messing around in the kitchen again. Get a Were close to death, and he does something domestic. Like cooking, or trying to do my laundry until I outright snarled at him to *leave me the fuck alone.*

Get a hunter close to death, and she gets the jumping jitters. No place for all that adrenaline to go except saw-ing along the nerves.

The coat dripped thick red and thin rotting blackness on the floor. I had to hose it off and dispose of it, trans-fer everything into the pockets of a new black leather trench. But I just stood there, shaking.

I could have died. If it wasn't for the Were I would have died. The 'breed had me hooked neat as a trout. He could have just reeled me in and . . .

The trembling refused to go away. From scalp to heels, the animal side of my body was taking revenge. It knew how close it had come to death, and wasn't fooled by my continued breathing and heartbeat. Mikhail called this part the "rabbit shaking in a hole" and had some long involved Russian prayer he would use whenever things had gotten dicey and we'd pulled through once more.

Me, I just shivered. And shivered some more.

I put the coat up on its rack, forcing myself to move. My laundry room was painted yellow, a nice sunshiny color. The sunsword was back at Galina's, in her greenhouse for charging all day tomorrow under the near-desert sun. She hadn't said anything, but her eyes had gotten big, and she'd taken the sword without comment.

I hadn't stayed in her shop long. Maybe I was afraid of what might happen *next,* for Chrissake. I was done. Stick a fork in me.

The floor in here was tiled, so I hooked up the hose and sluiced the tiles as well as my coat. By the time the water turned clear and went down the drain at the far end, I was jittering so bad my hands almost blurred.

I made it out into the living room, crossed it in long strides, and swung into the kitchen. The floor was cold under my bare feet. I reached up on tiptoes and got the bottle of Jack Daniels down. I had to grab for it a second time, and catch it when I knocked it off the shelf, actually.

"Steak. And onions. I'm not sure if you like them, but no steak is complete without. You need protein." Saul sounded amazingly calm. "And salad, I think. We don't have fresh bread, so it'll have to be store-bought wheat with butter. Sorry about that."

I twisted the cap off the bottle. Eyed the glasses on the shelf underneath the liquor.

Fuck that.

I took a long pull straight from the bottle itself. Most alcohol just goes straight through me—my metabolism runs so high now. It was a goddamn shame, because getting drunk seemed like a fabulous idea.

The bottle fell away from my lips. I had to breathe. Then I lifted it and poured a little more down. It *burned* all the way, and I could finally admit what was bothering me.

Oh, Jill, my pretty little Jillian, do you have any idea *what you are going to owe me when this is all over?*

The trouble was I *did* have an idea, and a good one. Negotiating with Navoshtay fell under the amorphous heading of "other services" that were covered in the bargain I'd made with Perry—at a price of a few more hours of my time. It wasn't going to be pleasant, especially if he decided to fiddle painfully or otherwise with the scar again.

Or if he decided he wanted my blood to flow instead of his. It was always a possibility.

I'm more worried about Perry than I am about the other hellbreed, and that's not right. He's wormed his way into my head, dammit. "Jesus," I whispered, and took another long pull.

Saul's hand closed around the bottle, pushing it away from my lips. "Easy there, hunter." He said it softly, almost kindly. "Easy."

Words I could never say boiled up in my throat, hit the stone sitting there, and died. *Easy? What's fucking easy about this? It's not going to be easy paying Perry what I owe. It's not going to be easy dealing with Navoshtay in my town. And it isn't going to be easy to get my hands to stay still and my brain to stop running in circles.*

I searched for something to say to get him away from me. To run him out of the house, if possible, or just get him to shut up and leave me alone to deal with this in my own way. My gaze snapped up to his. "There is nothing easy about this," I rasped. "Fuck off."

He overrode me, sliding the bottle's hard glass from my fingers. Something sizzled on the stove, but he paid no attention. He set the bottle down on the counter with a slight click, then did something very odd.

The Were took my face in his hands, his palms warm against my cheeks, and stared down at me. His gaze was dark, not the black pit of a hellbreed's but a human darkness, for all the unblinking patience of a cat lived behind it. I saw something pass through his eyes, a long low shape like a hunting animal, muscularly padding through sun and shade.

He didn't flinch. Most people find my gaze hard to meet because of the mismatch; it disturbs them on a deep nonverbal level.

The first time I'd opened my eyes after coming up out of Hell, I'd seen Mikhail bending over me, the bloody gem used to anchor me clasped in his fist and his mouth drawn tight under his hawk nose.

So, he'd said, quietly. *You come back with gift,* milaya. *Come, let us get you in bath.*

The sob startled me. I caught it behind my teeth, swallowed it. Smelled the musk of a male Were and the smell of food, mixing together. Good smells, both of them, and a heady pairing.

Saul's thumb stroked my right cheekbone. "Let it out." He crooned in the particular way Weres have of soothing an injured one of their own, a deep rumbling that shakes the bones loose and the muscles into jelly. "Just let it out, Jill. Let it go away."

He said it so kindly, and he didn't look away. He stared right into my eyes as if they didn't bother him a bit, as if they were normal and natural. Then he leaned down, his eyes not closing, and his mouth brushed mine.

I leapt guiltily, almost knocking foreheads with him, but his fingers tightened and I stilled, letting him touch my lips with his. As soon as I stopped struggling, one of his hands curled warm around my nape, and my mouth opened to his.

I had not been this close to anyone in so long. Not since Mikhail.

The smell of musk and male filled my nose, heat sliding down to detonate in my belly, my eyes fluttering closed as my fingers came up and wrapped in his hair. He pressed forward, his hands sliding down to flatten on my back, and I found myself with my back to the counters, balancing on one leg because I'd ended up wrapping the other one around him, his mouth open and greedy but curiously polite, as if he didn't want to press the kiss any further than I wanted.

As if he was *asking* me. He tasted like moonlight and the taint of whiskey passed from my tongue to his, came back laden with another, newer taste—the one we made together, a mixture of my own breath and someone else's.

My head tipped back. His mouth traveled down past my jawline, onto the curve of my throat, and hovered over my pulse. The low rumbling growl he gave out chattered the bottle against the counter and made the wood groan. The scar had turned hot and tight on my wrist under cold copper, and I realized I was naked under the T-shirt and his hands had roamed, and that I could feel the harsh material of his jeans against the inside of my thigh.

I turned into a statue. My breath stilled, stopped, and I waited for the violence to explode. I waited for pain, for the sharp strike of a hand against my cheek, for him to shove me to the floor, a kick catching me under the ribs with a sound like red fury. Red and yellow shapes tangled behind my eyelids, squeezed shut tight enough to ache.

Even with Mikhail I had sometimes frozen, despite his gentleness.

Saul froze too, a curious stillness, his warm hands flattened against my back and his face in my throat. I felt the hard prickle of a tooth through his lips, he'd paused right over my jugular.

Of course. That would be the most sensitive, most highly charged spot for a Were. The trust implied in letting his teeth near my throat was tremendous.

My fingers had turned to wood in the silky pelt of his hair.

My breath held itself as long as it could. He didn't move.

When I finally let the air free of my lungs with a small wounded sound, he stirred. Set me gently back on my feet, his arms still around me and my cheek pressed against his chest. The rumbling intensified, shaking through the channels of my veins, loosening my muscles, and calming the frantic racing inside my head. It felt safe to rest there, leaning against him, a safety I could never remember feeling anywhere else.

A safety I found I liked a little too much.

Cancel that. A *whole lot* too much. He was just a

country-boy Were full of disdain and thinking he knew everything, looking down his nose at me for making a bargain that allowed me to fight better. If he wasn't an enemy, neither was he a friend.

Then why was he holding me? Why had he spent all day bumping into me, herding me around?

He'd saved me with my own knife.

Coherent thought returned. *What the fuck just happened?* My heart pounded against my ribs like an overcharged motor. *Jesus Christ, what the fuck is this? Weres don't . . . they never . . . I . . .*

I couldn't even finish a sentence inside my own head.

His arms tightened briefly, squeezing my breath out. "You go change," he said finally, as if it was a foregone conclusion that I would. "I'll finish dinner. You need some ballast in you." He let go of me, after taking one last long inhale in the vicinity of my hair.

Smelling me. Taking me deep in his lungs, marking me in his memory. Weres did that while tracking, I knew. It was an oddly intimate thing, and I wondered what it *meant*.

I dredged real deep for something smart to say. I settled for spluttering. "What the *fuck*—"

"Jill." He gave me one dark look, shaking his hair down over his eyes and glaring. "Go get changed. I'm making you dinner."

Stubborn endurance has always been enough for me—too much, sometimes. But this time my courage failed me. I fled the kitchen and headed for my bedroom, and by the time I got there the phone on my nightstand was shrilling.

I scooped it up. *Please don't let it be Perry.* "Yeah?"

"Kismet?" An unfamiliar male voice. "It's Clarke, from New York. You set us to do some digging about a disappeared 'breed named Cenci? Real blonde, lots of trouble?"

Relief curled inside me, hot and deep. It wasn't Perry. Of course, it could be bad news in its own right.

That's the trouble with being a hunter. Some days, it knocks the optimism right out of you.

"Yeah." I cleared my throat, repeated it. "Yeah, I did. Do you have anything, anything at all?"

"You won't believe this." Click of a lighter and a long inhale; Jonathan Clarke was a smoker despite being a hunter. You don't live long in this line of work without *some* kind of stress-reduction vice, I guess. "Her name's Cenci all right, but that's only half of it. Guess who her daddy is."

I just got almost killed and kissed by a Were. I think my threshold of disbelief is a lot lower than I started out tonight with. "I give up. Who?"

"Navoshtay Niv Arkady. Old Ark-and-Bark himself. There's more."

He's her father? The strength ran out of my legs. I sat down hard on the bed, the mattress squeaking faintly. Saul had made the bed, neatly, and I felt a moment's guilt at screwing up the pristine blankets.

This just keeps getting better. "Take it from the top, Jon. I'm listening."

Harp called in as I was scraping the last bit of grilled onions up from my plate. I snagged the phone with one hand, licking the fingers of my other hand clean and reaching down to yank at my boots. "Jill here."

"Jill, it's Harp. Glad you're home. Listen, I—"

"Clarke from New York called. I have an earful for you." *Boy, do I ever.*

"Save it to tell me in person. You and Saul need to hightail it down here. We've found what we think is the main nest."

My pulse quickened, my breathing shallowing out. Saul took the empty plate from my hand with a nod. He'd been quiet all through dinner, neither of us meeting the other's eyes, the only sounds the scrape of forks and knives.

The fact that his cooking was good even for a Were was merely incidental. Just like the fact that I was a lot less shaky once I had some ballast in me.

"Where are you?" I must have sounded different, because the Were's eyebrows shot up, and he cocked his head. I saw this in my peripheral vision, unwilling to look directly at him.

She gave me the address—a house down on the south border of Ridgefield, the edge of my territory. "We're keeping the press off, but that won't last long. When can you be here?"

I did a few rapid mental calculations. It was a thirty-minute drive. "I'll be there in fifteen. Is Monty there? Get the ranking officer to tell the traffic detail I'm going to break a few laws and to get someone to cut traffic for me. How many bodies do we have?"

"Four for sure, but I'm not certain about anything else. There's sorcery here, Jill. I hope like hell you have some good news."

Sorcery meant something they needed a hunter to look at, something possibly deadly. I finished pulling my boots on. "News, yes. Good, no. See you soon." I smacked the phone down so hard I was faintly surprised the plastic didn't crack, and looked up to find Saul's eyes on me.

There was no time for talking about anything other than the current crisis. I am such a coward I was actually *relieved.* "Saddle up, furboy. Let's roll."

19

The Impala's engine cut off, its full-throated purr ceasing and the ticking of cooling metal taking its place. Saul managed to work his fingers free of the dashboard, and gave me a look qualifying as sardonic. "You're a menace," he said flatly, but I was already unbuckling myself. The windows were down all the way, and the sudden cessation of wind-roar was shocking.

"What, you don't like riding with girls in cars? I thought out on the Rez that was the main form of entertainment." *And having a touch of precognitive ability does help in traffic, you know.* I opened my door and stepped out into a predawn hush full of grayness. Prickling filled the air. We would have an autumn thunderstorm before long, the heat was already becoming close and dense.

"Riding I like. Committing suicide by automobile I don't." He actually did seem a little green, and that cheered me up immensely. He fell into step behind me.

The street was quiet and residential, with a few lush

greenbelts taking advantage of the river's proximity. I habitually calculated angles of cover as we walked toward the flashing reds and blues, yellow crime-scene tape fluttering as they roped off the entire yard. Forensics was out in force, and I saw three white coroner's vans.

Christ. The banter wasn't easing my nerves. "You're still alive, aren't you? I hope you didn't leave fingermarks in my dash."

He was again way too close to me, almost bumping me as we walked along, perfectly coordinating his steps with mine. "Next time, *I* drive."

I don't think so. "Dream on. Nobody drives my baby but me."

"Your baby?" Again, that faint tone of grudging admiration.

I ran my tongue along the inside of my teeth, wishing my cheeks weren't flush-hot. What was the matter with me?

What was the matter with *him?*

"I rebuilt her," I said shortly. "I drive her."

"You rebuilt her?"

I stopped and rounded on him, my second spare leather trench coat swirling. He stopped as well, with perfect balance, not running into me or even stumbling. The stormlight was good to his face, and silver winked in one of his braids. I took a closer look—it was the twisted remains of the silver bracelet from Galina's, tied into his hair like the charms tied into mine with red thread.

Nameless fury worked up inside of me. I throttled it, kept my voice steady and even. "Look. I don't know what game you're playing, but it stops *here*. I've got a job to do, and the less I'm distracted the less people will die. I want this goddamn rogue *and* this goddamn hellbreed off my streets, and safely dead if at all possible. Whatever you're doing, *quit*. I don't have time for it."

He studied me for a few seconds, his eyes humanly depthless. Not like a hellbreed's at all. "I'm not playing a game."

Then what the hell just happened? Or is that some arcane Were protocol I don't know about? I don't hunt your kind, I don't know all their ins and outs. "Whatever it is, stop." I figured that covered about everything. "I have enough to deal with."

"I'm here to help." Was that a scowl? He looked away, at the plain two-story frame house being swarmed by Santa Luz's finest. "There's Harp."

Just like a goddamn Were, looking away and changing the subject. "Fine. Just stay off my back."

"Huh." It wasn't affirmative or negative, just a sound.

Goddamn Weres and their goddamn noncommittal noises.

I wished the heat in my cheeks would go away, took a deep breath and looked up to find Harp standing, fists on hips, on the porch. She looked tense and furious, the feathers in her braids fluttering and her jaw set.

Great. I ducked under the yellow tape, nodding at the uniform on duty—it was Willie the Mouse, who flinched when his eyes hit mine, his left hand coming up to touch his right shoulder. A Trader had taken a chunk out of him once, before I could get there and put it down in a welter of blood and screaming, not to mention the stink of roasted flesh because the apartment complex had been burning down around us.

So many of my memories are tinged with smoke.

And blood.

I dropped my eyes as Saul ducked under the yellow tape behind me. "He's with me, Willie." I pitched my voice low and soothing. "How's the shoulder?"

Mikhail had once rescued him from two Traders and an *arkeus*. That was before my time. Poor unlucky Willie.

"Still hurts sometimes, Jill. Thanks." He didn't sound thankful—he sounded like he'd prefer I didn't talk to him at all.

He'd needed a solid two years of therapy before he stopped waking up screaming, I'd heard. The chasm between us yawned wide.

But at least he was still alive. That was worth something, wasn't it?

A knot of forensic techs swarmed around a particular spot in the dry grass of the yard. I saw Foster's sleek ponytailed head; he nodded and pointed up at Harp, a quick sketch of a movement.

In other words, *I'll catch you later, go see the Feeb.*

"Hey, Harp. What's a girl like you doing in a place like this?" It bolted out of my mouth, and her quick smile was iron-tense, a mere flicker.

"The usual. Blood and chaos. Smells like you just had dinner." Her eyebrows lifted a bit. "Sorry to miss it."

The edges of her tan jacket fluttered a bit as I hopped up the steps and got a nose-watering dose of the smell from the open front door. Rogue Were, hellbreed, and death; the mixed reek scraped across my nerves and turned them even more raw. "It was the only nice part of the night, sweets. You won't believe who's in town."

"At this point I'd believe just about anything. Come inside, I want to show you something."

"Harp." I couldn't put it off any longer. "Navoshtay Niv Arkady's here from New York; I came across him while I was cleaning out a Trader hole. Perry's off making amends and smoothing the troubled waters, since Saul knifed Arkady and I clocked him with a sunsword. The hellbreed we're looking for—our pretty blonde girl—is Navoshtay Siv Cenci. Navoshtay's daughter." *And I am going to have hell to pay the next time I visit Perry. Maybe even sooner.*

Harp actually went pale. Her eyes flickered up to Saul, who made some slight movement, having climbed the steps after me. Maybe a shrug, since his coat creaked a little. He moved closer to me, looming behind me and actually bumping into me again, softly.

Harp's eyes got as big as the plates down at Micky's. I moved away, irritably, and peered in the front door. "And there's even more, Harp. Hang onto your hat, because this one is *weird.*"

She still stared over my head at Saul. I waited a beat for her to give her next line—something like *well, life around you is never normal, Kismet.* But she didn't give it. Instead, she looked at Saul like she'd caught him eating babies.

The Were behind me responded by moving even closer, crowding me so I felt his chest touch my back. I stepped away, to my left, taking in the front door's white paint and two dead bolts. Whoever lived here had been cautious.

Fat lot of good it had done them.

Saul moved in on me again. "Quit it," I snapped over my shoulder. "What is *wrong* with you? Harp, did you hear me? The head hellbreed on the East Coast is in my city, and he's after his daughter. Who, I'm told, has been a very busy girl."

Harp shook her dark head, the feathers in her braids fluttering. Her mouth opened, shut as if she couldn't find the words.

I could relate. I dropped my other bombshell. "I also know why she's hanging around with Our Boy Carnivore. If another hunter hadn't told me I wouldn't believe it."

That seemed to shake her loose. "Jill—" But she stopped, still staring at Saul.

I've had about enough of this. It isn't like you, Harp. "Come on, Agent Smith. You show me yours, I'll tell you mine—and we might have a chance at stopping this thing."

Dominic greeted me with a nod. He crouched, low and easy, in front of the cellar door. I took in his stance and the alert shine to his eyes, the way he settled into immobility after the quick sharp movement.

He was standing guard in case the rogue came back to his little nest and found a bunch of humans here. I felt a chill trace down my spine at the thought.

The ground floor of the house was oddly pristine. Here in the kitchen, where the door to the cellar stood wide open, stairs going down and that smell belching up in waves, there were clean white countertops and a rack full of washed dishes with a thin layer of dust on them. A blue washrag lay folded over the arch of the faucet, dried stiff. The table was layered with papers. The garage, visible through a wide-open door leading off the kitchen, held two cars—one of them a minivan with car seats.

I didn't want to think about that.

The only sign of violence was one of the chairs pushed over backward and a single smear of dark liquid on the clean floor.

"Family of four," Dominic said when my eyes fastened on the chair. "Near as I can figure, someone opened the front door and got subdued, then was brought back here to where someone else was doing bills. Everything on the table's dated for last month. I think this family was the first to go down, and he's probably been dragging kills back here—there's another entrance to the cellar out back, Theron's out there. He's the one that found a trail in this neighborhood."

I nodded. Theron was the bartender at Micky's, a lean, dangerous Werepanther. Good backup, even if he was an arrogant twit. If he was out in the backyard, I didn't have to worry about the people out there. It was a relief to know.

Harp's voice came from the living room, slightly raised. Dominic's eyebrow twitched, an eloquently inquiring look expressed in a fraction of an inch.

"Don't ask me." I spread my hands, indicating innocence. "I don't know what the hell's going on. Your friend Saul seems to have a gift for pissing Harp off." *And I've got other problems.* "So there's car seats in the garage. What's upstairs?" *Please tell me I'm wrong. Tell me we've found the kids alive.*

"Three bedrooms. Two decorated for cubs, both with beds messed up like the little ones just got up for a drink of water." He tilted his head back slightly, indicating the cellar. His eyes glowed briefly, very sad. "My guess is, down there. I'd love to be wrong."

But it's not fucking likely, is it. I swallowed something suspiciously hot, tasting of bile. "Scene's been held for me?" *What else is down there, Dom? Drop the other shoe.*

The look he gave me qualified as scathing. "Of course. Harp and I took a look at it from the stairs, that's all. Something down there stinks of sorcery, and that's *your* job. There's enough in the yard and around the door to keep the humans busy for a while. Take your time."

My, that's awful sweet of you. But I just eased past him and through the door. Wooden steps went down, concrete walls dry-gleaming with oil under the gassy reek of bodies. The smell of dandruff and hot spoiled musk was eyewatering. I was glad I had stopped for a fresh copper cuff, the air itself was caustic.

Add the sweetish rot of hellbreed, and I suddenly wished very hard that I hadn't eaten dinner.

The memory of Saul's mouth on mine rose. I pushed it away with an almost-physical effort. Distraction was the last thing I needed. Shelves on my right held cans and jars—nonperishables, laid in for a rainy day. I caught sight of a can of Chef Boyardee and my stomach turned hard, thinking of two small rumpled beds upstairs.

My heart pounded thinly. *Of all the things about this job I hate, that's the worst. Kids are the* worst.

I wasn't the only one to feel that way. The hardest cases, and the ones the psych officers worked the hardest on, involved the very young. No matter how hardened or seasoned the cop, kid cases can cut you right down to bone and bleed you for months, if not forever, afterward.

I swallowed, my tongue sticking to the roof of my mouth. I kept an eye out for critters—they weren't likely down here in a concrete cube, but you never know.

The steps turned to the right, a one-eighty that slowly revealed a dusty disused cellar. In the back left corner, as far away from the stairs and the door to the backyard—a trapdoor, just like Auntie Em's—as possible, was a tangled mess of shapes.

Oh, God. White bone peeped through, glimmering in the dark. One electric bulb in the ceiling did nothing to dispel the darkness. A curtain of glaucous night shielded the corner, a shimmer like heat off pavement mixed with night's obscurity only pulling aside to show small glimpses of whatever lay beyond.

Tangled over the bodies was a sorcerous shell of concealment, laid with power and exquisite care. The shield drew tight, humming with alertness as my aura fluoresced in the ether, random points of brilliance swirling around me as the sea-urchin spikes of my personal borders poked through, sparked against the contamination of hellbreed, and retreated.

It nagged at me. Even with what Clarke had told me, something was wrong here. One instrument was out of tune, screwing up the whole symphony.

Deal with what you've got in front of you, Jill. Analyze later when the scene's safe.

The ruby warmed at my throat. Silver chimed in my hair, shifting and heating up.

I shut my dumb eye, my blue eye piercing the strings of sorcery, a shifting pattern of darkness and occasional bloody flashes. She did good work, this Cenci.

The copper cuff snapped free of my wrist of its own accord, tinkling down the stairs. The scar turned into a brand, wet heat tracing obscenely up my arm, following the branching channels of nerves and veins. I lifted my right hand, black fire twisting around my fingertips, crackling as I pulled etheric force through the scar and down my wrist, a low humming cycling through the concrete.

Pitch a levinbolt low enough, and you can actually shatter glass or work a hole in pavement. The drawback is, it takes a *lot* of energy—energy I had to burn now. One reason to be glad that I'd made my bargain with Perry, no matter how much I cursed it while I was in the Monde.

Oh, very nice work. If I push there, it traps me. If I take it apart here, the backlash knocks me down. Huh. You're a sneaky bitch, aren't you? Daddy must have taught you well.

I set my feet on the last stair. My coat flapped, a hot breeze lifting from nowhere, teasing my cheeks and the silver weighing down my hair. Sparks crackled, Mikhail's ring burning on my left hand, the ruby at my throat spitting again and again, warning me.

Levinbolt flames swirled counterclockwise, coming to a tapered point like a narwhal's horn. Cupped in my palm, the spire of etheric energy trembled, cycling up to a moaning cry of torched and distressed air.

More, Jill. Give it more. The whisper burned under my conscious thoughts, my attention centered on the levinbolt straining to wriggle free. It takes a particular relaxed fierceness to hold this much energy still, corralling it to one's will; sorcery isn't for those who can't relax and concentrate.

If Harp and Dominic had come down off the stairs, they would have triggered the trap. I'd have been looking at a severely wounded pair of Weres, maybe even critically damaged.

Good thing they've got me. I bent my knees, sinking down, compressing myself. The levinbolt whined, my fingers scorching where it pulled on the nerves and yearned to fly free. My coat pooled behind me, clinks and clanks and sparks trembling in the air as the silver in my ammo, knives, and jewelry responded to the contamination of a hellbreed curse in the air, straining toward me just as the bolt strained to escape my control.

Do it fast, Jill. Go for the quick tear.

I leapt, uncoiling, right hand flung forward, the bolt crackling through the first few layers of the sorcerous shield and piercing, stuck fast—then, *explosion,* all that contained force suddenly finding itself free. Potential became kinetic, like a lightning bolt lancing air and producing a sonic boom. The psychic thunderbolt smashed the shield wide open, and I landed, driven to one knee by the backlash of energy bouncing off concrete walls and buffeting my aura. A shower of sparks fell from my hair, one huge bloody point of light from the ruby at my throat, and I shook the deep hideous noise out of my head. It was like the world's biggest gong vibrating inside my skull.

Easy as cake, Jill. Your usual fine work.

A low thrumming growl slid under the ringing in my ears, my right hand spread against the cold concrete floor, my leather-clad knee soaking up a chill too. My coat pooled behind me, and I raised my head slowly. Very slowly.

Oh, shit.

It hadn't been a shield to keep the bodies from being found. It had been a protection laid on the rogue Were, sleeping in his nest of meat and snapped bone.

He wasn't sleeping anymore.

His eyes were flat with beastshine in the dim light, and he crouched on the slope of mounded bodies. He was halfway between his animal form and human, neither one nor the other, and as a result . . . well, most Weres are beautiful and graceful in their human forms, and just as beautiful in their animal forms. The state in-between is never someplace they linger, and it is just as graceful as the rest of them—but subtly *wrong*. Wrong like a nonhuman geometry. Wrong like a note no human instrument can produce.

Wrong like a hellbreed's face, when they drop the mask of humanity.

Wrong like something spoiled, gone rotten, all a Were's power and glory thrown away for the lust of the hunt and the consummation of murder. That's what *going rogue* means.

I stared into the rogue's eyes for a long moment, the bizarre insanity of its gaze terrible because of the near-humanity of its suffering.

Then it leapt for me, and I had no time to jump free. A hunter takes on hellbreed, that's true. But a Were gone rogue, gone berserk, is different. Just like for a Were, taking on a Trader is one thing, but fighting a full-fledged 'breed is something else.

Rogue Weres move with the speed that pulls muscle free of bone, a thoughtless scary speed married to weight and momentum that isn't trackable like a hellbreed's tearing through space. On most hunts, Weres run backup for hunters.

On a hunt for a rogue, hunters most definitely run backup for other Weres. Because if we don't, we tend to catch flak and die.

He collided with me, his claws out, the impact so immense I didn't even feel my ribs snap as I was flung against the concrete wall and into momentary, star-filled black unconsciousness.

20

Shouts. Screams. The coughing roar of a Were in a rage. Cold concrete against my spinning, motionless body. A shattering sound, another scream, I was picked up and tossed again, bones snapping as I hit another unforgiving surface.

The pain crested over me in a wave, and I yanked instinctively at the scar, flesh scorching as for one vertiginous moment I *pulled* on every erg of etheric energy available to me. The print of Perry's lips on my flesh turned molten with sick heated delight, and I flung my hand out as the rogue came for me again, a bolt of pure power boiling up into the orange spectrum at its edges as it streaked through the potential-path in the air and smashed the rogue ass-over-teakettle into the knot of Weres suddenly crowding into the cellar's dinginess.

The lightbulb broke, smoking dustmotes of glass peppering the air. Sparks hissed and flew, the ruby at my throat singing a crackling note like a crystal wineglass stroked just right before it shatters. Agony raced down my arm, exploded in my chest, tore itself through my belly and detonated in my left leg, where the femur had snapped.

—ohgodohgodgetup.Iillgetup

I *pulled* on the scar again. Did Perry feel it, wherever he was?

Right then I didn't care, and it hurt too much for me to feel the queasiness that thought called up.

Bones melded together, all the pain of weeks compressed into a single moment as the scar hummed to itself, chuckling a bass note that sounded so much like Perry my skin turned to ice, great drops of sweat standing out and soaking what was left of my blood-soaked clothing. I coughed, a jet of bright blood from my lungs mixing with fluid as my rib cage snapped out to its proper dimensions, jagged ends of broken ribs sliding free of delicate tissue.

*—hurts it hurts, ohGod, it hurts—*I tried to get up, to fight, to strike back at the thing hurting me. To *meet* the pain head-on, to smash at it, batter it away.

Yet another personality quirk, and maybe the one that made Mikhail choose me. I keep fighting *long* past the point any sane person would throw up their hands and quit.

Snarling. More screams, shaking the house. Dirt pattered down. An explosion of noise, snapping wood, a high chilling wolf-cry of agony. The noise was incredible.

Get up, milaya. Mikhail's voice boomed and caromed through my head, echoing through a corridor of memory turned into a Möbius strip by agony. *Get on your feet, and fight.*

I made it to hands and knees. Felt for a gun with my

left hand. My right was so hot I was afraid it would detonate bullets in the clip. A stupid fear, but I wasn't thinking straight.

A burst of fresh air blasted through the cellar, gray light flooding in. Shapes danced, the close thick reek suddenly returning all the stronger for the brief moment of freshness. Shadows fled out against the square of light.

I coughed, my eyes watering. Tears flew, and blood sprayed from my lips. *Losing a lot of the red stuff, Jill. Just think, the Red Cross could follow you around and make a killing. Get it, make a killing? Arf arf.*

Over that hysterical wash of panic, another thought, tolling in my head like a bell. *Get up. Get up and fight.*

"Jill." A familiar voice. Someone approaching, crouching down over me.

The gun came up, my shoulders hitting the wall. My boots scrabbled in blood. *My* blood, thick and slippery on the cracked concrete floor. Heaving breaths echoed as I shuddered on the knife-edge of murder. *Move. Fight back. Kill.*

The Glock pointed straight between Saul's eyes, less than an inch from his skin. I drew in huge gasping breaths, my fingers aching to clamp down on the trigger. Adrenaline sang in my mouth, pounded in my blood.

He didn't even blink. "You okay?" Looking past the gun like it wasn't even there. Like I wasn't crazed with fear and about to snap, sail right over the edge and fill him with silverjacket lead. A shot at this range would *kill* him, even if Weres aren't allergic to silver.

And oh, I ached to shoot something. Anything. When you live from one violent fight to the next, it becomes a habit. A *need* to pull the trigger, an instinctive, life-saving reflex. The animal in you clamors to strike out with claws, teeth, anything at hand.

He must have seen the murder in me. There was no way he could miss it.

Saul's eyes held mine for what seemed like eternity. Behind him, more swirling shapes coalesced. Other Weres. I heard a gasp, a murmur, and someone swore in a low fierce tone.

"It's okay, kitten." Saul's voice was even, soothing. "Everything's under control. It's all fine. It's all right."

My thumb came up. Clicked the hammer all the way back, eased it gently down. The small sound was very loud. The scar throbbed, full and flushed with wet poison heat. I heard a low sob, recognized too late it was my own voice.

Saul's fingers curled over the gun, pushed it aside. As if it was the most natural thing in the world, he took my shoulders and pulled me away from the wall. His arms folded around me, his purring rumble shaking through my bones again. "Easy," he whispered. "You okay? Say something."

My lips were cracked, my throat desert-dry. I heard another greased-skid muttering rumble of thunder in the distance.

I just got kicked around by a rogue Were. That's twice in twenty-four hours I should be dead. Dead. Even with the bargain, I would be dead. Rotting. Gone.

In Hell, probably. Almost certainly. That's where hunters end up, in Hell.

Or so the Church said. No Confession, no Communion, and no Heaven for those of us who come face to face with the nightside. The murders we commit and the foulness we witness remain with us even after death; it is a point of doctrine from 1427 onward. It hasn't ever changed, despite hunters' petitions.

Sometimes I wonder about that.

A shiver passed through me, muscles locking like a seizure. I pulled myself together with an effort that chilled fresh sweat on my skin. "Fuck," I whispered. "Where did he go? Where is he?"

Saul's weight shifted slightly, his arms tightening as soon as I spoke. "He bolted south. There's a full pack of Weres after him, Dominic went with them." His mouth twisted down for a moment, and my brain slammed into overdrive.

What's he doing here? He should be chasing the rogue. "Go." My lips were numb. "You're a tracker. Go."

An electric current bolted from his eyes to mine, something surfacing in his and shooting straight through my veins like a jolt of recoil. I almost flinched, the feeling was so strong. He should have gone after the rogue that killed his sister, but he'd stayed here to make sure I was all right.

Why?

I didn't know, and I didn't care. For that one moment, someone looked into my eyes and saw past every wall I'd ever built to protect myself. And I could swear I saw past every wall he'd ever built in his head too, and that something in me—something deep and buried, something bruised and battered but still strong—*recognized* him.

Knew him. Somehow.

What the hell?

"I'll be back." He rose in a swift wave, letting go of the gun, and was gone through the shattered door into the backyard, his shadow briefly made of black paper against the grayness of a thunderlit dawn. The air swirled with electricity.

I shut my eyes. *Storm coming. Probably hit this afternoon, I can feel the pressure shifting.*

Why did he do that?

The shrieking, gibbering animal part of me didn't care. Blood soughed in my veins, and my skin crackled with drying sweat and other slick drying fluids. I heard my pulse, clear and strong.

I was alive.

This is getting surreal even for me. And that's saying something.

"What the *fuck* is going on?" Harp's voice was loaded with a growl of its own, somehow all the more chilling because of the soft clear femininity of the tone. "Kismet? Care to clue me in?"

I heard my breath, harsh and jagged, leaned my head back against the freezing concrete of the wall. "Jon Clarke called from New York. He told me Navoshtay had trapped a Were for his own amusement, damaged him. But Navoshtay's daughter set the Were free and fled with him." My throat was raw, I tasted blood with the words. "We've got a major paranormal incident shaping up. God knows what she wants that Were for. And I've got a goddamn 'breed capable of a psychic nuke looking to make this more difficult than it has to be."

That was only half of what Jon had told me, but I knew better than to open my mouth about the rest of it.

That's bullshit, Jon. I'm surprised at you. The sick

thump under my breastbone wouldn't stop hatching thin traces of nausea.

I have it on the best authority, Kismet. Somehow, Arkady's daughter bred with a rogue Were. She's pregnant, and her daddy's after her.

What authority do you have it on? I'd persisted. Too many stars were moving into alignment, and the constellation they were making was disturbing, to say the very least.

The best authority, Kiss. Watch your ass out there. There's no telling what will happen if this situation gets out of control.

The trouble was, it was already out of control. Were don't like hellbreed, and hellbreed don't like them. But Jon wouldn't tell me this if it wasn't true. Hunters don't lie about this sort of shit.

Even a little white lie can kill a hunter, and there are too few of us as it is.

I should have been screaming in fear or sobbing with the snapback reaction of passing too close to death and clawing my way through once more. I *should* have been pushing myself to get up, clean myself off, and *do* something to stop this immense clusterfuck-in-progress.

Instead, I was thinking of Saul Dustcircle's eyes, and feeling the electricity that went through me at the memory of his skin on mine.

He *knew* me. Or for one brief, endless second he had seen right through me. It was the same thing. He had somehow recognized what I was, down at the bottom of my soul.

And he had still held me.

Get up, Jill. Get back on the horse. You don't have time for this.

Not while there were people dying and a rogue on the loose. Everything else could wait.

Cleaning up wasn't as bad as I'd feared. Most of the forensic techs had been in the front yard, poking at a suspicious patch of grass dying under the weight of a viscous, rapidly decaying fluid that might have been oil. I couldn't figure out what the liquid was, even after scanning it with my blue eye. It reeked of hellbreed and death, blackening the grass underneath. The techs took samples, but I didn't think they'd get anything. Hellbreed tissues break down quickly once they're damaged, and this stuff seemed no exception.

The rest of the cops hadn't seen the rogue shatter out of the cellar, or the collection of changed and unchanged Weres streaking after it.

Thank God for small favors.

The bodies in the cellar were being untangled by Forensics, gently and thoroughly. I couldn't see the cavalcade of blue rubberized bags going out the front door, but I heard it each time a coroner's van started up and the picture-flashes started popping. My skin would run with gooseflesh and I would repeat the promise to myself.

I will avenge you, whoever you are. I will grant you vengeance on the thing that did this to you. I left the copper cuff off, paying my penance with each eyewatering puff of stench striking across my sensitive nostrils.

I could even tell myself the hot water slicking my cheeks was just from the smell.

Harp leaned against the wall inside the shattered cellar door. I sat on the steps going up to free air and a day overcast with the promise of thunder, yellow-green stormlight drenching my shoulders from behind. She had settled into immobility, her eyes lambent with the weird light.

Mike Foster detached himself from the organized hive of activity and crossed over to us, peeling off his latex gloves. "You okay?" His sleek ponytail wasn't mussed, but his eyes were haunted, with dark circles to rival my own growing underneath.

"What's the count?" That wasn't what I meant. What I wanted to say was, *did you find the children? Tell me you didn't.*

"Thirteen." His eyes met mine, spoke for a long moment. "Two of them . . ." He didn't have to finish the sentence.

I made a slight movement, closed my eyes. The worst thought of all returned—that there had been dust on the counter and the dishes, and bills from last month on the table.

I should have known. I should have somehow saved them.

Mike sighed. "I think we've got everyone. We'll ID them if we can, there's no clothes or anything hanging around. That's weird."

Not so weird if a hellbreed is cleaning up afterward. It's like them to minimize the information you can get from a scene. "Not so weird." I hauled myself wearily to my feet. "Buzz me if you need me, 'kay?"

I wanted to howl and beat my head against the concrete. I wanted to take off blindly running south, after the rogue and the hunting pack of Weres trailing him. Hopefully he had already been brought to bay and dispatched.

Hopefully.

I rocked forward, standing up and opening my eyes. Foster, at the bottom of the steps, flinched as he met my gaze. The silver chimed in my hair, tinkling sweetly as leather creaked.

"Jill—" He stopped abruptly, tried again. "Be careful, okay? This is *bad*. The bodies, they've been . . ." His eyes cut over to Harp, and the sharp stink of human fear cut through the reek of death for a moment.

"Savaged," Harper said flatly. The feathers in her hair fluttered as she made a swift movement of distaste. "Chewed up. You'll find muscle mass gone and organs missing, as well as splintered bones."

Mike winced. His watch glittered as he reached up, raking his fingers through his glossy hair. "I wish your friends wouldn't tell me these things." He directed it at me.

I wish Pepper was back on duty. She had a higher tolerance for this sort of thing. Still, I couldn't blame Mike. This would bother any reasonable human being.

Should I be glad or upset that "reasonable" doesn't describe me? I almost shot Saul, and nothing I've done has turned out right on this job. I should have picked up on this long before now.

I reached out, blindly. Mike's hand met mine, and I squeezed briefly, gently. The scar pulsed on my wrist, sensing human flesh and high emotional distress. I reined myself in with a physical effort, more sweat slicking the waistband of my leather pants. Things would start chafing if I kept this up.

There was something in my throat, a difficulty like talking through mud. "Sorry, Mike. Give a call if you need me, and see the psych boys for some downers if you have to. Okay?"

"It's not me I'm worried about, Jill. It's you. You're looking a little worn out."

I wonder why. I made a face, freeing my fingers from his. "So they tell me. When the nightside slows down, I will too." I turned on my heel and was gone up the steps before he could respond.

Harp matched me step for step, and she waited until we were in the backyard before her fingers closed around my arm. "Jill."

I stopped, staring across the yard at the greenbelt behind the house. There were bushes back there, and a screen of trashwood trees. Dusty greens and grays ran together in front of my eyes, and I was suddenly sure it would be a good place to watch the house from. I caught no breath of *being* watched, but you don't live long as a hunter without checking the terrain.

Harp's fingers didn't loosen. She could break my arm without half trying, with a Were's strength.

Of course, I could heal in moments and repay her with interest.

What am I thinking? She's my friend, and she's a Were. I'm too close to the edge if I'm even thinking *like this.* But the engine in my head didn't stop turning over the probabilities, evaluating every single living thing around me.

When you can't turn that machine off, it's time to get

some rest. Unless, of course, you *can't* rest because the bodies are piling up.

Harp didn't shake me, but I got the idea she wanted to. "What's going on?"

I tried not to feel relieved. "I wish I knew. I only have half the pieces of the—"

Her face went through frustration, a flash of anger, and settled on impatience. "No. I mean with you and Saul."

Dammit. I suppressed a guilty start, knew she would feel it anyway. "Don't know there either. You're the one who sicced him on me. Besides, he thinks I'm tainted."

Good one, Jill. Why did he swap spit with you, then? And so nicely, too. I felt the flush creeping up my cheeks again, couldn't stop it. Cursed inwardly.

"He apologized. He didn't understand, and you know what Rez Weres are like." Harp's tone was so dismissive I felt my teeth want to grind together.

"Not so much. I never worked with a Rez Were before." I pulled away from her hand, achieved exactly nothing. Felt the temptation to grab her wrist and lock it, give the quick jerk to dislocate and bring my knee up . . .

Calm down, Jill. She's not the enemy here. "Let go, Harp. I'm not in the mood."

"He's acting possessive." In her *you-are-being-dumb* tone.

So I played dumb. "Who?"

"Saul."

"Is that what it is." Then, mercifully, my pager went off. I dug with my right hand in my pocket and fished the damn thing out. "Let go. It's Galina." *Thank God it's her. Anyone else calling, it'd be likely to be another body in the streets. The Weres are chasing the rogue, and that just leaves this blonde hellbreed and her loving daddy to deal with.*

She gave up, letting go of my arm and making a short noise of annoyance. "Just be careful, Jill. Don't break his heart."

I cannot believe I am having this conversation with you. Why don't you keep him away from me? "Weres don't date humans, Harp." I swung away from her. "Now I'm going after that goddamn hellbreed. Buzz me if you need me."

"You're not exactly fully human anymore, Kismet." She had to raise her voice a little, and thunder underscored her words. I took a deep breath of the dusty green smell of impending rain and hunched my shoulders.

Yes I am, I wanted to shout back over my shoulder. *I am still human, and humans don't date Weres.*

Yeah, the snide little voice of my more sarcastic side piped up. *But rogue Weres don't work with hellbreed either. And hellbreed don't make bargains with hunters. Pigs are going to start flying any moment now.*

21

Galina's shop was shut up tighter than an oyster, the sign turned to "closed" and the blinds on the front windows drawn. Her back door was closed and locked too, and the red-orange carapace of Sanctuary shielding wedded to the walls resounded uneasily, crackling with the charge in the air. The storm was coming in fast, breathless expectancy hanging thick under the clouds, pressing on pavement and hurrying people.

I knocked at Galina's red-painted back door for a long time, more uneasy than ever. I couldn't break in and poke around inside her house without dealing with the Sanctuary bindings, and if she wasn't answering she was either out or had retreated to her inner sanctum for some Work. The latter was most likely; Sancs don't often go abroad.

Then who the hell called me from here? And would Galina be out with a rogue Were on the streets? Not to mention the hellbreed action recently.

I thought about it, eyeing the porch roof over her back door.

A few moments later I was on the roof, and I cased it thoroughly, even sweeping behind the glass cube of the greenhouse where Galina grew all sorts of fun stuff. I mean, where else are you going to get your hellebore and mandrake, if not from your local Sanc?

I don't like this. Who called me? Where's Galina?

My boots creaked, dyed dark with dried blood. My coat flapped, lifting on stray breaths of breeze as wind flirted uneasily between earth and storm-laden sky. The scar pulsed, random little soundless chuckles of wet delight spilling up my arm from its puckered tissue.

Even the emergency hatch behind an AC unit was closed and stubborn. I moved to the edge of the roof and peered down the deserted street, not liking the feeling I was getting.

A slight prickling between my shoulder blades, as if I was being watched. Was it nerves? God knew I was having a little trouble with mental balance, lately. Getting almost-killed twice in one day can do that to you.

It's not the getting killed that's worrying you, Jill. It's a Were. Specifically, a Were who's "getting possessive," in Harp's immortal phrase.

It took a physical effort to get my mental train off *that* track. *Stay focused, Jill.*

I eased along the edge of the roof to peer down at the front of the store. Stray bits of paper rustled, skipping down the pavement. I caught a breath of diesel and a powerful hit of green-gray river water, and the ozone smell of approaching lightning. The street was deserted, lamps flickering into life in the gathering artificial twilight.

A glass and iron box a block up caught my eye, and my skin roughened instinctively. I felt cold all over, my breath shortening and my nipples peaking under my T-shirt, hard as chips of rock. *Phone booth. Galina's got her number stenciled on her front window, and my pager's not exactly a secret. I'm a goddamn idiot.*

The cloak of red-orange energy over the building shivered restively, like a horse.

I froze.

The click of a hammer cocking sounded very loud behind me.

"Don't move," Navoshtay Siv Cenci said, in a pleasant, light tone. "Keep facing the street, hunter."

I've been shot before, hellbreed. But I stayed where I was, my back alive with gooseflesh and the knowledge that a 'breed who had nearly eviscerated me and made mincemeat out of Harp was behind me, with a gun. The click sounded like a large-caliber model. Or maybe that was just my nerves again.

Behind me. She had to have come up from the porch roof. Had she been watching from down the street? How had she gotten my pager number? It wasn't a secret, but still—

Galina had better be inside her sanctum. If you've touched her I will kill you. Rage worked its way up inside me. Subsided with an effort that left me shaking, struggling to think clearly through the adrenaline haze. It wasn't logical—even a hellbreed couldn't harm a Sanc inside her own House. Galina was too smart to go outside, wasn't she?

Wasn't she?

I waited. *Patience*, milaya. *It is soft and quiet that catches mouse.*

Only this mouse had the drop on me, and a gun to boot.

"You've killed to find me. To flush me out of safety." Cenci's voice was calm and pleasant, with only the tinkling wrongness of it to tell me *hellbreed*. I could sense it now, the contamination in the air around her. Silver shifted in my hair, heating up, blue light running under its surface. Thunder roiled faroff, coming closer.

"The Were's being chased," I said to the street. "He'll be killed mercifully. You, however, are a whole different ball of wax." *Two children. And Jimmy Cheung, you bitch. Cleaning up? What kind of game are you playing?*

The silence behind me took on a predatory cast, the pause of a shark in the moment just after blood hits the water and right before frenzy. Galina's building thrummed underneath me, quivering with unease. Slowly waking up, catching the current of bloodlust passing between my unprotected back and the hellbreed behind me.

"I should kill you," Navoshtay Siv Cenci whispered. "We don't want trouble. I just wanted to be left alone to do what I have to do. Is that so much to ask?"

Left alone? "When your father's Navoshtay Niv Arkady? *Alone* doesn't happen, sweetcheeks. You're 'breed. You know that."

"So you're going to do his dirty work." Did her voice actually break? Amazing. I gathered myself. My right hand curled loosely around the whip-handle.

Keep talking, bitch. I'm a few seconds away from changing your whole religion for good. "I don't do dirty work. I avenge my people. Like the rookie cop you put in the hospital." *He'll never be right again, even with therapy and the best of care. You ruined a life, and you did it so easily.* I eased my weight forward onto the balls of my feet, a millimeter at a time.

"They shot at him." She dismissed it, I could almost envision her shrugging. "I was quick, I was *merciful* as I could be. But you, you're doing my *father's* dirty work." Yes, a definite break in her sweet, corrupt voice. Did she use it to hook her prey, like Arkady used his black, black eyes?

I rose, the flesh on my back crawling with the knowledge that a bullet might be coming any moment. If she was aiming for my head, this might all be over very quickly. I would find out if hunters really went to Hell when they finally got unlucky. "I'm doing what I should, to protect the citizens of my city. I'm a *hunter,* hellspawn. It's what I *do.*"

Another thought slid through my head. *She's not shooting me. Why? She's not acting like a hellbreed.*

Fat sizzling drops began to patter down dispiritedly. They made stinging quarter-sized dollops on the dusty, hot rooftop. Sweat pricked under my arms and at the small of my back, dried blood crackling as my clothes moved on the breeze. My fingers shifted slightly, ever so slightly, on the whip handle.

"I told you not to move." Cool, now. She'd made up her mind what she was going to do. Maybe I'd been premature in thinking she wasn't acting like a hellspawn. Maybe she was just playing with me, cat with mouse.

In other words, bad luck for you, Jill. But if you're a mouse, you're a mouse with claws. I polished my very best *fuck you* tone and flung it at her. "What are you going to do? If you shoot me, other hunters will take my place. Your daddy's in town, and he's pissed off because you stole his Were toy. There's a major incident shaping up over him even *having* a Were toy—"

"He isn't my father's!" she screamed. "He's *mine!*"

I spun, diving, the whip flashing free and my left-hand gun clearing leather. The whip's ribbon curled through the air, screaming, and struck across her face as she hung in midair, claws outstretched, her own gun falling unheeded to the rooftop as mine spoke. Time turned to gelatin, closing around me as I *moved*. Black hellbreed ichor flew in a flattening arc before she smashed into me, catching me in midair and throwing us both over the edge.

Wind whistled, and we hung in freefall, the silver in my hair spitting and crackling. She struck me across the cheekbone, a good punch if she'd had all or even some of her weight behind it, a hot gush of pain as her claws buried themselves in my chest, tangling in my ribs before she could jerk her wrist down and spill my guts. Back arching, scream bursting through my blood-slick lips, we fell in a thrashing tangle of tortured air and a sudden booming as the protections on Galina's house woke in a sheet of blinding crimson and orange flame.

She sure doesn't act like a pregnant woman. Maybe it's hormones. The thought was tinged with deep screaming hilarity over a well of panic that training shoved aside.

Cenci thrashed, but I had one hand fisted in her long platinum hair and I brought the gun up, pistol-whipping her across the face.

Falling and Fighting 101: brace someone's head when you're bouncing a gun off them. It hurts more.

More black ichor flew, spattering my skin in stinging drops. I got in another two shots on the way down before we hit pavement, a snapping in the structures of my skeleton—again and her claws were torn free, a hot gush of blood following them. *No wonder I need steak.* Another flash of a thought, there and gone in a moment that paradoxically seemed to last forever. *I'm losing iron left and right.*

Cenci rolled free, dazed and shaking her head. The smell of scorching rose, and Galina's protections flamed again, dilating like a camera shutter. A scream of toasted air boiled away from the shop, the plate-glass window in front bowing and making a wobbling noise.

The sky opened its floodgates on us both.

I rolled, *get away get away* shaking my right arm out as the scar boiled with acid, desire-laced pain and shot a jolt of power up my arm, sinking into veins and jacking through my system like a needle-load of something deadly. A sharp clarity bolted through me, I made it to my knees with both guns out, the whip slithering along the pavement with its metal bits tinkling as it landed, dropped like a bad habit.

My first two bullets caught her, but she collided with me again. There was no technique, it was sheer blind rage and overwhelming strength—which is a hellbreed's downfall.

They get so used to bullying humans around, they don't use their strength effectively. Hunters are trained to *never* stop thinking about how to most efficiently fuck up the nightsider giving us trouble right *now*.

Reflex had loosened my knees and let go of my right-hand gun. I socked my hip into her midriff, bootsoles squealing on pavement and a long trail of sparks hanging in midair behind her, and I didn't need to do much, just grab a fistful of her and *shove* to deflect a critical millimeter or two, her blind rush providing all the impetus necessary to throw her directly into Galina's plateglass window.

BOOM.

A wall of concussive force slammed outward, tossing me like a rag doll across the street and into the brick facing opposite. Heat bloomed, and superheated air broke the sound barrier, thunder rolling down the street. I slid down to the pavement, coughing and retching, and heard stumbling footsteps as the hellbreed fled.

Galina's defenses settled, rumbling through the pavement like a subway. Sanctuary rule numero uno: do *not* throw yourself at the Sanctuary's walls. The protections respond without any conscious effort, and the response is . . . energetic, to say the least.

Other footsteps, softer ones, approaching me at what seemed a very slow rate next to the rapid pitter-patter of little hellbreed feet. Noise returned through the white buzzing of my dazed ears. Rain pounded my skin.

"—ogodjillareyou—"

I am getting really tired of being flung around. I shook my head. Warm trickles of blood slid down my neck from my ears, dripped from my nose. I blinked more warm wetness out of my eyes. The pain came then, a great rolling breaker of it as my body coped with the damage.

I'm racking up one hell of a bill with Perry. Then, a small, noiseless thought: *I wish Saul was here. I'd like to see him.*

When had I started being happy to see a disdainful country-boy Were? When he'd kissed me? Or when he'd stayed to make sure I was still breathing after tangling with a rogue?

You've got bigger problems, Jill. Get up and start fighting. It's what you know how to do. So do it.

I blinked and looked up. Galina's hot mortal fingers pressed against my clammy forehead. "Get *up!*" she screamed, and thunder rattled. Coruscating energy sparkled in the air around her—she was actually *dividing her Sanctuary spell,* protecting me as ripples of power boomed and echoed, potential-paths opening as lightning blurred down, the sound like cannonades. Smoke boiled up, and the rain began to slash down in earnest.

I made it to my feet. Leaned on Galina as she half-dragged my heavy self—muscle-dense, hellbreed-strong, weighed down with leather and metal and ammo—across the street under lashing rain slicking down her hair and mine. She smacked the door to her shop open, and the bell tinkled merrily as she dragged me into safety. I collapsed on the floor near her glassed-in counter, next to a bookcase and a rack of candles. My body curled into a ball, and I decided on the spot to spend the next few hours shaking and drinking some of her spiced rum.

Alas, such was not meant to be. Because as soon as I shut my eyes and sagged against the floor, really wanting to shut the world out for a while, the bell tinkled again, and a soundless step filled the shop. The protections thrummed, a high mounting note of energy just aching to be unleashed.

Galina spoke with the sonorousness of church bells chorusing morning in some ancient, smoke-decked city.

"Take one more step toward her, Pericles, and you will be thrown back to Hell screaming." She paused, the heavy static-breathlessness of power not abating one iota. "And while you're at it, close the door."

Perry wrapped his long pale fingers around the steaming mug. It was peppermint tea, the vapor rising from it assuming angular screaming shapes before dissipating. Galina swabbed at the blood on my cheek while rain smashed against the skylight overhead. Her marcel waves were tousled and she moved with quick, sharp birdlike movements, her necklace glinting at odd moments as the protections fluctuated.

I took another jolt of rum. The scar on my wrist throbbed. Perry's blue eyes lingered on my throat, and I was suddenly very glad Galina had made him sit at the other end of her long scrubbed-pine kitchen table.

"The Weres lost him, you know." His words were underscored with a booming rattle of thunder, and every once in a while a small mouselike tremor would run under the surface of his skin, flickering and gone in a heartbeat as whatever shape lurked under his semblance of bland, almost-handsome male humanity responded to the raw energy in the air. Still, even Perry didn't dare make trouble in a Sanctuary, and he sat very still where Galina told him to. "He slipped their hunt. Rogues sometimes do, I'm told."

Not often, Perry. As a matter of fact, hardly ever. Just one more thing about this case that isn't what it should be. I set the bottle down on the table with a click. The scar flushed, a knot of poisoned delight. I wished I'd

tucked a spare copper cuff in my coat along with everything else, instead of leaving them at home. "I'm getting
blood on your floor." I sounded mournful. "I'm sorry,
Galina."

"No problem. I'm just glad I came out in time to see
what was happening." She grinned, her slanted eyes
dancing with merriment for a moment before she so-
bered, glancing back at Perry.

Who sipped his tea, quietly. And sat still.

*Hallelujah and pass the ammunition, there's a single
place where Perry won't fuck with me.*

The only trouble was, I couldn't stay here. I had too
much to do.

Galina's eyes caught mine. Her fingers were gentle as
she sponged more blood from my face. Silver buzzed in
my hair like a rattlesnake's tail, responding to the humming tension of the storm overhead and the echoes of
the Sanctuary protections' lunge into wakefulness, re-
verberating in the ether.

I took another jolt of rum. "I'm fine, sweets. Thanks."
*I had no idea you could divide your Sanc protections.
Still, that's not the question I'd like answered most right
now. Right now I want to know who called me, and
where Cenci was hiding. I should have felt her in the
neighborhood, especially after driving her off Harp. I
should have fucking smelled her.*

Which meant either she could cloak herself from me
more effectively than any other hellbreed, or she hadn't
been waiting for me in the neighborhood.

Galina made a small derisive sound. "Your pupils are
all over the place, Jill. I think you have a concussion."
She wrung out the washcloth, water dyed thin crimson

squeezing through her fingers. "What were you doing on my roof?" The question was casual, but her shoulders were a little too tight.

I don't even know what I was doing on your roof. "Someone—I'm betting it was this hellbreed Cenci— buzzed me. Maybe it was to lure me away from Harp and Dom, get me where she could at least put me out of commission for a while. Probably so she could get back and move her Were buddy." *The spell in the cellar was laid to protect and conceal him, neatest trick of the week. This just keeps getting more tangled the deeper I dig.* My eyes flickered across the table to Perry's, interested and bright over the rim of his cup. "Any light you can shed on this, Perry?"

He set the mug down, a slight smile playing over the corners of his lips. His linen suit was, of course, pristine and unwrinkled, though he must have been outside in the downpour. "I've interceded with Arkady for you. As long as we keep you out of his way, I think we can avoid further unpleasantness."

A flickering tremor slid through his face, as if something had shifted just under the skin. His grin widened a trifle as he adjusted his cuffs, his forgettable face turning sharp and predatory for a single moment.

Which doesn't explain what you're doing here. My skin chilled. Galina's mouth drew down sourly. She carried the bowl over to the sink, glanced at the water washing the window outside, and dumped the bloody mess down the drain. Her silence was full of the kind of loathing most people associate with pale wriggling things in spoiled meat.

"Very kind of you." I picked up the bottle, took another swig. Then, because not to do it would be weak, I met his eyes again. The scar turned to an agonized infected burning burrowing into bone, a reminder that he could tweak it into pain or pleasure as his mood called for.

"A pleasure." The smile widened, white teeth exposed. Electric light shone mellow in his sandy-pale hair; a flash of lightning outside bleached everything briefly. "Especially when done for my Kiss."

Do not call me that, Perry. I hate that. Again, I didn't say it. "Why did he come all the way from New York to fetch his daughter instead of sending you a request to have her sent back? You are, after all, the ranking hellbreed in the city."

His eyes hooded. "Especially since you recently thinned our ranks so drastically. You're gaining quite a reputation for impulsiveness." The sibilants slid over the scar, each sending a thread of soft poisoned delight into my flesh. The old carrot-and-stick approach.

I wondered which he thought worked better, the reward or the punishment.

"You're not answering my question." *That gives me wriggle room on our bargain.* Cautious relief warred with fresh unease.

A single shrug, infinitely evocative of nothing, pulled up his shoulders. His eyes flicked away, roving the surfaces of the kitchen, leaving a thin vibration of slime on everything they touched. "Other families and their dirty laundry hold no interest for me. He is here, he wants his earthborn progeny, under our laws she belongs to him." Perry's gaze flicked back to me, and the faint smile he had settled into now seemed a grimace of distaste.

"Earthborn progeny" means Navoshtay impregnated a Trader. A shiver of loathing went up my back, jingling the silver in my hair. It still didn't answer why Navoshtay was here to collect her personally. By what I knew of hellbreed customs, Cenci was born out of a human and therefore not pure 'breed. She had the same "legal" rights as a chair or a coffee mug and theoretically not as much power as a pure 'breed; it should have been a simple case of Perry cooperating with me to send her back trussed up like a pig on a spit, with an apple in her mouth—if it was necessary to send her back *alive,* that is. If he could control the unruly hellbreed of Santa Luz and the surrounding metro areas, he could apply enough pressure to find one troublemaking 'breed female and kick her ass over the river.

Then again, she was powerful. *Disturbingly* powerful. Navoshtay's spawn in a body that might be old enough to burn out some of its mortality . . . the thought was nightmare-worthy, and that's saying something. Besides, I'd never seen Perry unveil the extent of his power, not even when he marked me.

Sometimes I let myself think he might just be tricky instead of strong.

Perry paused for a moment, then went on, silkily. "She is making quite some trouble with the *human* law—of which you are still a part—and you have made it adequately clear that the trouble will not stop if she remains in my territory. There is no profit to keeping her here and angering Arkady. For all these reasons, I could care less *why* he wants her. My interest is that this matter be concluded quickly, so it doesn't interfere with my own pleasures more than it has already."

It was a nice pat explanation. Too bad I didn't buy it. It was *not* like Perry to merely obey another hellbreed, no matter how powerful. Hellbreed don't do obedience and they don't do charity. Their net of feudal obligation runs on one thing: fear. There's no trust among 'breed. They turn on each other at a moment's notice, whenever they think the benefit outweighs the risk.

Thank God it does, too. Otherwise they *might* rule the world, instead of just hanging in the dark corners and buying power and privilege.

"Well, thanks for telling me. I'll call you if I need you." I lifted the rum bottle again, touched it to my lips.

Perry's eyes fastened hungrily on the bottle's mouth, and by default on mine. "Are you dismissing me, my dearest?" One pale eyebrow raised.

Oh, goddammit, I am so not in the mood for this. "Why are you here?"

Perry slid off his seat. He looked about to say something, but Galina turned from the sink and regarded him, level and easy, her mouth a straight line.

"Don't make me, hellspawn." Her tone was just as even as her mouth.

He ignored her, but he didn't move forward. "I came to tell you the Weres lost their rogue. I *also* came to tell you Arkady will not pursue you. As long as you stay out of his sight, he will . . . forgive . . . your impoliteness."

"And you just *happened* to be in the neighborhood when I came by?" I tossed it at him as if it didn't matter. *Who did call me down here, Perry? If it was Cenci, why didn't she shoot me? And if it was you . . . that would mean that you knew she was in this area.* My brain pawed lightly at the problem, turned it over, and dropped it in disgust. I was too tired, blunted both by adrenaline fatigue and the shock of almost-dying so many times in a row. I needed some rest before I could even begin untangling this out.

"I can always find you, my dear." The grin widened again, white teeth showing their sharp pearly edges. I thought of shark's teeth when I saw him smile like that. "Think on that, for a while. See you soon." A nod to Galina, his sandy hair falling over his forehead in a soft wave—and he was gone, the Sanctuary shields settling back into taut humming alertness as the bell on the shop door downstairs tinkled.

I let out a sigh and put my forehead down on the smooth wood of the table. It felt good, cool against fevered flesh. *Great. Just . . . great.* Dried blood crackled on my skin, but my hair was still wet from rain.

"Every time I talk to him I feel slimy." She shuddered, a movement I could sense without looking. The shields shivered too, responding. "I don't know how you stand it."

I don't. Not very well, at least. I'm so scared he's going to get in, Galina. The more he plays with my head, the better he gets at taking me apart.

The better he got at that, the more dangerous it was for me and everyone I protected. "I don't stand for much. Thanks for bringing me in." I closed my eyes, tried to relax my shoulders. They wouldn't go down, tight and taut and aching.

The faucet started to gurgle. Was she refilling the bowl? She wouldn't be able to dab much more blood off me with just the one washcloth. "I had to," she said quietly. "We can't afford to lose you."

I took refuge in bleak humor. "I'd hate to be lost."
Thunder boomed again, the storm slacking despite the
massive disturbance of the roused Sanctuary shields that
had contributed to the instability of the weather pattern.
You can always tell when a Sanc gets pissed off, it gets
rainy over their little castles.

"Seriously, Jill. Perry was just up the street, I sensed
him as soon as I hit my doorstep. He was standing
around, waiting."

I lifted my head, bracing my chin on both hands and
slumping in the chair. She shut the water off, brought the
bowl to the table, and dipped the washcloth in again.

"Up the street?" I turned this over in my head and got
exactly nowhere with it, again. *He was waiting. If he
knew Cenci was waiting here too . . .*

What the fuck is going on?

"I wonder if he was going to ride in to save you." Her
touch was gentle as she sponged at the crusted blood
along my hairline. "Or if *he* lured you down here in the
first place."

Me too. My face wrinkled up, hard. I tasted blood and
the sourness of failure. "Thank you. I was trying not to
think that out loud."

"Just one more service I provide. You want something
to eat?"

"More rum, if you've got it." I finally succeeded in
pushing my shoulders down a little, unstringing the nervous tension in them. "Then I've got to go home. I'm
calling it a day."

22

My pager was battered and busted despite its padded pocket. The lightning hadn't helped; even insulated electronics can have a little problem when you start messing around with potential-paths in thunderstorms. I had a spare at home, courtesy of the Santa Luz Police Department, and I needed more ammo anyway.

And—I'll admit it—I was feeling a little shaky.

Cancel that. A *lot* shaky.

I pulled through silver curtains of rain into the garage, was out of the car in a heartbeat, and walked through the utility room. It felt good to be home, for the first five seconds.

Then I realized the entire place was buzzing and resounding. Unhappy Weres will do that.

I didn't blame them for being upset. If they'd lost the rogue they were likely to be a little *more* than upset. They'd be downright cranky. Which meant more food. It's a wonder they weren't all butterballs. Damn Weres.

Of course, their metabolisms run high and hot, like

mine, and the *change* is metabolically expensive. I just had a hellbreed scar working on forcing my body to heal fast enough to stand up to the abuse I was taking.

I was hanging up my coat when I discovered they were arguing, and not quietly either. The acoustics of my home are good for a *reason,* I like to know when even a roach is scuttling in the walls.

Not that I have a roach problem. Sorcery is *occasionally* a practical thing.

"How am I going to tell your mother this?" Harp's voice, raised as it seldom was, edged like an axe and flung at someone.

"You won't have to." Saul Dustcircle's tone was quieter, but no less sharp. I hadn't heard this particular tone from him before, and I was glad of it. "I am not a kit, Harper. I'll tell her my damn self, like I should."

"What are you going to *do?*" Harp hit a pitch usually only reserved for a screaming-meemie fit at Dominic during a bad stakeout or shadowing. I couldn't remember ever hearing her sound this upset, even that time they came out to help Mikhail deal with the hellbreed who *used* to run Santa Luz.

The one who had declared it open season on Weres, and did his best to turn the barrio into a death-hole. I hadn't been allowed out onto the streets during that, since I'd barely started my training. But I'd heard plenty, and seen enough of it to fill in most of the blanks afterward—especially in my nightmares.

Saul's voice, again. "I'm going to do what I *should,* for once. Don't push it, Smith. I've made up my mind."

"You're a stubborn, arrogant, self-centered—"

I came around the corner out of the utility room to

find Dominic leaning against the wall in the short hallway. His hair was pulled back into its leather-wrapped club, but a single tendril fell in his face, a sure sign of exhaustion. He nodded and laid one long finger over his lips, then made a pushing-down motion with his hand.

In other words, *stay out of this one, Jill. It's Harp on the rampage again.*

"That's *enough*." I almost didn't recognize Saul's voice. A touch of growl to it shook the walls and rattled the *ikon* of the Virgin hung in the hall, a gift to Mikhail from Father Gui over at Sacred Grace Seminary. I'd only heard this tone from a Were once or twice, usually an alpha snarling at a pack member who'd stepped out of line in a big way. "I didn't ask for your editorial. I did not ask you what you thought. I told you what I'm going to do, and that's final. I'm of age, I'm legal, and I've made up my goddamn mind. End of story."

Harp changed tactics. "Your sister—"

"Don't you dare." Saul's whisper was more effective than a shout. "Don't bring the dead into the business of the living. You know better."

Dominic saw his moment and took it. "Hey, Jill." He didn't have to say it very loudly, they all probably knew I was here. That's the drawback to good acoustics; everyone knows when I'm at home.

Unless, of course, I don't want them to.

I folded my arms to disguise the way my hands were shaking. Dried blood crackled in my hair and along my hairline as I lifted an eyebrow. "Heard the rogue slipped through."

"Only a matter of time. Weres are patrolling the entire city. When we flush him again, it'll be the last run he'll ever have." His dark eyes traveled down my body, and his nostrils flared a little. "You look awful. What happened?" He jerked a thumb at the end of the hall and lifted both eyebrows, an eloquently silent warning. Good old Dominic.

"Got tangled up with our rogue's girlfriend. Tossed her into a Sanctuary's window." *With Perry waiting down the street, for some nefarious purpose, no doubt.* I didn't mention that part. I also didn't mention that I'd been lured down there by one of them, and I wasn't sure yet which one.

Dominic actually laughed, a mellow, relaxed sound. He had a nice face, attractive in a strong-jawed way. His sidearm was briefly visible as he reached up to tuck the one stray strand of hair behind his ear, an absently graceful motion. "You have all the fun. I just ran my ass off after a rogue who seems to know how to disappear."

"Yeah, well, it's been rough all 'round today." I followed him out into the south end of the living room, wishing the house was empty so I could start shedding clothes. A shower sounded *really* good right about now. Along with a nap, and a case of hard booze—and a flamethrower to take care of some unruly hellbreed.

Harp dropped down on my couch, pale with anger. Even the feathers in her hair seemed bleached, and they were slightly askew—just as shocking, in its way, as Dominic's mussed hair. They were both so contained and precise that the small imperfections blared like a bullhorn.

Saul, his arms crossed over his chest, dropped his hands to his sides. His face was pale and drawn under his coppery coloring, and his eyes were live coals, more like a cat's than I'd seen before. He looked literally spitting mad as he glared at Harp, and I had the sudden mental image of a housecat with every hair on end, eyeing a dog. Since they were both feline Weres, the image was even funnier.

I managed not to laugh. But it was a close call.

Saul's eyes met mine, and the entire world stopped for a moment.

It was still there. That electric sense of *contact,* as if he knew something about me. Saw something about me, something nobody—even Mikhail—had ever bothered to look for.

It wasn't fair. What gave him the right to look at me like that?

"You okay?" Saul's gaze didn't move, but he would have had to be blind not to see that I'd been dipped in blood and air-dried, then dumped in again and run through a downpour once or twice.

Rain beat at the roof, splashing and overflowing the gutters. We would have flash floods out in the desert, and maybe a brief blossoming. Greased ball bearings of thunder fell through the roulette wheels in the sky. Maybe God was gambling with human lives again, hoping for a better turnout.

"Been worse." I seemed to have lost most of my breath. *I wish he'd stop staring at me like that.* "You?"

"Been better." The corner of his mouth quirked up. I could feel it in my own lips.

Oh, yeah. Something strange is going on here. I got a good deep breath in. We looked at each other. I could almost feel a taut line humming between us—me leaning back away from the connection, him shifting slightly forward, pursuing it.

"You hungry?" The fur had gone down, and his tone softened.

I still got the idea that wasn't what he was really asking.

"I could do with a bite." I didn't look away. I got the idea that wasn't what I'd really answered.

"I'm on it." He turned sharply on his heel, his coat flaring briefly open. Stopped. Swung back, as if he'd forgotten something. "I'm glad you're all right," he said, abruptly. Like a challenge.

Not now. Don't pick a fight with me now. "Me too." I could have slapped myself, it was such a stupid answer. I was *trying* to be conciliatory, a new skill for me. "I'm glad you're okay, too. I mean. Yeah."

Who said you couldn't teach an old hunter new tricks?

Dominic made a slight muffled noise. When I swung around to look at him he wore an angel's innocent face, his mouth pressed down tamely and his eyes roaming away, searching for something to fix on.

"You two." Harp leaned back on the couch, the curve of her throat exposed and her arm flung over her eyes. A single feather fluttered out of her hair, came to rest on the orange Naugahyde, and I suffered a deep acute flash of shame for the shabbiness of my house. "Can we please have some answers here? What the *fuck* is going on?"

Just like the forensic techs; she didn't deal well with this kind of uncertainty either.

I took a deep breath. Saul's eyes were very deep, very dark, and quiet.

I dropped the bomb. "I saw Cenci, at Galina's. She didn't initially try to shoot me." That got me everyone's attention and a full ten seconds of silence, which I broke by dropping the other shoe. "I think she might need help. I think she and the rogue are together, and I have it on good authority that the 'breed female's pregnant. She might be carrying a hybrid."

23

Harp shook her head. "I don't believe it. It's *not possible.*"

What's that Sherlock Holmes thing about the impossible? "It's only a theory." I gulped another mouthful of scorching amber alcohol. The smell of chicken frying wafted under the green oily curtain of rain and the ozone of lightning strikes. "You've got to admit, it fits better than anything else we've got. It also explains why Navoshtay's hot to trot out here and drag her home personally. I hear he's big into experimentation."

We were at the breakfast bar. Saul moved around the kitchen, each step graceful as a dance. He'd shed his coat, and I tried not to watch the movement of muscle under his black T-shirt.

Harp knocked back her glass of Jim Beam and frowned into the dregs. "Experimentation." She shuddered, mussed feathers quivering in her glossy hair. "Someone should kill that son of a bitch."

Yeah, someone should. But right now he's further

down on my list than you'd think. "It's been tried. Several times. Not very successfully, I might add."

"Why is he experimenting? And for what? A hybrid? Assuming that's even possible, genetically speaking." Dominic set his beer down, stretched his hands out with fingers interlaced, stretching. His ponytail lay tame against his neck, raveling down his back now that it was free of the leather thongs.

"There's legends about Were females raped by 'breed." My mouth felt dry and clumsy, even mentioning it. "It could be Navoshtay's looking to find the truth of those legends."

"There *is* no truth to them." Harp moved, a sudden sharp twitch like an irritated cat. "Besides, we're human. They're not."

"Still . . ." Dominic drummed his fingers on the counter, thoughtfully. "Navoshtay's a sadist. Who knows what his real reason is for this . . . experiment? Assuming it is one, and we're not just going down the garden path."

"Who knows why hellbreed do anything?" I muttered, staring into my glass. My eyes weren't focusing properly. Exhaustion weighed down every limb.

"Hunters." Harp didn't sound mollified. If anything, she was sharper than ever.

If we knew that much, we wouldn't have people vanishing into the nightside. "Even the best hunter can only make an educated guess, Harp. Don't ride me." I reined in the flare of irritation. She didn't mean a word of it, she was just frustrated and probably as tired as me.

That got through to her. She sighed, leaning forward and resting her chin on her hand. I could smell the sharp iron-tang of dissatisfaction mixed with her peppery female musk. "I'm sorry. I just . . . we *had* him, and he slipped through our fingers. More people are going to die, and all I can do is sit around and *wait*."

"A rogue Were runs on instinct. He shouldn't be this hard to predict *or* catch." Saul set a plate in front of me, and another in front of Harp. "Eat, both of you. Don't sharpen your claws on each other, they'll wear down."

I stared at the wheel of food in front of me. Fried chicken, new potatoes with rosemary, a small mountain of greens, and actual biscuits. I could *smell* the iron in the greens, craving waking up behind my palate. I'd lost a lot of blood.

Dominic made a small sound of pleasure as Saul handed him a plate.

Everyone blessedly shut up, which gave me a moment to think. *We've got a rogue who isn't behaving, really, like a rogue should. We have a hellbreed covering his tracks and trying like hell to keep him away from Navoshtay—not that I blame her. I wouldn't want my worst enemy trapped in one of Arkady's games.*

Well, maybe Perry. That would be nice, and I would sleep a whole hell of a lot better. The colors on the plate blurred together as my eyes narrowed, both of them trying to pierce through time and matter to find the pattern, catch the rhythm and anticipate my opponent's next move.

Opponent? No. Prey.

Still, something was bothering me.

You're doing my father's dirty work. . . . He's mine. Odd words for a hellbreed. Clarke swore she was pregnant, and swore he had it on good authority.

Pregnant with *what?* Another one of her father's experiments? Dark stories were whispered about Navoshtay, even darker than usual horror tales hunters like to swap. Most hunters are men, and love to bullshit endlessly over brewskis.

Stories about New York's oldest hellbreed were *always* whispered, though. Even Mikhail had referred to him as "one scary motherfucker, *milaya.*" Nobody wanted to talk much about Navoshtay. I was frankly surprised Clarke had called me back so soon.

If there's something a hunter won't talk directly about, you *know* it's bad news. Something a hunter won't mention unless it's daylight and the doors are bolted is the worst news around.

Pregnant with what?

Do I really want to know?

And who lured me down to Galina's, and why? Why is Navoshtay here to pick up his bastard daughter himself? And last but certainly not least, why is she protecting the Were? That's what she's doing. It's the only way her actions make any shit-for-sense. The kaleidoscope of events shifted this way and that as I tried to figure out what the pattern was—or even where the blank parts in the pattern fell enough to give me a glimpse of the underlying cause of this whole huge mess.

Saul's voice broke my trance. "Jill? You don't like it?"

"Huh?" I surfaced, blinking irritably. My skin crawled with sweat, the residue of rain, and dried blood. I suddenly wanted a hot shower and a long uninterrupted thinking-session.

"I thought you'd probably like the chicken." He leaned

on the counter, his dark eyes level with mine because he was bending down, hunching his broad shoulders. The silver bracelet lay tangled in one of his braids, winking wickedly at me, as if it knew a secret. "You look a little pale, kitten."

"Oh. No, I was just thinking."

The silver glittered, sharp darts of light. Why was he wearing it?

"About what?" he persisted.

Well, if you want to hear it out loud I might as well. It might help me think. "About how this doesn't add up, any of it. All I have is one question after another, and the deeper I get the more weirdness crops up. By now I should be getting some *answers,* not more goddamn questions. Which can only mean one thing."

He nodded, took a hit off his beer. A Corona, and he'd even rubbed the mouth of the bottle with a slice of lime. He'd make someone a fine wife someday. "What's that?"

"It means I'm barking up the wrong trees. It *also* means someone's lying to me." I picked up my fork, took a mouthful of butter-drenched potatoes. *My God. Weres can usually cook, but this is* really *good.*

"Do you know who?"

I wish. The pattern still refused to make sense. "No. But I know what about."

"What about, then?" Soft, logical, reasonable, as if he'd done this before, giving me the questions to help me shape everything inside my head out loud.

I began with the central question. "About what exactly is going on between Cenci and this Were. Who doesn't even have a name yet, and that's another thing that bothers me. His kin should be looking for him too. You said the first murder was out in Massachusetts, but I'm willing to bet it wasn't. Harp, I need you to get on the horn with your boss and get them tracking all the kills following a certain profile."

"You really think we've been off-base?" Harp took a gigantic bite of fried chicken. She must have been hungry, and Weres need more protein than the rest of us.

My brain settled into functioning again. It was going to be a short-lived burst of productivity—I needed some rest in the worst way. "I don't think you've been off-base. I think you've been misled. Navoshtay's capable of hushing some things up on the state level but might not have his pretty fingers inside the Martindale Squad. Though I wouldn't put it past him. If there's something he doesn't want us to find out, it's going to be in New York. Have them liaise with Clarke and see what they dig up, and for God's sake give the hunters out there some protection while they do it."

"It's a good idea." Dominic's tone said just the opposite. "How much of this is based on what that hellbreed told you?"

"Practically nothing," I admitted. *It's what Perry didn't tell me that has me curious.* "Which is why I'm probably on the right track." Thunder muttered softly behind my words, echoing in the warehouse's spaces. Windows vibrated a little, bouncing under the sound.

Harp finished chewing. "So what are you going to do next?"

The only thing I can. I braced myself. "Call on Perry to set up a meet for me. I'm going to do my best to drag something useful out of Navoshtay. *Before* then, though,

I'm going to do something I haven't done since Mikhail was alive."

The feathers in her hair fluttered as she made a sharp restless movement. She visibly restrained herself from waving a denuded chicken bone at me by sheer force of will. "What, go out for a movie? You're killing me here, Jill."

I winced. *I wish you wouldn't say things like that.* Picking up a chicken wing, I bit into it. Chewed thoughtfully, and swallowed. Licked my fingers, and stared at the white meat under the crust of breading. "I'm going to go *between.*"

No sound except rain dripping, splashing through the gutters, swirling on the roof. "You're going to what?" Saul said it very quietly, as if he didn't understand.

He probably didn't. Harp had gone still. I took another huge bite of chicken, stalling for time. Then indicated my blue eye with a quick sketch of a gesture, still dangling the chicken. "I came back from Hell with a sort-of-gift. I've got a dumb eye and a smart eye. One can see the normal world. The other sees *below* and *between.* If I need to, I can see more of the *between.* All it takes is blood." *And since I've spilled so much already, I might as well.* I let out a soft sigh. "I just need someone to hold the other end of the line for me while I go down. Mikhail's not here, and I doubt Perry can be trusted with that. Maybe Galina, or Avery."

"I'll do it." Saul's tone had stayed soft, but there was an edge to it. "If you're really determined to do something so risky."

I don't think I'll let you hold the other end of that line for me, Were. I don't know you enough. "Nobody involved in this is going to tell me the truth, and none of my guesses satisfy me." I laid my fork down. "The rogue's going to kill someone else. Or *she* is. Or Navoshtay. I want the killing to stop."

"But . . . *between*." Harp, out of all of them, sounded like she understood what I was talking about. "Jill, I don't know if that's such a good idea."

What about me facing down both Perry and Navoshtay? Between I can handle. Hellbreed who each want to take a bite out of me I might have a little trouble with. "Screw *good idea*. I want *results*." I stared at my plate some more, wondering how on earth I was going to get the food in me. "And I want 'em yesterday."

"You won't get anywhere on an empty stomach." Apparently Saul had decided to get all Jewish-mother on me. "It won't stay hot forever, either."

I picked up my fork again. *If I go* between *I'll probably lose everything I ever felt like eating in my life. Not to mention dealing with Perry and what he's going to ask in return for setting up this meet. Might as well enjoy something while I can.* "Guess not," I mumbled.

"You're not really intending on . . ." Dominic took a quick mouthful of potatoes when my eyes met his. He also shut up in a hurry.

The warehouse clattered with the sound of rain and the static of tense, unhappy Weres. *I'm not exactly happy about this idea either, guys.* "If I don't do it, who will? I'm the resident hunter."

"You should take better care of yourself." But Saul dropped his eyes, and the words didn't have the usual sting.

"Hard to do when I'm running from one goddamn

thing to the next." I settled down and applied myself to my plate. "But I'll keep it in mind. Maybe I'll even learn how to cook."

For some reason, both Harper and Dominic laughed their fool furry Were asses off at that. Dom laughed so hard he almost choked on a potato. It's a damn good thing he didn't spit it across the kitchen.

Harp and Dom headed back to their hotel room, needing a change of clothes and some sleep. Even Weres get tired.

I had other plans.

I started dialing Perry's number three times, hanging up in the middle each time. I dialed *four* times before I could let it ring through without hanging up.

Getting braver all the time, eh, Jill?

I told that voice inside my head to go away. I didn't think it would, and I was right.

One ring. Two. Three. The shadows of rain reflected all through the room, ghostly dapples against the wall and my skin, a mottling like hellbreed contagion in an aura.

My aura. The scar turned hot and hurtful, straining in anticipation. My pulse thundered so loud I almost couldn't hear the ringtone, kept my breathing even only by sheer stubbornness.

No, that's not true. My throat had closed to a pinhole, that's why my breathing was shallow. I shouldn't have been doing this, I was too tired. I was going to make a mistake.

Mistakes are not allowed, Jill.

He picked up. "Hello." A silky, smooth, bland voice that raised both my hackles and gooseflesh the size of eggs on my arms.

My mouth was bone-dry. Dry as a chickenbone in the desert. Dry as my palms were slick and wet. Still, I sounded good. Steady, even. "Perry."

"Oh, my dear. I've waited ages for you to call me." His voice crackled through phone wires, diving underground to come up and bleed into my ear like snakes aiming for my brain. He chuckled, a warm pleased sound, and I felt condensation collecting on my skin again, the touch of a scaled, rough tongue too flexible to be human *or* animal.

"Can the sentiment, Pericles. I want you to set up a meet for me." The words came out hard and fast, just as if I wasn't scared out of my mind. "With Navoshtay Niv Arkady."

Silence, crackling like lightning. I got the idea he didn't think too much of the request.

Tough luck, hellbreed. "I've got questions that need answering. This is *my* town, after all. You'll set up the meet and keep my skin whole through it. It'll count toward the time I owe you. And you'll keep your nasty little maggot fingers off me the whole time, too."

More silence. When he spoke, it was the rasping of sharkskin against the palms of a drowning diver. "If I am to perform this miracle, it will *not* count toward what you owe me. That's ridiculous, my dear."

A hot jet of nasty satisfaction curled through me. *He didn't say no outright. Thank you, God.* I tossed the dice. "Ridiculous or not, it's what's going to happen. You're not coming clean about something, Pericles. That violates our agreement. You can either be in violation, or you can set up the meet and have it count toward my balance."

More silence. I prayed I just hadn't opened up a can of worms, and I further prayed he wasn't thinking up a lovely way to get back at me for outwitting him this once.

I don't care. I'll put up with it. The important thing is to stop the killing. My palms ran with fear-stink sweat, a trickle of ice sliding down my back. I couldn't tell if it was sweat or merely dread. I did not close my eyes— I didn't want to imagine him on the other end of the phone.

The shadows dappling my bare arms had all turned angular, though the water falling on the skylight hadn't changed its shape.

"Very well." Sharp and curt, the words were knives. "I shall arrange it, and go to some trouble to ensure your safety. I will further allow you some leeway on your repayment. Don't think you've avoided me, my dearest. I do this because it pleases me."

You do this because you think you can worm your way into my head a little more, and because you are *in violation—you* haven't *come clean with me. I've won this round.* "Go borrow a quarter and call someone who cares. Call me when you've got the meet set up. And Perry?"

A long exhalation of hot diseased air I could almost smell vibrated over the phone line. My skin flushed with heat, then chilled, pearly drops of sweat re-wetting my torn, dirty, bloodstained clothes.

"Yes?" Quiet, but with an edge.

I suppressed the urge to scream-laugh like a maniac. A terrified maniac with one hand on the trigger and the gun under her chin.

The laughter receded, and when I spoke I was steady. "The next time you lure me into a setup with a mad hellbreed I'll send you back home, and it won't be a pretty trip."

"I was watching over you, Jillian. Protecting my very *dear* investment." Each word frosted with black ice. Thunder boomed overhead, more lightning crackling. It was turning out to be a hell of a night.

Sure you were. "Yeah. Fine fucking job you did too, since a Sanctuary had to rescue me."

"You are still alive. Don't press your fine luck, hunter. I like this conversation less and less." His tone had dropped from a tenor to a baritone, the throbbing of Helletöng rubbing hurtfully underneath. The warning was clear.

He's already mad, you might as well. I couldn't help myself. "Poor little hellbreed. I could almost pity you." Then I slammed the phone down, before he could respond.

My legs trembled. I sat down hard on my bed, my knees spilling out to either side and my arms turning to wet noodles, every muscle shuddering and rubbery. My pulse beat high and thin in my throat. A sharp bloody noise trembled on my lips, burst free, and echoed like the voice of a bird battering at the side of a cage.

An iron cage, with horsehair cushions and old rusty stains crusting the elaborate scrollwork, while sick remembered pain roiled through my nerves and the scar puckered and prickled, tingling.

You did it. Good job. Very fine work, Jill. Now stop shaking. Stop it.

My room was dark except for the reflections of rippling water covering the walls, stippling my forearms. The shadows had relaxed, no longer full of sharp edges. Gooseflesh remained, hard and cold, swelling up through my flesh like a disease.

Are you listening, God? I was actually wringing my hands like some bargain-basement Lady Macbeth. *It's me, Jill Kismet. I just pulled the tail of a huge sleeping dog. I'll be lucky to get out of this without losing a few more gallons of blood. Not to mention a few pounds of flesh.*

There was a small sound, like an indrawn breath or a restless movement. My nerves were scraped so raw I almost flinched.

"How much did you hear?" At least my voice was still steady. I had to hold myself very still, denying the urge to reach for a gun.

A patch of wall near the door rippled. He laid aside the camouflage trick, the one Weres use to keep from being seen by ordinary humans. But I could see the blurring of the real world, with its strings of energy, underneath the mere refraction of light.

If I'd just kept to that little skill and told Perry to go fuck himself when he offered that bargain, would I still be alive? I'd certainly be a lot more cautious—and there were a lot of people who might be dead instead of just traumatized.

Was it worth it?

"I smelled fear." Saul's voice was quiet. "That was the hellbreed? The one you made a bargain with?"

My fingers knotted together. *If he makes one snotty comment, I swear to God I'll . . . what? What will I do? Something I'll regret. Make him go away.*

That was the goddamn trouble. I was unpredictable even to myself when Perry started playing with me. And just because I'd come away the winner in this round didn't mean anything. Next time would be just as uncertain.

I brushed my lips with a dry tongue, wished the spit in my mouth would come back. "Just leave it alone." *Just leave* me *alone. All I want is to lie down and shiver for a bit. I'm getting a little sick of the merry-go-round.*

He paced into the room, one slow step at a time. "You're shaking."

No shit, Sherlock. "Really? I hadn't noticed. Leave me alone. Go bake some cookies or something."

"Did he scare you like this before the bargain?" Saul sounded curious. The marred light slid over him, his eyes glinting a little as he sank down into an easy crouch, halfway between the door and the bed, not getting too close. For once, observing my personal space.

I shut my eyes. The darkness was not comforting. *Go the fuck away.* "Of course he did. But Mikhail . . ."

"Your teacher." Soft and easy, the same tone I suspected he'd use on a frightened animal.

Well, I was certainly one half that description, wasn't I. The other half . . . well, who knew? You had to be a little bit of an animal to work this job. "I loved him." My voice broke. My fingers ached, I tried to yank them apart and couldn't. "I still do. But he's gone. I wasn't strong enough or fast enough when it counted, even after the goddamn bargain. And now—" My voice rose. "Now

I've got this mess on my hands and nothing's going right and I can't even keep my people from being killed in the streets and my God, there were two *kids* and the scene was a month old, they've been here for at least three weeks if not the whole goddamn month and I didn't know, I've been so busy but there were *kids,* for Christ's sake, just *children,* fucking *children*—" The words spiraled up into a gasp that wasn't a scream because I bit it back, swallowing it. Pushing it down, pushing it away.

It didn't want to go. It had been waiting a long time, this cheated howl. For six months at least, ever since I'd stood beside my teacher's pyre and felt the chill wind against my tear-slick cheeks, as the sobs I couldn't let go bolted down into my stomach and turned into a steady red flame of rage. Against hellbreed, against Sorrows, against Mikhail—yes, I committed that sin. I raged against my teacher for leaving me alone.

But most of all, I turned that blowtorch of agonized grief on myself. Because I had failed to save him.

And now, here I was.

"Shhhh." Saul was on the bed next to me. I flinched, throwing up an elbow—but he caught the strike with one broad hand, shoved it down without missing a beat. His arms circled me, a cage I wanted even as I leaned away from it. "Let it out. Let it go."

"I *can't.*" Heat and water slicked my cheeks. A sob broke the second word halfway, and I went rigid, leaning away from him. "I've got w-work to d-do tonight—"

More hellbreed holes to torch. Because tonight's as good a night as any to do a little murder in the name of getting Perry's voice out of my head. I don't c-care if I'm too t-tired—

The thought trailed off into a hoarse gasp as he pulled me off-center, into the shelter of warmth and the sound of someone else's pulse. Were filled my nose, a musky boy scent mixed in with something that was one of a kind, his, unique. When had I started recognizing that smell?

An even bigger question—when had I started liking it? When had it become *safe,* as safe as Mikhail's long-gone odor of pepper, leather, vodka, cordite, and foreign skin?

That was what broke me, finally. The remembered smell of my teacher, a powerful sensory memory of the only man who had ever protected me. Gone forever now, buried with him, nothing of that ephemeral imprint of a soul remaining except in my faltering human recollection.

My cold, comfortless, pitiless memory of everything I would rather forget.

I clamped my jaw down over the sobs. Swallowed them one by one as they rose, juddering me like an earthquake. My own personal set of seizures, rocking me off the face of the earth. I made no sound. He was silent too, not even thrumming the deep hum Weres use for wounded animals. He stroked my hair, silver chiming and tinkling; slid his hand under the heavy weight and cupped my nape, his thumb moving soothingly just under my ear. He simply breathed, and held me.

The shakes quieted bit by bit. Thunder in the distance. There would be flash floods out in the desert, the gullies and channels cut through Santa Luz would be full for once, liquid pumping through the city's dry veins. The simple fact was, there was nothing I could do tonight, even if I wanted to. If I went *between* in this state I'd get lost, my focus gone. If I went down into a hellbreed hole I'd end up getting myself scorched. I was too tired, too nerve-strung, and too goddamn edgy.

I'd just hit the wall, big-time.

Finally I rested against Saul, awkward, my upper body twisted and my cheek pressed against his shoulder. His hand had moved down from my nape, stroking my back evenly. Stopped, his fingers playing with the arch of a rib. Came back to my spine, tracing muscle definition through my T-shirt.

"I don't even like you," I whispered mournfully into his shoulder. Could have kicked myself, taking a deep breath of him. Then one more. Maybe just one more. *You do much more of this, Jill, and you're not going to want to stop.*

He didn't take offense. Maybe he even understood. "Give it time. I'm told I grow on people."

"Why are you doing this?" I squeezed my eyes shut until starbursts of red and gold burst, my blue eye still seeing the complicated strings of energy in his aura that shouted, *Were.*

A shrug, careful not to dislodge me. "Because you need it. Because I want to." A careful tone, giving nothing away. "Good enough for now?"

Not nearly good enough. I don't even know what it is you're doing. You're fucking up my head and I need to be clear for this. "You need to stop." I couldn't make the words louder than a whisper. "I can't afford this." *I can't afford any of this.*

"No strings, no payment, no bargains. I'm not hellbreed." Was that a new coolness in his tone?

I hoped so, and I didn't hope so. "I didn't—"

"Shut up." No anger, just flat finality. His pulse beat steady under my cheek.

I did. He held me, and for a while it was enough. Long enough for me to promise myself a hundred times that this next breath I took of him would be the last—and to break that promise, each and every time.

24

You spend a lot of time on rooftops as a hunter. The high ground is always best, it's another cardinal law.

Of course, when you're tracking someone else who hangs out on the roof as a matter of habit, it can get a bit tricky. But my quarry didn't even look up. He glided through shadow and streetlamp light, flickering through belts of orange glow, pausing only to catch the rhythm of a street before sliding along on the tangent least likely to draw notice.

When you have the preternatural sensitivity of a hellbreed, you can afford to stay far back. But the scar burned and prickled so much, the welter of sensation so deep and terrible each time, Mikhail had suggested covering it up. Galina had copper cuffs, and they seemed to work just fine . . . but I could still hear the slight scrape of Mikhail's boots against concrete, his pulse hammering. I could almost taste his pheromones on the air, a lingering trail of phosphorescence.

I hung back, just at the very edge of his sensing range.

But he wasn't watching for a tail—who would follow him?

Nobody except a stupid girl, that's who. Just finished with her training, and curious about where her teacher had taken to disappearing so frequently. Curiosity might have killed the cat, but satisfaction brought it back—that was one of Val's sayings.

I tried not to think about Val.

The new coat made a slight flapping noise and I cursed silently, stopping still. But my teacher didn't even break stride. He had a bounce in his step, and plunged into a network of alleys at the fringe of the barrio.

What was out here for him? I fell further back, following him only as a faint faraway song, more a pressure against sensitive ear membranes than music.

It was wonderful, and I couldn't wait to surprise my teacher with this new dimension to the mark we'd bargained so hard for. Although how I could do that without him knowing I'd tracked him . . . that was the question.

I was so busy thinking about it I almost stepped over the silent edge of Mikhail's field of awareness. He had stopped in a deep well of shadow in the lee of an alley, and the air itself listened when he told it to.

Silence folded itself around me, my heartbeat smoothing out. I dropped into a crouch and drew that silence like a blanket around my shoulders. It was a trick he himself taught me, and the small burst of pride inside my chest from performing it so successfully warred with caution and growing unease. What was he doing?

Did it matter? He had a right to privacy, didn't he? That was why he wasn't sleeping in the same bed with me anymore. I had my own room and my own blankets now.

A slim shadow unmelded itself from the end of the alley. I would have held my breath, but training had me in its grip—you do not rob yourself of the advantage of oxygen while you're on a rooftop watching a shadow in an alley. You just don't.

She swayed toward him, blue silk whispering, and my mouth gaped open, both to provide me with soft shallow breaths and also so the shock could escape my throat in a soundless puff. Long dark hair and pale, pale skin, she was willow-graceful and must have smelled of incense and honey.

Under that smell of female attractiveness was an edge. It was rusty, blotted with old iron blood, and somehow wrong. My left eye twitched and watered, seeing the strings under the surface of the world resonate in response to sorcerous pulsing.

Whoever she was, she wasn't wholly human. But Mikhail stood still, light gleaming in his pallid hair, as she swayed toward him, moving so supple and soft I could imagine anything but legs under her skirts. A faint murmur reached me, satin-soft; she was talking to him.

My hackles rose.

Mikhail reached for her like a drowning man grabbing at buoyant wreckage, and they drew back into the alley's shadow. The clink of his belt buckle unloosing under those pale fingers was as loud as a shot to my tender ears, and I looked away, my face and ears burning with a shame that poured down my throat in a river of bitterness.

The soft sounds—her murmurs, his gasping for breath, the wet sound of lips and tongues meeting—tore across my eardrums like copper spines. Heat and shame alternated with burning cold, laid on my skin like a heavy fur coat. The scar prickled, running with gleeful vicious pain.

Was it my anger? Or was it that I was even now, nailed to the edge of this rooftop in an easy crouch, obeying my training and staying quiet and still as an adder under a rock?

Mikhail's little snake under the rock. The trouble was, there were more things under this rock than just snakes.

I eased back, one step at a time, but not quickly enough to escape hearing the climax. I knew that full-throated hitch in Mikhail's breathing, the body brought to bay, the way he would stiffen and sometimes drive his teeth into my shoulder to muffle any sound.

Training doesn't stop in the bedroom, either.

I thought it was because of the mark. *The thought came from nowhere, rising to fill my head like bad gas in a mineshaft.* I thought he didn't want me because of the scar.

A hard, cold truth surfaced underneath it. Is he Trading? That doesn't look like a hellbreed. First you've got to find out what it is, Jill. How would you do that?

I knew how. First a visit to Hutch, the man with the library of rare texts. Then dropping by Galina's and casually, oh so casually, asking a few questions.

Then what? What the hell was I thinking? He was my teacher.

I eased away. Soundless, even my coat didn't flap.

Alternating hot and cold waves started at my crown and ran through to my soles. I was burning and freezing to death at once, but my body kept moving, training becoming instinct.

I did not run blindly. I just kept moving through the city, leaping from roof to roof with my coat flaring behind me, no sound except a huff of effort when I landed, etheric force pulled tingling through the flushed hard knot of the scar until I ended up under the granite Jesus atop Sisters of Mercy, hunched over, arms crossed tight and squeezing down to hold my heaving ribs in. Hot salt water slicked my cheeks, and now that I was out of the danger zone I heard soft weak sounds spilling from my throat.

I was sobbing.

The terrible thing was, I swallowed each sob, and they sounded like a woman in the ultimate crisis of sex, helpless shudders racking me. Each sound was a weakness, and reminded me of my teacher's body clasped against something in a dark alley, the stabbing motions of any cheap john taking a hooker against the wall.

The shame was worse than the anger, because both were marks of how I'd failed once more to be what a man needed. If Mikhail was Trading, how could I trust him? How could he trust me, with a hellbreed scar turned into a hard knot of corruption on the inside of my wrist?

I never told anyone, but that was the moment I truly became a hunter. Because I suddenly knew I could not even rely on my teacher—if he was Trading with something inhuman, he was a question mark until I figured out what was going on. He had taught me well, and the logic was inescapable. He was hiding something, and I wouldn't be able to rest until I knew what it was.

Until the rock was lifted and I saw the pale squirming things underneath.

I had not been an innocent when he found me, but the last dregs of whatever innocence I had left me under the granite Jesus. Because even while I cried, I was planning.

The tears would not last nearly long enough.

25

I flipped on the radio next morning to hear the bad news, and only relaxed a little when no messages or news of murders came in. Autumn floods had arrived with a vengeance, and the rain lasted long enough to spring a leak in my ceiling. I stuck a large plastic tub I used for soaking blood out of leather under the silvery drops and promptly forgot about it. I had other things to worry about.

Galina was regretful. "I can't, Jill. I've got serious Work to do in my sanctum for the next three days, I'm closed down and tapped out. I would, but this is for the shields, and—"

I said I understood. And I did.

Avery was a bust too. "The exorcisms are kicking my ass. I'd slip, Jill. I'm not strong enough and you know it. Eva and Benito are out too, we had to sweep the whole city last night. It's turning into a madhouse out here."

Guilt, a hot rank bubble, rose in my throat. "I'm working on it, Ave."

He made a short sound of annoyance. Behind him, phones rang and someone shouted something. It sounded like he was up in Vice, probably bullshitting with his buddy Lefty Perez. "Since when do you stop working on it? Can the martyr trip, Jill. Clear your head out and get this bastard sewn up so we can have that beer together."

I made my goodbyes and hung up, chewing at my bottom lip. Saul handed me a cup of coffee. "No breakfast?" he asked for the third time.

My stomach clenched into an iron fist. "Not before something like this."

"I told you I'd anchor you. I wouldn't be much of a tracker if I couldn't." He'd showered, and his hair lay glistening-dark against his shoulders except for the twin braids on either side. It was a good look for him, framing the classic purity of his cheekbones, balancing out the line of his jaw. He wore the same T-shirt, and I wondered how light he traveled. I hadn't seen a suitcase yet.

"I don't know you that well. No offense."

An easy shrug, as if I couldn't offend him. "None taken, but it looks like I'm all you've got. Harp's not a tracker, and Dom's her mate."

In other words, she wouldn't like it if Dom got close enough to anchor me. I could call Theron, I supposed. I could even scare up a few more people if I had to, including Father Guillermo down at Sacred Grace.

But Gui wasn't strong enough for something like this. Anyone else I could call in would be a risk—and *at* risk, not only because I'd be vulnerable, but because the process itself was so dangerous.

I studied Saul in the fall of sunlight through the skylights. It was pale, washed-clean light, fresh and bled white by the storm last night. The weather report said the storms were moving in, coming from a ridge out in the desert meeting another ridge coming up the Rio Luz's broad slow muscular bends. We'd have heat lightning tonight and more rain tomorrow when the weather finished rolling up like a parade of barrio low-riders.

Saul's jaw was set, his eyes sleepless and fierce. The silver twisted tighter against one of his damp braids pulling the hair out of his face. I didn't ask him where he'd slept last night, because my bed had smelled like both of us this morning. I smelled a little like him too, the tang of Were mixing with cordite and silver and leather, and the faint trace of hellbreed and death that clung to my skin. It was a heady mix.

The bracelet was unrecognizable now, twining through his hair like a morning-glory vine through a fence. I stared at the gleaming metal for a moment, memory boiling up under my skin.

He paused in the act of taking a sip from his own coffee cup. Steam drifted up, touching his face. "What?"

The blonde hair, and the red hair, twisting around each other. I set my coffee cup down and bounced to my feet from the rumpled bed. I moved in on him so fast I half expected him to flinch, but he kept still, watching me. His eyes were very dark, and very deep.

The silver was warm from his heat. I touched the metal, running my fingers over the tight curves married to the silky texture of wet hair. "Did you do this? Make it bend like this?"

"It happened." He didn't move, but I sensed a shrug. "It happens. So what?" The faintest hint of a challenge, his chin lifting just a fraction. Mulishly defiant, and a startlingly young look for a Were so contained. How old *was* he?

I ran my tongue along the inside of my teeth, shelving the question. Something else bothered me, the shape of an idea just under the blanket of my consciousness.

He isn't my father's . . . he's mine. "So what does it *mean*, Saul?"

His fingers flicked. He caught one of the charms tied into my hair with red thread and gave it a slight tug, his eyebrow quirking meaningfully and his mouth firming into a straight line.

Knowing Weres, that was the only answer I was going to get from him. I'd have to talk to Harp about it. Something about the two hairs twining together bothered me. Or not precisely bothered me, but gave me the tail end of an idea I didn't much like, one I had to tease out with an hour or so of hard thinking. An hour or so I didn't have right now. The unsteady feeling behind my pulse told me this thing was wending its way to a conclusion, and not a pleasant one.

You don't live with adrenaline and intuition, not to mention sorcery, for very long without getting a feeling about when a situation's going to blow sky-high. I let out a soft breath, frustration blooming sharp under my breastbone. My palms were damp again. "All right. You'll anchor me. I hope to hell you know what you're doing."

"I usually do." He let go of the charm, patted my hair back into place. The look of defiance was gone, replaced with calm steadiness. "Don't worry. I won't let you fall."

It was oddly comforting to hear him say it.

"It's not the falling I'm worried about. It's the climbing back up out of *between*." I eyed the coffee cup longingly, heat from the mug burrowing into my fingers. Handed it back to him. "Let's do it before I lose my nerve."

"I can't imagine *that* happening," he muttered as he turned away.

Ridiculously, I was hard-pressed not to smile.

I rarely used this narrow room, as the padlock and the chain on the door proved. It was little more than a closet set to the side of my practice-room, the empty wall opposite that had held Mikhail's sword lying under a rectangle of thin sunlight. I made a mental note to pick up the sunsword from Galina's and led the Were through the door. Darkness swallowed us, broken only by a faint silver glow.

The altar was at the other end of the room, and the walls were covered with an intaglio of spray paint, blue and black, protection-symbols from almost every religion since the dawn of time. Fat lines of paint shifted like tentacles, responding to my presence, and the air hummed as my eyes adapted, pupils flaring wide.

Cut into the hardwood floor was a double circle, spiky symbols carved between the inner and outer rings. The pentacle, inscribed just as deeply, glowed with silver hammered into its sharp lines. Hardwood inside the circle was stained darker than the surrounding floor, the silver pale and drained but glittering faintly, like a half-busted neon sign.

"Huh." Saul peered over my shoulder, his heat burning through his T-shirt and mine. "Nice."

If you think so. My fingers tightened on the knife I carried, the only weapon I had on me. I felt damn near naked. "Mikhail did it. As a present." *And also so I don't have to use a church to go* between, *since most churches are tactical nightmares when it comes to defense and I'm vulnerable while I do this.*

It was the last present he'd ever given me. The warehouse, and this little room, hours of work and love I hadn't thanked him properly for. Three days later, he'd been dead, bleeding out through slashed jugulars in a cheap hotel room as the Sorrows bitch he'd fallen in love with fled with his amulet and I kicked in the door just a quarter-minute too late, unable to save him.

Oh, Mikhail. The familiar bite of shame turned bitter in my throat.

"He must have spent some time on it." Saul pushed past me, lingering for a little longer than absolutely necessary as he touched me, and stepped away to examine the circle, giving it his full attention. There was barely enough room for it, but it was complete, the carved lines deep and still fresh.

A swift pain lanced through my heart. I could remember Mikhail with his arm over my shoulders. *Is for you,* milaya. *Use wisely. Some day old Mischa might not be here to protect his little snake under rock, eh?*

I missed him. I missed him so much, even the slaps and the kicks as he trained me. Even the fear in the middle of the night. You must love your teacher as deeply as you hate him; the love will bring you back from Hell while your teacher holds the line. That love will also save you if you lose your way in the shifting forests of suicide and screaming that are the border between Hell and our world of flesh and light. The love is necessary.

The hate is to make you *strong*. Out in the wilds of the nightside, there is no second chance, and your teacher has to make sure you can survive on your own. It's bad to lose a fellow hunter, there are few enough of us as it is. Losing an apprentice is much, much worse.

So it's love, and hate, and need. All twisted together and made into a rope, a bond, a chain. A fetter each hunter wears with pride, and the reason why we don't lie to each other. You can't lie to someone else who's been loved like that.

No matter what secret your teacher keeps from you. No matter how deep the betrayal.

"He did," I whispered. *He spent weeks on this. Did he know he wouldn't be here forever? Sure he did. He was already old, and he had to know . . .*

Had he known the Sorrows bitch would turn on him? He *had* to have known, Mikhail taught me everything I knew about the Sorrows and their worship of the Elder Gods, their Houses where incense hung heavy in the air and women became hive-queens, their collective energies focused on bringing back the Elders through the veils that kept them from the "real" world. I had to go to Hutch only because I hadn't smelled one before.

Mikhail *had* to have known. So why had he trusted her? Why hadn't he *told* me?

Deal with what you have in front of you now, Jill. Quit stalling.

Saul stepped into the bare space in the middle of the pentacle. I inhaled, deeply. Then I reached up and unclasped the ruby from my throat. Its sharp edges dug into my sweating palm as I slid past the Were. I stepped delicately over the double circle and turned to face him, my back to the altar. His face was shadowed, only the glitter of eyes and the glint of silver in his hair reflecting the spent light from the pentacle below.

I held up the chain. The ruby dangled, bloody sparks drifting in its depths as it sensed the event looming toward me. "This is my line back." My voice sounded normal, except for the pain riding each word. "It'll get slippery, and it'll fight you. *Don't* let go. If you let go, I'm lost."

He nodded, solemn. Silver winked in one of his braids, his fingers brushed mine as he took the gem, its chain dipping and swaying. "I won't."

Jill. Time's wasting. I turned my back on him, walked the four steps to the altar. It was bluestone, quarried in Britain somewhere and shipped here on the hush-hush by one of Mikhail's friends in "exports." A simple thigh-high rectangle of stone, it resonated as I laid my hand on it, cold burning my fingertips. "O my Lord God," I whispered. "Do not forsake me when I face Hell's legions. In your name . . ."

That's the trouble. I'm not doing this in God's name. I'm doing this for me.

I hopped up on the altar and spent a few moments arranging myself. The chill of stone reached even through the leather pants, and my T-shirt was no barrier to it at all. I didn't wear my weapons, except the one small knife with a leather-wrapped handle. I lay on my back, arranged my booted feet carefully, and wriggled my head a little until the silver charms didn't dig so hard into my skull.

My left hand was pale, my apprentice-ring glittering as I lifted it. The knife-hilt was in my right hand. I swallowed dryly.

Don't do it, Jill. Don't. You know what this is like. Don't do it. Find some other way.

There was no other way. If there was, I wouldn't be here.

Determination took shape under my skin. A spark crackled from the ring, a point of lightning-white in the gloom. The spray-painted sigils ran wetly on the walls, whispering like bruised fingers rubbing each other. By now the door of the room would be invisible from the outside, sealed shut. Inside, womblike dark was broken only by the eerie glow of the silver pounded into the pentacle's lines.

Go for the quick tear, Jill.

My breath whooshed out past my teeth. I set the knife-edge against my palm and *cut.*

The smell of blood exploded in my nose. Bile scorched the back of my throat. I dropped the knife to the side, heard it clatter behind the altar, and whipped my left hand out as the scar tightened on my wrist, rumbling a low dissatisfied note.

An arrow of etheric force from my palm smashed into the ruby, an attraction older than time. Blood calling to a bloody, blood-sensitized gem. My back arched, and the rope of force tautened.

Saul had caught the other end. It strained, and I sensed him going down to one knee inside the pentacle, his fist tight around the ruby and blood—*my* blood, transferred through space—welling slick and hot between his fingers. He leaned back against the pull, and I *dropped*—

—*into howling wind, buffeting increasing as I fell, a scream like the slipstream past a jet's windows filling the world. Falling, naked flesh stung by air turned hard with velocity. It was dark, the utter dark of blind closed eyes at the bottom of the sea at night.*

In this space there is no up or down, despite the sensation of falling. We call it between *because it is; between life and death, earth and Hell, physical and spiritual.*

Between present and past.

The greatest danger is forgetting who and what I am, falling into chaos and dispersing, the psyche unable to contain itself without an outside border. But the bracelet of agony closed around my wrist, crimson light spilling between my fingers as the etheric copy of the jewel closed in Saul Dustcircle's fist almost snapped free of my grasp. A long huuuuuuuuuuungh! *of mental effort burst out of me, the taste of copper filling my mouth to the brim, and I swallowed. With the jerk of arrested motion came the consciousness of who I was, what I was doing here, what information I sought.*

Time means less than nothing in this space, and so does distance. I became an arrow, translated between one spot and the next without the benefit of moving, the reflex of a physical body turning my stomach inside-out. Gagging, choking, trying desperately to remember that I was not in a real body but between *and therefore without a goddamn stomach to reject food, I slammed through the barriers and found myself in a howling ash-choked wasteland with pale copies of skyscrapers glittering through a fog that tore into agonized screaming faces at my approach. Flying, through walls and jets of bright psychic moments crystallized by emotion, until the location that pulled me came into view.*

It was a mansion, its physical shape common enough for the super-rich and paranoid. Its etheric shape, though, was a howl of suffering and pleasure in that suffering, the psychic fume of death and corruption like the belch of an old cancerous dragon, tinted with dark flame having its origin in hell. Into this maw I flashed, the not-me holding a bloody jewel that twisted like a live snake in my grip, trying to break free of this place of horror and flee back to its real physical home.

The mansion swallowed me.

There they were. The hellbreed was a pale sword of diseased brightness, and the rogue Were a twisted mass of fur and flesh, crouched at her feet. The images overlapped with Cenci's face, hair whipping in pale strands as she fought to contain a massive force spilling through her, lips pulled back in a grimace of agony.

It is its own kind of agony to see between. *There is no difference, once you are sideways in that not-space, between the face and the mind behind it, the vessel and the wine. People become smears of reaction, hellbreed spreading vortexes of contagion, hunters straight disciplined arrows of brilliance each with a screaming child on the inside. It is a vision of inner truth that can drive you mad, if you have not been trained—and even then, sanity is not certain.*

Cenci knelt, the Were bleeding at her feet. The floor was tessellated patterns of darkness, black and white linoleum squares stretching to infinity. Don't worry, *she* whispered to the hulk of shattered fur and animal growl. I'll take care of you.

The Were screamed with fury, but her slim strong arms came around him—and then, Navoshtay Niv Arkady came.

A tidal wave of etheric force slammed into me, a bat hitting a baseball with the cracking of a sweet swinging-for-the-fences bonebreaking home run. The slippery line between my fingers slid a few inches, my hand loosening, opening, my self flung through nonspace, skidding for the edges of reality.

If I went over that edge . . .

I heard, from very far away, Arkady's voice. I knew it was his because of the black weight of ice it carried, and the unmistakable stamp of black oily eyes and coppery skin, a hook nose and the smell of heatless acid fire. This is unacceptable. Each sibilant carried a dagger of ice, plunging for the beating heart of whatever living thing it could find. You are my vessel, and I will break you if I wish.

Comprehension blazed through me as I lunged away from the sound of that voice. A hellbreed that old can sometimes see between, and if he caught me spying inside his secrets even Perry might not be able to call him off.

The jaws of the mansion slammed shut as I streaked through, shoulder screaming in pain as the ruby pulled, and my fingers slipped again, hot blood torn loose from my hand in a painless gout as the gem squirted out of my slippery palm.

Falling. I had gone too far, the cord sliding between nerveless fingers, stunned and dazed by the impact.

Comprehension flashed through me too late, a map of cause and effect stretching back to one image—slim white arms, bleeding from a hellbreed's claws, clasping with more than human strength as a red-haired man struggled and screamed in agony, his flesh cracking and madness bleeding through.

I fell. And fell. Heart stopping, brain bleeding, breath turned to a death-rattle, I fell.

And was caught, deceleration slapping hard against every atom of me.

—come back—

I hung pinned for excruciating eternal moments like a butterfly, the world wheeling underneath with a sound like rushing hungry waves. Then another jolt, as someone wrapped both fists around a bloody gem and hauled with every muscle and erg of strength, pulled until lungs and heart both strained, eyes bulging and a cougar's coughing roar smashing against spray-painted walls, a pentacle shifting silver and the line snapping, ripping, tearing me back into a body that glowed with a spiky clear aura, a blot of shining darkness on its right wrist like a live coal.

The part of me that went between *slammed back into this body, convulsing, choking, flung sideways like a rag doll, falling—*

—until my head smashed into the wooden floor. I lay crumpled in front of the altar, hearing my own hoarse screams as my legs jittered and flopped.

The retching eased, every muscle in my body seizing up and relaxing in waves. I could finally *breathe* again. I lay against the altar, my eyes closed, vibrating with pain. The scar pulsed, a wave of sick delight spilling up my arm and curling down my back, as if a warm, manicured hand had just stroked along my spine, a linen cuff touching my skin gently.

Of as if a scaled tongue too wet and warm to be human had touched the vulnerable hollow behind my ear.

I flinched, without the energy to cower away. Got myself up on hands and knees, my left hand singing a thin note of pain before the cut, sucked bloodless, closed. I realized, through the ringing noise in my head, that Saul was calling my name, his voice hoarse as if he'd been shouting a while.

"Goddammit, answer me!" He sounded frantic, and the silver light pulsed as if he'd tried to step over the pentacle's borders. It held fast, singing a warning note of crystalline power.

"Hold . . . on . . ." I managed through a fresh set of retches and the howling in my head. It was a good thing I hadn't had breakfast.

He subsided, but the rumbling growl coming from him shook the walls. He was one unhappy Were.

Well, I'm not too happy myself. I struggled for a laugh and couldn't find one.

My arms and legs trembled, as if I'd just pulled through a fever. I managed to sit up, propping myself against the altar, and made the gesture that released the double-circle and the pentacle. Silver light folded away, its hum diminishing as it bled into the ground.

Saul's feet slid and slipped in the spreading pool of my blood as he launched himself, the silver glow turning bloody as he broke the weakening barriers and landed next to me, almost crashing into the altar. He fetched up hard and went to his knees, grabbed my shoulders, and shook me, my head bobbling back and forth. Sounds came out of him that I only vaguely recognized as words. I was too busy shaking, choking back more retches, and hearing the roaring noise of *between* fade too slowly out of my ears.

I'd made it. The knowledge I'd brought out of the space *between* thrummed in my veins, spilled through my head, and the whole monstrous pattern became clear.

I began to cry as Saul cupped my face in his bloody hands, the ruby a hard hot edge against my cheek. I sobbed until my ribs ached, howling, and when he kissed me I couldn't stop weeping but I also started to scream, and he swallowed my cries as I found out I was once again alive.

26

I splashed cold water on my face again, flung my head back. A charm chimed against the mirror, whipping at the end of a long strand of hair. The phone shrilled, and I reached it just as Saul appeared in my bedroom door. My guns lay on the nightstand, each with a full clip and one in the chamber.

It was Harp. "We've got him, Jill. His name's Billy Ironwater, and he hails from Connecticut. He went to visit kin in upstate New York—the Alleghany pack—and disappeared about half a year before murders started popping up, murders that until now have been 'lost' in a stack of paperwork. The Alleghany canines have been looking for him and running up against blank walls. Most of those walls lead back to hellbreed, and in *that* state it only means one thing."

I felt the click of a pattern slide under my skin, resounding in my bones. "Arkady," I breathed. I couldn't call him anything else, now. Not when I had brushed him *between* and seen his true face.

"Yeah. We're in the barrio, at the Criz in the Plaza. Can you bring Saul? We've found a trail, and we need him. The entire Were population except for cubs is on this." She was straining and eager, now that she had her prey in sight. Now it was time for the hunt, and all uncertainty was over.

It was a relief. My brain slid into overdrive, the plan crystallizing in a moment. It was a good plan, and might even get me out of this alive. "I'll give him my car keys." Shocked silence rang on the line. I slid one gun into its holster, then the other. "What? I can't go into the barrio, I'm a *gringa*. Besides, I've got shit of my own to do."

"You're giving him your car keys?" She sounded, for once, taken aback. The hard note of glee was gone.

I felt sorry for raining on her parade. "How else is he going to get down there in time? This is worse than you think, Harp. Get moving; he'll catch up." I slammed the phone down and turned to Saul. "Harp needs you, down in the barrio. They've found a trail, and just found out who our mystery boy is. Name's Billy Ironwater and he's a canine Were from Connecticut." My hand shot out, and I tossed the jingling clatter of my spare set of car keys at him. I picked up my next spare leather trench coat from the bed, shook it experimentally, and shrugged into it. I'd put in my tiger's eye earrings, and they tapped my cheeks as I shook my head, freeing my silver-laden hair from the collar of the coat. The blessing in the stones flashed blue for a moment, subsided.

"I thought nobody drove your baby but you." He said it mildly, slipping the keys in the pocket of his jeans.

"If I can trust you to hold the line while I go *between*

I can trust you not to scratch my goddamn paint job," I snapped. *Get him out of here, Jill. Hurry up.*

Do it quick.

"What are you planning?" His dark eyes had narrowed, and I allowed myself a few moments of looking at his cheekbones, the shape of his mouth, the loose grace of his hands. He was beautiful in the way only a Were can be, each line arranged for maximum effect.

Like something human, only better, stripped of imperfections. All the flaws burned out, instead of scored in with a hellbreed's kiss. The distance between us yawned wide as the chasm between ordinary waking life and the screaming winds of *between*.

"I'm going to finish my end of this, and you and the Weres will finish yours." *After that maybe it's time for a vacation. I wonder what Tahiti looks like this time of year. Ugh, maybe not. I've had all I can stand of heat and rain.*

He took two steps into the room. "I wonder . . ." The sentence stopped itself, and his eyes met mine. The stinging communication returned, deeper than ever, the line between us wide open now and humming with force. It felt too good, too familiar.

"Don't wonder. Get going. You can find the barrio from here, and once you get there you can follow your nose." My hands had turned into fists. The scar pulsed, my agitation plucking at it.

Another two steps toward me. *God in Heaven, can't you just go?* I wanted to scream it, folded my mouth against the cry. Clenched my hands even tighter. Silver clinked and jangled in my hair.

He approached me cautiously. When he was within

arm's length I made a restless movement and he stopped, his feet poised. "What's wrong?"

What the fuck do you think *is wrong?* "This isn't going to work," I told him flatly. "You have to go. You *have* to. Right now."

His mouth compressed into a thin line. He reached up, and I thought he meant to touch my cheek. I flinched away, but his hand flicked, and one of my charms dropped into his palm, neatest trick of the week.

"Hey—"

Saul retreated swiftly, paused in the door. He held up the charm—a silver wagon wheel, tied to a long lock of my dark hair. His claws had sliced through as effectively as a razor.

I stared at him. That close, and that quick, it could have been my jugular opened instead of a lock of hair sliced. The worst part was that I didn't care. If he was close enough to kill me, he was close enough that I could breathe in that smell of safety, of something too good for someone like me.

"You're not hellbreed," he said softly. "And I'm not rogue. It might work."

There. It was out in the open, it was said. I opened my mouth, let my half of the flawed equation slip out. "I'm contaminated. I'm not willing to take the chance." *Now will you please get the hell out of here?*

"You've been wrong before." He stepped back, his fist closing over the silver charm. His boots made no sound, and it hurt to see his fluid grace, and the way his eyes moved over my face, as if he saw something precious there.

"So have you. Get going, Were." *Go and find yourself*

a nice pretty Were girl on the Rez and raise nice cublets. Forget about all of this.

"I've only been wrong once, hunter." Then he was gone, the space in the air where he'd stood crying out to me.

I stood wooden next to my bed, my eyes shut, listening. When the garage door opened and my car's engine roused my shoulders sagged. When I heard the purr of the Impala receding along the street, I finally opened my eyes.

My cheeks were wet. I swiped at them angrily and slid the replacement pager into its padded pocket a moment before the phone shrilled again. I was starting to hate that goddamn noise, and had a brief satisfying vision of emptying a clip into the fucking thing.

I couldn't waste the ammo. I hooked the headset up out of the cradle. "Talk." I sounded a little less than welcoming, even to myself.

"So glad to find you at home, my dear." Perry's voice had turned from bland to venomously gleeful. "I am calling to inform you the meeting you requested is scheduled for dusk, here at the Monde. It is the only place I can be assured of your safety."

You sound so happy I'm going to bet my safety isn't on the agenda tonight. My mouth had gone desert-dry and sandy inside. Cool sweat rose up on my forehead and prickled at the small of my back. I was about to use my own body as the lure in a trap, for the five hundredth time in my life.

As usual, I took refuge in sarcasm. "Gee, Pericles. That's awful swell of you. Do I get a pony for Christmas too?"

"Do not bait me today." The words rattled around my ears, each spilling their load of cool poison. "There is a limit to what I allow you, Kismet."

My temper broke with a brittle snap. "Get one thing straight, hellbreed. Your end of this stinks, and if you want to keep your nice cushy little existence in my city you *will* keep in line. You fuck with me, and there won't be any profit in this for you. It'll be all loss, and I'll personally take pleasure in filling you with silverjacket lead right before I burn your web to the goddamn ground with you in it. Is that clear enough for even your thick little head?"

Amazingly, he chuckled. The sound was so warm and rich my hands began to shake. "You're coming along quite nicely. See you at dusk, my dear." A sound that might have been a kiss breathed into the telephone, and the line went dead.

I checked the clock, picking up my knives and sliding them into their sheaths. Dusk gave me roughly six hours to nerve myself up for what I had to do.

Get going, Jill. Come on.

I got going.

27

The next wave of stormy weather had begun to move across the city by the time I reached Galina's. I didn't go through the shop. Instead, I leapt across a narrow gap between the Italian restaurant next door and the rooftop of her building.

Galina's greenhouse glowed with failing light as I cast my glance over the roof again. Concrete was gritty and oily underneath my boots, their leather still dark with my own blood. The stain in the closet next to my practice room had gotten deeper, wine-dark inside the double circle.

How long are you going to keep bleeding, Jill?

Another useless question.

I lifted up the latch and ducked into the greenhouse. The cloak of Sanctuary shields had no reason to stop me, which told me Galina was out of her sanctum and in the house somewhere.

Probably sensing me overhead.

Most certainly waiting. The entire world was breathless with waiting. The pattern, seen with striking clarity in the buffeting nonspace of *between,* had its own momentum now. All that remained was for me to do what came next.

And not get my stupid self killed. *That* was going to be the hard part.

The sunsword lay on a slim table scattered with gardening tools under a shelf of blue frilly orchids. Dozing, drowsy heat encircled me, the scar on my wrist pulsing under its carapace of copper, clipped on just this morning. I smelled decaying organic matter in the potting soil, the healthy powerful scent of green things growing, the sharp pungency of just-watered earth. I closed my hand around the hilt.

The Sanctuary shields shivered, tensing. My skin chilled.

"I'm not going to do anything," I said without turning around. "I just want to talk to her."

"I don't know if that's a good idea." Galina spoke from the trapdoor leading down to her bedroom. She never did like to be far from her plants. "I'm sorry I couldn't tell you, Jill. It's the nature of the Sanctuary vow."

You keep my secrets just as thoroughly, I suppose I can't blame you. I nodded, deciding to piece it together. "Understood. She came here with him, didn't she? They were desperate, looking only for a way out by now, since they couldn't run anywhere else; Arkady was too close. Ironwater suggested a Sanctuary, probably as his last hope."

"I'm always a last resort, Jill. Just like you. I couldn't help him. He had some periods of lucidity, but . . ."

Heaviness tinted her voice. "She's here now, asking for a weapon to kill you with—one I won't give her, by the way. He's gone, broke all her protections and fled. The Weres are hunting him now?"

So he ran away even from her, at last. He must want to die. There would be no torture more thorough for a hellbreed-broken Were with intermittent periods of sanity than to know that he had broken a whole clutch of their oldest taboos and tasted human flesh. "You know they are. This time they'll catch him, because she won't be there to mask his trail and slip him free." I slid the sunsword into the soft leather sheath through the side snaps. The clicking of the snaps was very loud in the stillness. The walls hummed their song of Sanctuary. "I wouldn't have put the pieces together, except I went *between* this morning. I saw what she's hiding from, and I know she wouldn't shelter with any hellbreed. That's why I couldn't flush her out by burning hellbreed holes. She moved him around as much as she dared, and she hid the last place anyone would suspect—with a Sanctuary. A *human.*"

It's official. Perry called me here to flush her out of hiding, but didn't pursue her. Why? What's his game?

Even with all I now knew, that part was still murky. It was enough of a wild card to give anyone cold sweats.

"I took my vows." Her voice didn't tremble. "And I'll keep her here to give you a head start. I don't want any more fights on my roof, and you're my friend as well as our hunter, Jill. This city can't stand to lose you."

Mighty nice of you, Galina. "I just want to talk. That's all."

I sensed the sad slow shake of her head. "I said that's

not a good idea. You'd better get out of here. Once the Weres catch him there will be hell to pay."

A chill touched the base of my spine. "There's going to be hell to pay all right." I picked up the sword, buckled the diagonal strap so it rode my back, a heavy comforting weight. "But she's not going to be dealing it out. I am." The glass walls rattled a little, responding both to my voice and the cycling-up of the Sanctuary shields.

Did Galina think I was going to turn on her?

A hunter is supposed to be unpredictable. Still, a Sanctuary should have no doubts about my trustworthiness. But Galina knew I'd been too late to save Mikhail—and maybe she suspected *why*.

You can't lie to yourself as a hunter. But I still couldn't decide if I had been too late because of some lingering traces of trust and respect for Mikhail keeping me too far back when I followed him that night, or if I had hung back because some part of me knew something was going to happen—and wanted to punish him for betraying me, not as a teacher or as a father, but as a lover.

Did it matter? I had been too late, in any case, and Mikhail had bled out, choking on his own blood. Melisande Belisa, the Sorrows bitch, had stolen his most precious amulet, the one that should have gone to me, and fled into the night.

And now here I was.

"You should go," Galina repeated softly. Conciliatory, but with a core of steel.

For fuck's sake. Can't you see I'm trying to finish this and stop all the killing? "Tell her this, Galina. I've got a meet with Perry and Arkady tonight at the Monde. Arkady started this whole mess. He's liable, but I can't take him on without help and Perry's about as useful as tits on a boar hog in this situation. He'll be too busy trying to figure angles for himself. Billy Ironwater's death will be clean and merciful. If she goes with me up against Arkady, I promise her revenge on her father— and a clean death, as painless as I can make it." My voice caught. I turned, and saw Galina standing at the edge of the trapdoor, her green tilted eyes alight with sorrow and raw power. An ageless look, and one I almost felt sure my own face was wearing.

Galina was in full Sanctuary robes, gray silk with the wide hood thrown back, the undersleeves of crimson glowing eerily. Her necklace—quartered circle, serpent shifting—glittered with hard darts of light. "I'll pass it along. Now get out." She held a gun, her slim fingers loose as it dangled by her side. Was it for me, or for the hellbreed brooding below? I almost imagined I could *feel* Cenci's breathing in the hot stillness.

Waiting, like a pale blind adder under a rock. Were we both snakes hiding under the same stone?

No. I'm not hellbreed. I backed toward the door, feeling my way with each footstep. "No hard feelings, Galina." She was, after all, a Sanctuary. She had no choice.

Just like I had no choice.

"None on my end either, Jill. I'll hold her until you're gone. Be safe out there."

I finally said it. "You know I can't. It's not in my goddamn job description." I eased out of the door, closing it behind me with a click. The sunsword vibrated on my back. My boots ground the rooftop as I took a running leap and launched myself out into space, landing on the street below and pulling etheric energy through the scar, streaking away.

Clouds covered the city under a yellow-green dome, heat held close and breathless under glass. Out in the desert there would be heat lightning, and animals scuttling to shelter. Here in the valley, in my city, there was scurrying to get under cover too. Even the humans could feel something lurking in the heat and the boiling sky.

Something with teeth, just looking to close on the unwary. No wonder they sought cover.

My pager went off four times. Harp, trying to track me down. I didn't respond. The game was set and the pieces were moving, and there was nothing to do now but see how it finished out. I had my own moves to make.

I sat for a long time in my usual back pew at Mary of the Immaculate Conception, watching candleflames shudder as uneven currents of storm-charged air brushed them. If Perry was watching me, I'd drawn him away from Galina's house to here, where I usually came before I braved the Monde to make my monthly payments. My eyes drifted across the crucifix, Christ hanging with his attenuated limbs and peaceful face. A quiet, aesthetic representation of a death gruesomely paraded in front of the faithful for centuries—I wondered why they hadn't chosen the Last Supper instead. Religion might be a little more civilized if a picture of a feast instead of a Roman torture was pasted up in the churches.

Still, I know better. Humanity doesn't go in for gentle gods. I wished Mikhail was alive; I would have wanted to hear what he would say about my forays into philosophy. Probably something practical, like how all the philosophy in the world wouldn't stop a bullet.

Oh, Mikhail. I loved you. I love you so much.

Did I kill you? Even now I didn't know.

It all boiled down to simple starkness. There was light and there was darkness; and there were those in the light who fought the dark. It made us worse, sometimes, than the darkness itself. We were so close to that edge. It was impossible not to step over sometimes, whether from momentum or choice.

Did that mean we should stop fighting? What decent person *could,* even if the job itself wasn't decent at all?

You know better than to think that, milaya. It was Mikhail's voice, a baritone purr. *I do not force you. You force yourself.*

"Bullshit," I whispered. But he was right. He had lifted me out of the snow, a battered and broken girl still clawing and fighting back with her last vestiges of strength. He'd fed me, and sheltered me, and would have turned me over to social services for therapy and reclamation; indeed, had tried to several times. I'd *chosen* to stay with him, stubbornly sleeping on his floor and following behind him as he did his daily practice until he took me on. There was no obligation laid on me. There never is, on hunters. We can give it up and walk away at any moment. Nobody, not even the Church, blamed us if we did.

Sure you can walk away. Now that you know what's out there in the night preying on the weak, you can turn tail and head for the hills. You can move to another city and take up tatting lace for fun and dealing blackjack for profit.

Sure you can.

He had saved me because I'd let him. Because I didn't want to die in the snow. I wanted to *live*.

Had I killed him for it? Had I been deliberately late?

I sat very still, my hands white-knuckled on the back of the pew in front of me. Raised my eyes once again to the crucifix, silver tinkling in my hair from the slight movement. The scar gave out a throbbing murmur of dissatisfaction edging on pain.

My eyes traveled up the long nerveless legs, past the loincloth and the tortured chest, paused at the throat, and watched the slice of dreaming face I could see under the heavy tangle of thorns and curly wooden hair. No glitter under his slackened eyelids answered mine. He was asleep. "I don't do this for you," I whispered. "I never have. Is that my sin?"

Or is my sin greed? I want something for myself. I always have.

I felt Saul's mouth on mine again. I still smelled, a little, like him. When he went back to his life, I was going to keep the sheets unwashed for as long as I could stand it. I would take deep lungfuls of that scent every time I needed to, until it faded like everything did, especially everything good.

There was so little unmitigated good in the world. The corruption crept in everywhere. How long would it be before I could no longer lay claim to my own soul?

Had I just made the same mistake Mikhail had, trusting a woman who wasn't truly human, tainted with hellbreed? Did that mean that everyone who trusted me had made the same mistake?

Did I kill you, Mikhail? I wish you could tell me. I need *to know.*

I leaned forward, my clammy forehead on my tense and clutching hands. Dusk was coming, I could feel it like a compass must feel north. Thunder rattled; the storm would probably wait until nightfall and the great gush of cool nightly wind from the river to unleash its fury. Somewhere in the city the Weres were hunting a rogue, and they would be kind when they caught him. He wouldn't feel a thing.

But for me, it was going to be vengeance. Whether Cenci took my bargain or not, it was going to be fury and hatred and messiness, spilled blood and screaming.

After all, that was what I lived for, right?

Just stop it. Mikhail's dead no matter what you intended, and you have a job to do. Just be happy Saul is out there somewhere in the world, that he even exists. Quit moaning and get on with it. This is your big night, you don't want to be late.

I could have been happy with being a *little* later. But I stood up, and I did something I hadn't done since my teenage years.

I approached the altar with slow steps, climbed the steps, and stood right next to the bank of candles and flowers, in the midst of their heady fragrance. They adorned what in pagan times would be a site of bloody sacrifice, whether done kindly or cruelly.

Times have changed a lot less than we think.

I looked up into the wooden face of the man on the cross, under the shelf of carved hair and runnels of painted decorative blood from jagged thorns. A great howling cheated scream rose up inside me, was savagely repressed, and died away.

What could I say to a God who had never spoken to me and a Son who slept?

"You give out redemption, don't you?" My whisper sounded very loud in the silence, broken only by the hissing of candleflames. "If you're not too busy right now, I could use a handful. Maybe even just a pinch."

I was still begging. Just like the girl I had been, before. The weakling.

I'd been taught a better prayer, hadn't I?

O my Lord God, do not forsake me when I face Hell's legions. In Thy name and with Thy blessing, I go forth to cleanse the night. My lips shaped the words, and the candleflames flattened. The scar on my wrist grumbled uneasily, a hot hard knot under the skin, infected.

I shut the thought of Mikhail away, along with the thought of Saul. It took a physical effort, a tensing of every muscle. When it was done, I inhaled, let out a long huff of air.

The click sounded inside my head. I'd never told Mikhail about this switch in the very bottom of me, the one I could now flip. I could lift off, shutting away everything but the job that had to be done, the shining path of vengeance laid out before my feet. That road might eventually end at Hell's bony clutching gates, but at least I'd take plenty of the predators who preyed on the weak with me. Maybe a few innocents would survive a little longer because I was out getting dirty.

Enough whining. The night could use some cleansing. I was just the girl to get it done. *If* the Weres kept the rogue out of my way, and *if* Cenci's need for revenge on her hellspawn father was greater than her need for revenge on me, and *if* Perry's interest in me would keep him from interfering, and *if* . . .

I was counting on a lot of *if*s, and on a lot of hellbreed jealousy. I was also counting on Navoshtay Niv Arkady being killable, which was by no means certain.

"Only one way to find out." My voice echoed in the church's cloistered quiet, the sunsword ringing softly underneath it. The ruby at my throat was warm and comforting. I had never seen a priest in here, but the doors were always open. I was glad on both counts; if I did see a priest now, I wasn't quite sure I could control my sarcasm. It would hurt too much to be respectful, and in any case I've never done submission well.

Did the man on the cross mind? Did he forgive me for it, knowing I was as I'd been made? By the same hand that had made him, the same hand that abandoned him to be nailed up for sins he didn't commit? Sins he had no choice but to pay for, over and over again?

Was memory a curse for the man on the cross too?

Quit fucking around, Kismet. Get your ass moving.

I did. But as I left the church I felt comforted, for once. I pushed open the doors and stepped out into an early evening eerily dark with storm clouds covering the sky's bright eye. In the west was a crimson streak. Dusk was coming, the sun sinking under the rim of the earth and night rising to start its games.

28

I didn't have to walk out to the Monde *or* take a cab.
I wasn't more than four blocks away from the church
when a pristine black limousine detached itself from
parking up the street and crept toward me.

It was absurdly anticlimactic.

I got in, taking one last drowning breath of heavy
muggy air crackling with approaching thunder before
air-conditioned calm and the smell of hellbreed closed
around me. I had to unbuckle the diagonal strap and lay
the sunsword across my knees, a bar between me and the
blue-eyed 'breed who lounged, patently unconcerned,
across from me on the white leather seat. The blondness
of the interior matched his sandy hair, and the scar on
my wrist leapt with sick hot delight under the copper
cuff.

"Alone at last," Perry greeted me. His suit jacket was
unbuttoned, and the stickpin in his pale blue tie was a
diamond. I suspected it would have a flaw like a scream-

ing face in its depths. "That is an exceedingly undainty tool for such a pretty thing as yourself, my dear."

You're not the first man to tell me that. I stared out the window as the quiet residential streets around Immaculate Conception flowed by.

The driver was behind a pane of smoked glass, and Perry sat with his back to the driver and regarded me. "No word for your faithful slave, dear Kiss? You're even surlier than usual. I've decided to forgive your insubordination this time as well. Comforted?"

There's nothing you can do that would comfort me, Perry. Except stop breathing, and maybe not even then. I wouldn't put it past you to rise from a grave or two. I caught myself, focused my eyes out the window. Mikhail had always told me a woman had an edge in this kind of bargain.

I was about to use that edge for everything it was worth. Besides, my head was full of colorless gasoline fumes, and all I needed was a spark. I hoped I was as dangerous as I felt right now.

He fell silent for a short while. I could feel his eyes crawling avidly over me, leaving behind a sparkling, oozing trail like the wetness coating a hot scaled tongue.

The driver was taking the direct route to the Monde.

Like that's a blessing, Jill.

The scar turned warm. Heat oozed up my arm, a pleasant bath of sensation. I set my jaw as the limo turned left, bracing my foot against the floor.

"You make this so difficult." He managed to sound mocking and contrite at once. I didn't dignify it with a response. "I've done what you wanted. Arkady is waiting at the Monde, enjoying such blandishments as might make him a little more amenable. I've spent a great deal of time and effort soothing his ruffled feathers and persuading him to overlook—"

Now, Jill. Go on the attack. "Bullshit." My voice slashed through his. "You've convinced him I can be used as bait for his daughter, since you've deduced—or maybe you even *know*—that the Weres are hot on the rogue's trail. Can the act, Perry. I'm tired of this game."

"There are other games to play." His eyes halflidded, a movement I could sense, though I kept my gaze out the window, by the sudden heat brushing my cheek. Every nerve was agonizingly aware, waiting for the violence. "You should take that abominable thing off. I like to hear your pulse."

"The cuff stays on, Perry." *At least until I start getting my ass beat by Arkady.* The limo's engine opened up, accelerating up the slight hill of Mendez Road.

"You're harsh." Delicate, dainty as a cat. "What have I done to deserve your ire, avenging one?"

You're here instead of in Hell, Perry. And you're fucking with my head. Watch me fuck right back. "Just don't start with me. I'm not in the mood."

"Changeful woman," he murmured. I sensed his eyes lighting up with predatory glee. The scar prickled, burrowing wetly into my skin. "It's your prerogative, I suppose."

Keep going, you scumsucking hellspawn. I was an idiot to think I could manipulate a hellbreed, especially one like him.

Still, even idiots get lucky sometimes. I felt lucky tonight. Or maybe just reckless.

He kept his voice low, thoughtful. "You've grown quiet. And very thoughtful."

I glanced at Perry. His profile was presented to me, he glanced out the opposite window, one leg crossed over the other, his hands folded on his knee. He looked like a mild-mannered businessman.

I let him have it with both barrels, a mismatched stare and my seeming-full attention fixed on him. "I'm wondering how far you can be trusted when Arkady decides he wants to rip my throat open." *Or just use those eyes on me until I do it myself.*

Perry's head slowly turned. His blue eyes met mine, a shadow of indigo clouding the whites. "That is one thing you *don't* have to worry about, Kiss. You're signed, sealed, and *mine*. Navoshtay Niv Arkady isn't what you should fret over." His colorless tongue stole out, touched his bottom lip in a flicker of motion. "You should worry more about satisfying me once this meeting is over. You've put yourself right into my hands."

Oh, have I? Amazingly, I felt the corners of my mouth tilt up. It was a crazy, suicidal smile, and I heard Mikhail's voice from a long time ago—it seemed like centuries. *When you stop fearing them,* milaya, *you have made first mistake.*

"That's what you think, you hellspawn fuckhead," I informed him sweetly as we bumped across railroad tracks, the limo braking. The Monde was less than ten minutes away, along an extended stretch of road packed with slaughterhouses and warehouses, as well as rumbling bits of railroad track freighted with commerce. I'd never approached the Monde from the meatpacking district before.

It put a whole new shine on things.

Perry paused, his head tilted to the side. The indigo swelled through his eyes, and his hair stirred slightly, lifting on a breeze that came from nowhere because the interior of the limo was still as a drowned mineshaft. "I am going to enjoy breaking you," he whispered.

Then the night turned red, and chaos descended from above. I was ready for something to happen, but it still took me by surprise.

29

The limo was a burning mass of fragments, and the fingers in my throat were pure iron. I thrashed, the sunsword clattering to the ground just out of my reach—I'd been holding it when the limo swerved and the bolt from the heavens descended, tearing through metal like it was paper and igniting like a Molotov cocktail.

Navoshtay Niv Arkady crouched over me, his shoulders hunched and hellfire in the yellow spectrum dripping from his oily, curly hair. His eyes were black from lid to lid, and the sheen of oil on their tops was scorchhot, sucking at me as I went down, black water closing over my head. His teeth were serrated edges of pure ivory bone, and they champed as he sizzled at me in Helletöng, the rumble making the silver in my hair crackle and scorch. A bloody spark spat from the ruby at my throat, and he hissed back. The silver chain against my neck began to *burn*.

He'd gotten tired of waiting for me, despite whatever promises he'd made to Perry. I'd thought that might happen. Powerful hellbreed are touchy about hunters who make them look bad in front of their peers. Sometimes they can't contain their little tempers.

What a joy, I've finally figured a hellbreed out.

The copper cuff clanged on pavement as I surged up, fighting with almost-hellbreed strength. He bore down, grinding me into the pavement. *"You."* His voice was the death of stars, was the cold bleakness of space, his sterile breath scouring my face as I gagged and fought for air, the fingers of my left hand scorching too as I tried to pry his grip loose. He had his foot on my right wrist and he ground down, my scream lost and bottled in my throat. *"You stink of the beast!"*

A secondary explosion rocked the burning limousine. *"Animal."* A load of disgust and hatred made his voice stagger even under its awfulness. His weight, like the pressure at the bottom of the ocean, crushed down on me, my bare skin crawling with acid and loathing. His eyes dug at me, slicing, burning, nerves dying, the rope at my throat and the knife drawing up my arm, riptides of black oil sucking me down.

His breath roared hot and rancid over my face as he *sniffed* me. *"You reek of it!"* he screamed, and I remembered the tang of Were that overlaid my scent.

I realized too late that Navoshtay Niv Arkady was utterly and completely fucking insane, and that he had a big problem with anything smelling like Were. Like I did, now, after hanging out with them—and sleeping in the same bed with one.

If he hadn't intended to kill me before, he certainly did now.

The limo exploded once more, shrapnel flying. Lightning sizzled, thunder sounding very small when compared to the noise in my head. My eyes rolled up, and I dug for every erg of strength I possessed. I convulsed, pitching to the side, trying to throw him off, and got exactly nowhere.

I'm going to die oh shit I didn't plan for this think of something oh my God I'm not ready yet I didn't even tell Saul—

Arkady paused, his wetly gleaming head coming up like a lizard's, his tongue sliding out and poking the air. His cheek was scarred under its copper tones by the sunsword's finials.

FOCUS! Mikhail's voice roared inside my head.

My left hand stopped its fruitless digging and flashed down, closed on a gun.

I had almost cleared leather, my fingers suddenly clumsy and black spots crowding in on my vision, when Cenci simply resolved out of the air with the unholy screech of a basilisk and knocked dear old daddy on his ass.

I rolled onto my side, coughing and choking. The noise was terrific. I was glad the street was deserted, because Arkady slid across pavement, bumped up the curb, and flew right into the side of a warehouse with a snapping sound like a really good bowling strike. Cenci vanished, flung back by the strike her father dealt even as he flew, a long coiled serpent of pure force.

Crap. Now she was out of the picture.

Get up, milaya. Mikhail's voice, tender and pitiless. *Get stupid ass moving, woman!*

I did, dropping flat again from my half-crouch and rolling as the side of the warehouse exploded and

Arkady stepped out, siding and drywall—not to mention glass—whickering through the air. Little bits peppered the street; my coat made a snapping sound as the blowback pushed at its long flow.

My fingers curled around the hilt of the sunsword, and Arkady moved. He didn't so much seem to walk as to sidestep through space, as if he folded the street like a cloth and stepped from one wrinkle to another. He kicked me, and the massive impact against my side flung me back across the street, pain exploding and no more breath in the world, lungs starving, almost into the shattered burning heap of the limousine.

He could have snuffed me out. Arkady was playing with me before he killed me.

Now would be a really good time to have Perry on my side. Hell, I'd settle for anyone. The cough drove splintered bits of bone through my lungs, and the scar on my wrist turned almost as hot as the roasting from the burning limo. I smelled cooking hair and my entire body seized up, bones crackling as a long strangled sound of effort burst out of my blood-slick lips.

I was vaguely surprised I had the breath left to still try screaming.

I'm getting really tired of bleeding. Someone stop the world, I want to get off.

But the sunsword was still in my hand. I managed a walloping painful breath in, sucking at it like wine. Even tainted with hellbreed and burning metal, that breath was the sweetest I'd tasted for a long time. My ribs snapped out, and I screamed again as Arkady stepped mincingly nearer, the pavement groaning under his weight of insanity.

More thunder arrived, shatteringly close. I had my legs under me and a complete lungful of air as Arkady reached down, his fingers curling in my hair and hauling me up, probably to throw me around again.

The silver in my hair woke in a coruscating whirl of blue-white etheric flame.

He inhaled a scream like a black hole sucking in a star, dropping me. I landed on my feet, and pumped four shots into him at point-blank range, my shriek lost in the massive noise of his. Blood gushed from my ears and slicked my upper lip under my nose.

Then I brought the sunsword around, and slashed at him as the blade sputtered and burst into flame. I would have hit him too, if Cenci hadn't collided with him from the side again, her face twisted up in a mask of hatred and her claws making a snapping sound as they dug for his black eyes.

Her momentum slammed them both back into the wreck of the burning car, great gouts of oily smoke gushing up. I didn't hesitate, unhealthy strength flooding me from the burrowing burning of the scar, a tidal wave of heat and etheric force jolting up my arm and through the rest of me. My hunting cry mixed with the guttural scream the hellbreed female made, a chorus of female destruction.

I threw myself into the burning wreck of the car, my boots smacking down on something that crunched wetly as I swung the sunsword, flame suddenly belching in a white-hot blowtorch arc. This wasn't just sunfire—this was nuclear fission, the very soul of flame itself, responding to evil and to my throat-cut yell as I drove the length of bright whiteness into Arkady's chest.

He backhanded me, a fist narrow and hard as a crow-bar landing on my cheekbone, snapping my head aside and flinging me out of the inferno. I landed hard, teeth clicking together with a snap that would have taken a piece of tongue out if I hadn't almost swallowed it while sucking in breath to scream again. The gun clattered and spun out of my left hand, and I scrabbled back, erasing the skin on my palms in my haste, as the flames made a sound like the world ending.

I saw her, in the middle of the conflagration.

Navoshtay Siv Cenci crouched on her father's chest, her face a mask of keening inhuman rage as she tore at his face. His eyes were already deep gaping holes well-ing blackish ichor. Lightning smashed down, a gunpow-der flash etching every detail into my retinas.

Slim female hellbreed with long pale hair and a nose that echoed his, her eyes mad and alight with crimson as she hunkered down in the middle of fire crippling for an ordinary 'breed, ignoring the weak jerks and twitches as Arkady's old, immensely strong body fought to live, not knowing the battle was over. She held up the eyes with one hand, each with its long string of raveled nerve root, and her mouth opened once, twice. Dribbles of darkness spilled from the corners of her mobile mouth, and I saw the flames flinch away from her. Her other arm reached up, fingers clasped around the hilt—slim fingers, black-ening and curling at the touch of holy sun-fired metal.

I sat in the middle of the street with eyes that felt as wide as plates, staring like a child listening to a fairytale too horrible to be unreal.

The sunsword sang a high keening note of agony before the fire—even the burning gasoline—flattened and died with a *wump,* as if starved of oxygen.

I felt around blindly with my stinging hands, the reek of burning gas and scorched paint in my nose. Found my lost gun. My legs didn't want to work, but I pushed myself up, shaking, as the first spatters of rain began again. More thunder caromed through the sky's unhealthy orange cityglow. Lightning spattered between clouds.

The sounds Cenci made as she ripped even further at decaying hellbreed flesh brought everything I'd ever thought of eating up to the back of my throat. I doubled over, heaving so hard black spots danced in front of my eyes again.

There's even a limit to what a hunter can stand, I thought, amazed. Shotglass-sized drops of rain dotted the cracked asphalt. Crazy loops of scorching and cracking marred the entire surface of the street. Had I done that, or had the dueling hellbreed done it? The road was a mess. I spotted two lampposts and a telephone pole down, and a couple more buildings smashed. Down the street there were lights, and I caught the distant sound of sirens.

I'm alive. I didn't believe it even as I thought it.

Hands were at my shoulders. "It's over." Perry sounded very pleased with himself. "There now, my dearest. That wasn't so bad, was it? One little thing left to do, and we will go home."

My forehead left a bloody, soot-grimed streak on his immaculate, linen-clad shoulder. Not a hair out of place. He wasn't even bruised, or scorched.

The sounds behind me ceased. Tension tightened between the raindrops. I jerked away from Perry, whose hands dropped back to his sides.

Cenci stood amid the wreckage of the limousine. Ice now marred the edges of shattered steel and broken glass. I thought I caught sight of the driver's body in there, but my gaze locked on Arkady, who was swiftly collapsing into runnels of foulness.

They rot quick, when they're older. It was a comfort to imagine Perry like that. More of a comfort than I liked.

Navoshtay Siv Cenci's eyes met mine. They were crimson, glowing, and entirely crazed, but I saw . . .

No. I thought I saw . . .

No. I *saw.* I saw comprehension in them, and devouring grief, and shattering pain. I saw agony in those eyes, and my guns dropped to my side.

The anguish burning in her eyes was almost human.

"Kill her," Perry whispered, sweetly. His breath touched my cheek, hot and laden with moisture. "Kill her now, hunter. She murdered your people."

Blackness smeared Cenci's chin. Her clothes were smoking rags, and I wanted to look down, see if her belly was curved. I suspected not. I remembered the pool of oily viscosity in the front yard of the death house, and I thought of her crouching in the dark of night, her arms crossed over her midriff and her eyes gone crimson just as they were right now while she bit her lip so as not to make a sound, as one of her father's filthy experiments slid out of her body and onto the mortal grass.

She's not human! She killed them! Kill her! Kill! My brain shrilled it at me, but my hands were limp and cold. The guns dangled.

No. Not human. The body bags loaded with bits of

her ravaged victims I'd seen screamed for vengeance. That was my function, that was my job. To put her down like a rabid animal, no matter what I'd promised.

But I didn't shoot. I held her eyes, and I thought of Saul. I thought of a rogue laid under spells of concealment and protection, and I thought of the trail vanishing each time.

Because *she* had protected a Were whose name I now knew. Billy Ironwater.

My muscles strained between the two urges—the urge to kill, to do my job and be the vengeance of her victims, and the small still voice of my conscience, trying to speak through the soup of rage and destruction. Trying to show me the way.

I hesitated, on the knife-edge. Why was I not killing her? Which was the right path to take?

Did I even care?

Then Perry made his mistake. The mistake that put the last piece of the puzzle in place.

"Do as I *tell* you!" he hissed, vibrating with rage and impatience. *"Kill her, you stupid bitch!"*

I came back to myself with a jolt. Uncertainty vanished, and my conscience spoke with the voice of brass trumpets. I knew the right thing to do, and what Perry wanted me to do, and found with relief that I could still make that choice.

No. My lips shaped the word, without breath to make a sound. It was wrong. Just how I couldn't say, but I *knew* it was wrong.

If I killed her, I would no longer be a hunter.

I would be as bad as Perry if I cut her down now. Worse, even.

Had that been his game all along?

Certainly, something deep whispered inside me. *He's been watching and waiting to trap you, and Arkady gave him a perfect opportunity. It's just another game for him, maneuvering you into taking a life you shouldn't. Damning you just like a Trader, and taking his payment. Then it won't be him in the rack, screaming.*

It will be you. And he will not let you go.

Cenci nodded. It was a slight movement, her chin dipping faintly. Then she turned, the rags of her clothing fluttering on the sudden sharp rain-laden wind, and was gone, into the black mouth of an alley. Masked as thoroughly as ever a hellbreed was.

Perry twitched.

I threw myself back and to the side, avoiding his clawed hand. The guns spoke as I squeezed both triggers, staggering them. Each shot hit him full in the chest. Once, twice, three times. Four. Black ichor burst out, his diamond stickpin vanishing in a mess of gore.

He snarled, lightning etching sharp shadows into his face. They were the lines of an ancient inhuman hunger, and for a moment I saw beneath the screen of blond bland humanity and glimpsed the truth, as if I was *between* again.

I *saw* him, and my heart stopped, sanity struggling with the flash of revealed evil before my brain mercifully shut it away, unable to remember the full horror. My breath stoppered itself in my chest, heart struggling to function.

A clotting, cloying reek of spoiled honey and rotting sweetness boiled over me before the rain flashed through where he had been standing, and I heard retreating footsteps. Perry ran in the direction of the Monde Nuit, and I lay on the cold street as the slashing fat needles of water soaked through leather, cloth, and my scorched hair.

My breath came back, spilling into flaccid lungs. My heartbeat kept going, the stubborn muscle not knowing when to quit.

Thank God. Thank you, God.

If I lay there with my face upturned to the rain, the shaking juddering sobs wouldn't matter. I had very little time to cry, because the sirens were getting closer, and I had to find a phone.

30

It took an hour for me to clear the scene, mostly waiting for Montaigne to get there so I could tell him to start the paperwork for a major paranormal incident. The shattered hulk of the limousine, full of the water falling from the sky, was hauled away, and I used Monty's cell phone to reach Harp as I stood in a doorway, looking at the yellow tape and flashing red and blue lights. Monty palmed a handful of Tums while Harp's cell phone number rang.

"What?" she snarled, and I cleared my throat. I felt like I'd tried to swallow tacks instead of Monty's antacids.

"Harp. It's me." I coughed, each breath a broken husk. I was soaked to the bone, and would have been shivering if I'd had the energy.

"Jesus *fucking* Christ! Where the fuck have you *been?*" She was coming unglued.

That meant the job was done. Billy Ironwater was dead, the hunt had been successful. "Arkady's dead," I husked. "Where's the pyre?"

"The barrio. Barazada Park. Jill—"

"I'm on my way. Don't start until I get there."

"It's *raining,* Jill. Where the *fuck* have you been?"

"I will explain. Later." It hurt to talk. I tasted blood. "Hold the fucking pyre for me, Harp. It's necessary."

Silence, crackling. Thunder spilled through the clouds again, reminding us little mortals below of angels bowling and lightning striking.

I'd been so close to falling into Perry's trap. The idea that he'd used this to set up a snare just to catch me made me feel weak and sick.

The idea that I'd been so *close* made me feel even sicker.

What had stopped me?

"All right. Get here soon." Then she hung up, and I thought privately that her cell phone had probably been flung at a tree. Harp always got a little nervy after a successful hunt. She was coldly lethal during, but all the tension snapped like a rubber band afterward.

We know someone else who functions like that, don't we, Jill? Someone else who needs just a little push to go over the edge. Someone who almost fell right into a hellbreed's trap.

I ignored that voice in my head. The sunsword was a cold weight against my back, spent and icy. Working it free of the shattered metal and the pavement underneath had been hard for even my hellbreed-strong right arm.

Monty's bald spot glowed under the glaring lights. "Is it over?" He hunched his shoulders miserably under the assault of the rain.

"It's over." I would have sounded relieved, if it hadn't been for the broken glass scraping in my throat. "No more bodies, unless there's a site we haven't found yet. It's done."

"I don't even wanta know." He was pale. Fishbelly pale, and the water on his skin wasn't all from the rain. "You okay, Jill?"

The question was so absurd I almost laughed. I didn't only because it would have hurt too goddamn much. My ribs were tender, and I was so tired of being flung around and breaking them. The blood was washing off my face, and I was tired of losing it.

My throat was on fire, and I was tired of talking. I was just plain *tired*.

"Right as the fucking rain," I croaked. "I need a ride to Barazada Park, on the double. Can you?"

His tired, mournful eyes met mine. Lightning flashed, another tattoo of brightness. The bright yellow slickers of the emergency personnel wavered like fish at the bottom of a pond.

"I can do that," he said. Someone yelled his name and he waved fretfully over his shoulder. "Anything else you need?"

Another laughable question. There was so much I needed, so much I would never have.

But look at what you've got, Jill. A big fat pile of nothing. Isn't that grand?

At least I still had my soul. That, I now knew beyond a doubt. I had not fallen into a hellbreed's trap. I might be tainted, but I wasn't gone.

I was not damned. And if I wasn't now, had I ever been?

It was enough. For now.

"Not a thing, Monty. Thanks." Then I shut up and

let him make the arrangements for a black-and-white to break a few traffic laws getting me down into the barrio.

There's a corner of Barazada Park that butts up against a graveyard, the Church of Santa Esperanza sitting gloomily off to one side. Weres don't have much use for Catholicism—and they have their reasons, the Inquisition in the New World being a big one—but they understand the symbol of the sacred as well as anyone.

Bile and slick copper lay foul in my mouth. My throat still throbbed. My hellbreed-enhanced healing capability had other things to worry about, like replacing the few gallons of blood I'd lost lately. Little things like a sore, bruised throat were last on the list.

I sent the black-and-white with its nervous rookie driver away, hunched my shoulders against the driving curtain of cold downpour, and plunged into the park's pines, aiming for the back corner. I crashed through the brush without trying to move quietly—after all, they were Were. They'd hear me coming.

I tumbled out finally on the top of a low rise, looking down into the shallow depression where a stack of brushwood lay slick and dark, a long male shape arranged atop it. Lightning flashed somewhere else, spilling light and silver shadows onto the wet grass.

I felt them watching, from the trees. Lambent eyes and glitters of teeth. But none of them came out. Had they guessed, or was it just a courtesy they paid me? Where was Saul?

Just as I thought it, another shape resolved out of the

trees beside me, avoiding each wet clinging branch easily. Tall and broad-shouldered, two bits of silver glittering in his hair, Saul Dustcircle stopped short, staring at me.

I heard more branches crackle and whirled, held up my hands. *"Leave her alone!"* My harsh crackle of a voice was a crow's unlovely scarring on the sweet silver sound of rain and the clean roll of thunder. *"Leave her alone! She's not here for you!"*

Thank God, they retreated. A pale glimmer showed between the trees. The bone-splintering growl of threatened Weres rose under the collage of storm sounds.

Saul moved restlessly. "Jill?"

The growls died down. It took a while.

"Let her be," I managed through my swollen throat, struggling to pitch it loud enough to be heard. "I promised her."

He stepped away, twice. Both quick graceful movements. According to Were custom, it was his right to light the fire, since his kin had died at the hands of the rogue.

Water dripped icy down the back of my neck. I stared at the pale glimmer in the trees, willing it closer. Finally, Cenci stepped out.

She looked different, without the insanity of crimson glowing in her eyes. She had been washed clean, all the black ichor and scorching sluiced off. Her rags fluttered as she walked past, head held high with a hellbreed's pride, and stopped, staring down at the pyre.

Her face crumpled, once. That was all. She darted me a glance, and her eyes were dark without the shine of 'breed. Her throat swelled as she swallowed. She was taller than me by a good head, and so thin I saw the shadows of her bones.

Finally, she spoke. "Was it quick?"

I nodded, but it was Saul who answered for me. "Quick and painless." His voice was tight, almost as throat-locked as mine. Another restless movement on his part, and I stepped forward, steeling myself as I came within range of her claws. I kept my hands loose and free with an effort.

I hope I'm not being stupid.

She shot me a look that might have qualified as amused, if not for the sheer veneer of mute madness. Her profile was classic and serene, despite her father's nose. The damned are beautiful, all of them. Except maybe Perry, and he wasn't ugly.

The thought made my breath catch and my stomach go tight with stark terror. I'd shot him, and outwitted him by the barest of margins. If I'd fired on Cenci like he'd wanted me to, I probably could have killed her with a headshot. But what would have happened? *Really* happened?

I could guess, but I never wanted to know. I *never* wanted to find out. I never wanted to be that close to the abyss again.

Too bad, Jill. This is your life.

"I suppose you want an explanation." Her jaw set, her eyes flicking past me. Down to the pyre, as if she couldn't wait to get started.

"Don't need one." The rasp in my voice was better. I longed for a cold beer, for a hot bath, for a decent meal and a week's worth of sleep. "Arkady had a toy, and he had you. You did something hellbreed don't do."

"I'm one of his *experiments,* too. He impregnated a human. A *Trader.*" Loathing burned through her heatless voice. The sound of thunder retreated, the storm sweeping through and relaxing. The rain would be over soon, and fall would begin treading through the desert. Which meant colder nights, and the occasional seventy-degree day, and not much else here in Santa Luz.

The nightside doesn't take vacations. Neither do I.

"It doesn't matter." I didn't say that I knew, that I had seen it, in the way of things I saw *between.* A sudden flash of comprehension, and I'd understood so much more about her. Another toy, kept for some of Arkady's games, and a Were driven to madness after being trapped and subjected to God alone knew what.

They had done the impossible, both these broken creatures, and relied on each other. I didn't know if I could call it love. I would swear on a stack of Bibles that hellbreed can't love.

Yet she had put herself in danger, for a Were. Protected him as best she could, moving him across the country one step ahead of Arkady's search for them—because hellbreed do not like their toys to escape.

She had protected the Were the only way she knew how—with her sorcerous ability, and with spilled blood. His periods of lucidity grew less and less until he no longer recognized her—had that been a particular type of torture? And when he broke from her and ran, brought to bay at last by others of his kind, what was left for her?

Nothing but this.

"Are you ready?" I tried to sound kind, probably failed miserably.

"I'm ready." But she paused. "You know of Hell, hunter." It wasn't a question.

I shivered, not from the cold. Nodded. Rain peppered her skin and mine. She stared at the pyre still, her entire body leaning tensely forward, down the slope of the hill.

"Do you think he'll be there?" Abruptly, she sounded very young. I don't know how I knew who she meant, unless it was the human softness in her voice.

The rock in my throat wasn't just the swelling from being half-strangled. "Wherever you're going, Billy's waiting for you, Cenci."

She nodded. Stepped forward, and I noticed her feet were bare and battered, bleeding sluggish black that didn't look like hellbreed ichor. It was too thin, and though it looked black . . . well, blood often does, at night.

Human blood, at least.

Dear God, let this be the right thing to do. Let this be enough.

Her right hand was curled into a blackened claw—and I saw it again, her holding the sunsword's hilt, keeping her father pinned amid the gasping flames.

I stumbled. Saul's hand closed around my upper arm, kept me upright. The hillside was slick and treacherous as we picked our way down.

A Were pyre is lit with the peculiar practical sorcery they use. The flames aren't crimson, or black, or any of the spectrum of hellfire, banefire, or levinbolt flame. A Were pyre burns clean and hot, and it is white, with a dancing leaping thread of joyous yellow in its heart.

Saul Dustcircle stood beside me after lighting the wet

wood. The tapering rain hissed and splatted, underlit white smoke billowing as the Weres lifted their voices in an ancient chant wishing peace to the departed. If you have ever heard it, you don't need it translated. It is the very color of grief.

Navoshtay Siv Cenci, her white arms closed around the slumped body of a Were, made no sound as the flames crawled through her flesh.

And I don't want to talk about that anymore.

31

Harp's jaw jutted tensely, and the feathers rebraided in her hair fluttered. She wasn't speaking to me.

The platform was a chaos of noise and activity. Bright sunlight glittered on the ranked cars—Weres very rarely fly. They don't like it, so it was the train for all three of them. Harp and Dominic would drop Saul off near the Rez and use the rest of the trip to eat up a few days of recuperation time. They deserved it.

Harp and Dom had finished the small mountain of paperwork to report an interstate major paranormal event, and I would get a lump sum from the FBI's back-stairs funding. With a little bit of fudging, the official story held up; a rogue Were was put down and a med-dling hellbreed toasted. Cenci wasn't mentioned except in passing. All in all, it was a neatly tied package.

Perry still hadn't called me.

Dominic glanced at Harp, who had drawn away down the platform. "She'll get over it," he murmured to me. "Thank you, Jill. I mean it."

Same old Dominic, still smoothing things over for her. I nodded, silver shifting in my hair and my dagger earrings swinging. The bright sun was an excuse to wear wraparound shades, and I'd left the sunsword, blackened and still icy, at Galina's. If it ever recharged enough I might use it.

Or I might not. I shuddered at the thought. My replacement black leather trench creaked slightly with the movement, and I had my next pair of boots on. I hoped I could get through a week without bleeding on them.

Then again, the town had quieted down enormously. Maybe my reputation was finally scary enough to keep it that way. "Don't mention it, Dom. Why don't you come out some time when there's *not* an impending apocalypse? It'd be nice to just have a barbecue or something." My tone was far too falsely bright. I coughed into my hand, as if my throat was still troubling me.

"Sometime." Dom grinned. "I'd better go get Harp on the train. She'll call you in a few weeks."

I doubted it. She wasn't the forgiving type, and my putting a hellbreed on a Were pyre must have rubbed her hard the wrong way. Probably some other Weres, too.

I don't care. It was the right thing to do.

At least Dom agreed with me, in his own quiet way. Saul . . . he didn't say much one way or the other. It could have been that I was avoiding him.

If *could have been* meant *definitely,* that is. "See you, Dom."

He gave me a salute, sketching the motion with two fingers, and turned away. Harp had moved further down the platform, and I saw him slide an arm over her shoulders as he hustled her onto the train. They were a beautiful couple, I saw a few admiring glances tossed their way.

Saul stood with his hands in the pockets of his leather jacket. His eyes were on my face.

I studied him behind the sunglasses. My heart hurt. My head hurt. The pain ran through me.

"I guess this is goodbye," I said brightly. Blinked furiously behind the shades.

He shook his head a little, glancing across the platform behind me. The silver wheel and the twisted unrecognizable bracelet threw back sharp darts of reflected light. I tried to memorize everything about his face, storing it up like a thief.

"Take care of yourself," I added. I babbled. Like a complete idiot.

His jaw set, his mouth thinning. He nodded, privately, as if wrapping up a long internal conversation.

Saul's right hand came out of his pocket, and he held up something I had to squint at to make sense of. The shades didn't help, and neither did the water in my eyes.

It was a leather cuff, with buckles. Just wide enough for a wrist; for my wrist. He held it out, and I took it. I was helpless not to, my hand just flew up and grabbed it.

"That should last you longer than the copper." He stuffed his hand back in his pocket and cocked his head, regarding me. The departure announcement began blaring in the background, as last goodbyes were said all around us and people hurried to file onto the train. "When it gets worn or the buckles snap, I'll make you a new one." His voice dropped, as if he had something in his throat too. "I have to go home. My mother deserves to hear from me about . . . everything."

"I know," I jumped in. "Don't make it worse. Just go. Get the hell out of here." *Don't go. Stay. Please, stay.*

But I couldn't say it. I closed my teeth against the words. There were so many reasons why he shouldn't stay. He was Were, and I was human—tainted with hellbreed.

Corrupted, even if I retained my soul. No matter how hard I fought it, I was going to Hell eventually. And I'd just had an object lesson on what could happen to Weres once they tangled with anything hellbreed.

It wasn't fair. It was monstrously, hideously, absolutely unfair.

It doesn't matter, I told myself. *God, just make him go. Keep him safe.*

His eyebrows drew together, stubbornly. It just made him handsomer, the richness of his skin almost too real under the sunlight. "I have to say something."

Oh, Christ. Don't draw this out. "Just *go,* will you?"

"I'm going." His shoulders hunched. "But I'm coming back. You can't cook worth a damn."

With that he was gone, flowing away with the peculiar Were economy of motion. I stayed nailed in place, buffeted by a stream of people who were heading for the exits now that everyone was safely stashed on the train. When his feet left the platform and he hopped up into the carriage Dom and Harp were already in, the snap of his feet leaving the ground of my city echoed in my chest like a broken guitar string.

I turned blindly away. It was a miracle I was able to make it to the parking lot and my Impala with the cuff clenched in my sweating fist. The tears blurring my eyes and sliding down my cheeks didn't stop even when I dropped into the driver's seat. I put my head down on the steering wheel and heard the lonely sound of a train whistle blaring as the five o'clock special pulled out of the station and chugged out of town.

Epilogue

*L*ife went on. I cleaned out a nest of Assyrian shape-shifters, busted a ring of child-pornographer Traders, and wasn't thrown out of Micky's the next time I ventured in for beers with Avery. Theron simply nodded to me from the smoky dark lounge in back. I actually got to have beers with Ave every week, and we even went to see a horrible movie about zombie-slayers once. It was that calm. Unfortunately, I caught myself playing with a knife-hilt halfway through the film, and one of the supporting actors had shoulder-length dark hair and broad shoulders, not to mention a supple grace that was human enough to bring tears to my eyes. Avery didn't notice.

The weeks rolled by, and it came time for the payment. I finally nerved myself into a visit to the Monde on a gray Saturday night when fall had settled a blanket of sere monochrome over Santa Luz. Perry didn't act surprised to see me—but then again, he never did. In fact, he didn't talk much at all, beyond ordering me to strap him into the frame and use the long flat silver flechettes. The sounds he made were almost worth it, and I was so close, so close to cutting his throat. It would have been easy.

I could have killed him while he was strapped down. I *could have.*

I didn't. I don't know what stopped me, but I suspect it was the memory of silver in a man's dark hair, and his hand holding mine as yellow-white flames burned and the Weres sang their ancient, sad melody.

Cenci wasn't the only one a Were had saved. I could finally admit as much to myself.

By the time the hour was over, I was sweating while I cut, thinning black hellbreed ichor spattered over the frame and the white, white enamel floor of the room Perry reserved for his little games with me. I left him hanging in the frame, bleeding, and headed for the door, the flechette falling from my hand and chiming as it hit.

The edge was there, the temptation to kill him overwhelming. But he was strapped down, and if I murdered him now, or even tried to . . .

He spoke again. Just five little words. "Come back," he whispered, the sound sliding through the air and kissing the scar with a finger of soft delight. "Finish the job."

I did not pause. I ran, and his silky laughter followed me, falling from his bloody mouth. I knew his mouth was running with blackness because I'd punched him hard enough to make his lips a mess of meat.

When I finally got home that night I stood in a hot shower, sobbing and scrubbing at myself with coal-tar soap until I was raw all over, the water sliding down the drain turning ice-cold and running pink and red. I collapsed on my bed afterward, hugging sheets that still smelled faintly of a man's smoky musk.

Nothing had changed.

Everything had changed.

No rest for the wicked. I cried myself to sleep, got up the next night, and went back to work. But not before I visited Mikhail's grave with another bottle of vodka.

It was a relief to finally know I had not killed him. If I'd hung back, purposely waiting, on that night, it was only because I loved him. Had it been otherwise, I would have pulled the trigger on Cenci. You are either damned or you're not, and if you're not, you can stop worrying about your teacher's death in a shitty little hotel room.

Whatever responsibility I carried for Mikhail's death, it was not because I had deliberately robbed him of backup that night. I could swear that much with a clear conscience now, and if the keening infection of grief under my heart didn't stop, at least it got easier to bear.

Things picked up after that. There was a scare about a scurf infestation moving up from Viejarosas to the south—Leon's territory. We found a few *arkeus* who had a nice little Trader stable specializing in rape and extortion, busted it up. I took almost half a clip of heavy ammo before Leon knocked out one of the Traders. He told me later he'd thought I was a goner.

Not yet, I told him. *I'm too mean.*

He laughed, thinking I was joking.

There was the regular rash of exorcisms around Halloween, and I finally nabbed the hellbreed flooding the city with adulterated cocaine. Right after I beat him to a brackish pulp another one moved in to sell adulterated heroin, and I lost a few pints of blood teaching *that* hellspawn that if you were going to import drugs into Santa Luz, cutting them with shit wasn't good business sense.

Then came damn near a month of almost-quiet, and I roamed the streets at night looking for trouble and not finding any.

It was a good feeling, but also a faintly unsteady one.

I came home on a chill winter night. The mountains in the distance were wearing their hoods of snow again, and as soon as I pulled into the garage I knew something was different. I slipped out under my closing garage door and padded around to the side entrance, silent as death.

The door closed quietly behind me. I had the whip loose and easy in my right hand, the Glock in my left, and I eased down the short hall, the warehouse creaking and booming with wind coming from across the desert, laden with cold and the smell of sage.

There was another smell. I sniffed cautiously, then deeper. My chest hurt with a swift deadly pain before ice closed the feeling away.

What the hell?

The lights were on in the long living room. I edged out into the open, caught a flicker of movement in the kitchen, and leveled the gun.

He didn't even turn around. He wore a long-sleeved black thermal shirt and jeans, and he was barefoot. The sheaf of hair that used to touch his shoulders was shorter now, shorn, glowing red-black under the kitchen lights. He hummed a little as he added something to the saucepan.

My heart pounded so hard I thought I would faint. I actually considered it.

"It's late," Saul said over his shoulder. Silver glittered, threaded into his hair with red thread. He'd picked up a few more charms, and the glints looked good against the silky darkness. It would look even better once some of it grew out. "Or early, with you working the night shift and all. So I thought, omelets. Hope you like pepperjack cheese; it's hard to find decent pepperjack back on the Rez. I was craving it. And hash browns. Baked, this time. You don't have the right oil for frying them. Did you throw out *everything* in the fridge?"

My jaw was suspiciously loose. My ribs ran and boiled with pain that burrowed under and into every vital organ, but most of all my heart. I was having a heart attack. Jill Kismet, kickass hunter, dropping dead of cardiac arrest over an omelet.

He looked back down at the stove, the back of his neck oddly naked without a Were's long hair. "It took a little longer to finish up out in the Dakotas than I thought it would. I was going to call, but then I thought you don't answer your phone much."

I dropped the whip. Closed my mouth with a snap, and kept staring at him as the leather slid onto the floor, metal flechettes tinkling.

He was in my kitchen. Again.

Oh, God, I am not strong enough for this.

He shut off the stove, picked up the pan. Flipped one omelet off onto a plate arranged just so on the counter, repeated the process with a slightly bigger saucepan. Fragrant steam rose. "I'll leave salt and pepper to your discretion," he said, and I realized he sounded a little nervous, for the very first time.

I cleared my throat. That was the sum total of my conversational ability.

He turned, holding my battered plastic thrift-store spatula. "We're going to have to talk about your taste in kitchen utensils, too." His eyes met mine, dark and level, and he dropped his hand. The spatula dangled easily, loosely.

I summoned up every scrap of courage I had. "I'm no good at this sort of thing," I managed, in a squeak that sounded more little-girl Minnie Mouse than confident hellspawn-murdering hunter.

"I got that," he answered gravely. He didn't look away.

My heart cracked open inside my chest. *Please, God.* The prayer was no more than that, an incoherent mass of longing right behind my breastbone like Monty's indigestion. "I'm not a nice person." *I kill, Saul. I kill hellbreed and Traders and other nasty things. I'm corrupted. I'm tainted. You have no idea what I was, or what Mikhail made me, or what I am now. What I almost did, how close I came to handing over my soul to Perry. It's not just in the stories that people get taken by hellbreed.*

He sighed. Laid the spatula down on the counter. I remembered I was holding a gun, and holstered it. The creak of leather sounded very loud.

"Mikhail wasn't the only man who gives a damn about you." Saul said it very quietly. "No bargains, no deals. We'll see what happens."

One choked word struggled to get out. "Why?" *Why*

me? Why this? Why couldn't you have come here before Perry? Before I was a teenage streetwalker with a serious rage problem? Before I was broken?

He shook his head slightly, as if I'd just asked a stupid question. "Because you need me. Because I want to," he said softly, and because he was a Were and he said it so quietly, it made *sense.*

God help me, but it did make sense. He was here *now,* he was saying. He was right here. In my kitchen.

With omelets.

The bubble of tears broke in my throat. One slid down my cheek, hot and accusatory. "I don't know how to do this." That finished up all my ability to speak, because if I said anything else I was going to start screaming.

He shrugged. Picked up a plate, and I saw with a kind of mad hilarity that he even had a sprig of parsley stuck in each neat mound of hash browns.

"It's not that hard, Jill. You just sit down and eat something. Then we talk."

"Urgh," I managed, with a slight inquisitive sound at the end. What I meant was, *talk about what?*

And God have mercy on me, but he understood. He smiled, a sweet slow smile as he stood under the lights, and I lost every bit of good sense I had left.

"We can talk about anything, kitten. Come on, it won't stay hot forever."

Glossary

Arkeus: A roaming corruptor escaped from Hell.

Banefire: A cleansing sorcerous flame.

Black Mist: A roaming psychic contagion; a symbiotic parasite inhabiting the host's nervous system and bloodstream.

Chutsharak: Chaldean obscenity, loosely translated as "oh, *fuck.*"

Demon: Term loosely used to designate any nonhuman predator with sorcerous ability or a connection to Hell.

Exorcism: Tearing loose a psychic parasite from its host.

Hellbreed: Blanket term for a wide array of demons, half-demons, or other species escaped or sent from Hell.

Hellfire: The spectrum of sorcerous flame employed by hellbreed for a variety of uses.

Hunter: A trained human who keeps the balance between the nightside and regular humans; extrahuman law enforcement.

Imdarák: Shadowy former race who drove the Elder

Gods from the physical plane, also called the Lords of the Trees.

Martindale Squad: The FBI division responsible for tracking nightside crime across state lines and at the federal level, mostly staffed with hunters and Weres.

Middle Way: Worshippers of Chaos, Middle Way adepts are usually sociopathic and sorcerous loners. Occasionally covens of Middle Way adepts will come together to control a territory or for a specific purpose.

OtherSight: Second sight, the ability to see sorcerous energy. Can also mean precognition.

Possessor: An insubstantial, low-class demon specializing in occupying and controlling humans; the prime reason for exorcists.

Scurf: Also called *nosferatim,* a semi-psychic viral infection responsible for legends of blood-hungry corpses, vampires, or nosferatu. Also, someone infected by the scurf virus.

Sorrow: A worshipper of the Chaldean Elder Gods.

Sorrows House: A House inhabited by Sorrows, with a vault for invocation or evocation of Elder Gods.

Sorrows Mother: A high-ranking female of a Sorrows House.

Talyn: A hellbreed, higher in rank than an *arkeus* or Possessor, usually insubstantial due to the nature of the physical world.

Trader: A human who makes a "deal" with a hellbreed, usually for worldly gain or power.

Utt'huruk: A bird-headed demon.

Were: Blanket term for several species who shapeshift into animal (for example, cougar, wolf, or spider) or half-animal (wererat or *khentauri*) form.

Acknowledgments

Thanks for this book (and the series) go first and foremost to Miriam Kriss, who read the first half-page of a Kismet novel and insisted I finish the damn thing. Miriam, you are stellar. And I must also mention Devi Pillai too, who is all the things an editor—and, more important, a friend—should be.

Thanks are also due to family and friends: Maddy and Nicky for providing a core of strength; Gates for reminding me that miracles can occur even in the most benighted life; Mel Sanders for being the other half of a writerly brain; and the Mighty F-List for massaging my cortex each morning. And Saint Peter Honigstock, for being the wonderful geek he is.

Last but definitely not least, thanks to Chelsea Curtis, Sixten Zeiss, and Christa Hickey for coffee, love, and everything else. Including stockings. And Bukowski. And did I mention the coffee?

Finally, as always, thank you, dear Reader. Without you I am merely a voice in the wind. So let me thank you once again in the way we both like best.

Let me tell you a story . . .

extras

orbit

meet the author

LILITH SAINTCROW was born in New Mexico, bounced around the world as an Air Force brat, and fell in love with writing when she was ten years old. She currently lives in Vancouver, Washington, with three children, a houseful of cats, and various other strays. Find her on the Internet at http://www.lilithsaintcrow.com.

introducing

If you enjoyed NIGHT SHIFT
look out for

HUNTER'S PRAYER

Book 2 of the Jill Kismet series
by Lilith Saintcrow

It's not the type of work you can put on a business card.

I sometimes play the game with myself, though. What *would* I put on a business card?

Jill Kismet, Exorcist. Maybe on nice heavy cream-colored cardstock, with a good font. Not pretentious, just something strong. Garamond, maybe, or Book Antiqua. In bold. Or one of those old-fashioned fonts. High-class, but no frilly Edwardian script.

Of course, there's slogans to be taken into account. *Jill Kismet, Dealer in Dark Things. Spiritual Exterminator. Demon Slayer.*

Maybe the one Father MacKenzie labeled all females with back in grade school: *Whore of Babylon.* He did have a way with words, did Brimstone MacKenzie. Must have been the auld sod in him.

Then there's *my* personal favorite: *Jill Kismet, Kick-ass Bitch*. If I *was* to get a business card, that would probably be it. Not very high-class, is it.

In my line of work, high-class can cripple you.

I walked into the Monde Nuit like I owned the place. No spike heels, but the combat boots were steel-toed and silver-buckled. The black leather trench coat flapped around my ankles.

Yeah, in my line of work, sometimes you have to look the part—like, *all* the time. Nobody takes you serious if you show up in sweats.

So it was a skin-tight black T-shirt and leather pants, the chunk of carved ruby at my throat glimmering with its own brand of power, Mikhail's silver ring on my left third finger and the scar on my right wrist prickle-throbbing with heat in time with the music spilling through concrete and slamming me in the ribs. With my hair loose and my eyes wide open, maybe I even looked like I belonged, here where the black-leather crowd gathered. Bright eyes, hips like seashells, chains around slim supple waists and glittering jewelry, silken hair and cherry lips.

The damned are beautiful, really. Or here in the Monde they always are. Ugly 'breed don't come in here, even ugly Traders. The bouncers at the door take care of that.

If it wasn't for my bargain, I probably would have never seen the inside of the place shaking and throbbing with hellbreed. Even the hunter who trained me had only come here as a last resort, and never at night.

I might have come here only to burn the place down.

Nobody paid any attention to me. I stalked right up to the bar. Riverson was on duty, slinging drinks, his blind eyes filmed with gray. His head rose as I approached, and his nostrils flared. He could See me, of course. There wasn't much that Riverson couldn't see. And I burn in the ether like a star, especially with the scar on my wrist prickling, the sensation tearing up my arm, reacting to all the brackish hellbreed energy throttling the air.

Plus, a practicing exorcist looks *different* to those with the Sight. We have sea-urchin spikes all over us, a hard disciplined wall keeping us in our bodies and everything else *out*.

Riverson's blind, filmy gaze slid up and down me like cold jelly. "Kismet." He didn't sound happy, even over the pounding swell of music. "Thought I told you not to come back until he called."

I used my best, sunniest smile, stretching my lips wide. Showing my teeth, though it was probably lost on him. "Sorry, baby." My right hand rested on the butt of the gun. It was maybe a nod to my reputation that the bouncers hadn't tried to stop me. Either that, or Perry expected I'd show up early. "I just had to drop by. Pour me a vodka, will you? This won't take long."

After all, this was a hangout for the damned, higher-class Traders and hellbreed alike. I'd tracked my prey almost to the door, and with the presence of 'breed tainting the air it must have seemed like a tempting place to hide, a place a hunter might not follow.

It's enough to make any hunter snort with disgust. Really, they should know that there are precious few places on earth a hunter won't go when she has a serious hard-on for someone.

I turned around, put my back to the bar. Scanned the dance floor. One hand caressed the butt of the gun, sliding over the smooth metal, tapping blunt-ended fingers against the crosshatch of the grip because I bite my nails. Pale flesh writhed, and the four-armed Trader deejay up on the altar was suddenly backlit with blue flame, spreading his lower arms as the music kicked up another notch and the blastballs began to smash colored bits of light all over the floor.

Soon. He's going to show up soon.

I leaned back against the bar, that little patch of skin between my shoulder blades suddenly cold and goosebumped. The silver charms braided into my hair with red thread moved uneasily, a tinkling audible through the assault of the music. I had my back to Riverson, and I was standing in the middle of a collage of the damned.

Life just don't get no better than this, do it, babydoll?

"You shouldn't have," he yelled over the music as he slammed the double-shot of vodka down. "Perry's still furious."

I shrugged. One shrug is worth a thousand words. If Perry was still upset over the holy water incident or any other time I'd disrupted his plans, the rest of my life might be spent here leaning against the bar.

Well, might as well enjoy it. I grabbed the shot without looking, downed it. "Another one," I yelled back. "And put it on my tab."

Riverson kept them coming. I took down five before the air pressure changed and I *moved*, gun coming up, left hand curling around the leather braided hilt at my waist and the whip uncoiling.

People have got it all wrong about the bullwhip. In order to use the whip, you've got to lead with the hip; you have to think a few seconds ahead of where you want to be. Like in chess. You get a lot of assholes who think they can sling a whip around ending up with their faces scarred or just plain injured, forgetting to account for that one simple fact. A whip's end cracks because it's moving past the speed of sound; little sonic booms mean the small metal diamonds attached to the laces at the end can flay skin from bone if applied properly—or improperly, for that matter.

Despite his ethnic-sounding name, Elizondo was a dirty-blond in blue T-shirt and jeans, dirty boots, his hair sticking up in a bird's nest over the face of a celluloid angel. His eyes had the flat hopeless look of the dusted, and I was willing to bet there was still dried blood under his fingernails. What he was doing here was anyone's guess. Was Perry involved in the smuggling? It wouldn't surprise me, but good luck proving it.

The whip curled, striking and wrapping around his wrist; blood flew. I pushed off, my legs aching and the alcohol igniting in my head, the butt of the gun striking across his cheekbone. *Not so pretty now, are we? When I get finished, you won't be.* I collided with his whip-thin, muscular body, knocking him down. Heat blurred up through my belly, the familiar adrenaline kick of combat igniting somewhere too low to be my heart and too high to be my liver.

He went sprawling, landing hard on the dance floor, the thin graceful figures of Traders and hellbreed suddenly exploding away. They were used to sudden outbreaks of violence here, but not like this. It wasn't the usual dominance game.

No, I was playing for keeps. As usual.

I landed hard, the barrel of the gun pressed against his temple, my knee in his ribs. "Milton Elizondo," I said, clearly and distinctly, "you are *under arrest*."

I should have expected he'd fight.

Stunning impact against the side of my head. Judo stands me in good stead in this line of work; I spend a distressing amount of time wrestling on the floor. I got him a good one in the eye, my elbow being one of my best points. He had a few pounds on me, and the advantage of being a Trader; he'd made a good bargain.

Still, I put up a good fight. I was winning until he was torn off me, his fingers ripping free of my throat, and flung away.

A pair of blue eyes met mine. "Kiss." Perry's voice was even, almost excessively so. "Always causing trouble."

I made it up to my feet the hard way; pulling my knees up and *kicking*, back curving, gaining my balance and standing up. It was one of those little things you see in movies that's harder to do in real life but worth it if you want a nice theatrical touch. Nobody ever thinks a *girl* can do it.